**S0-AVI-745**

DATE DUE 2, AUG 05

| SEP 23 05 | | | |
|-----------|--|--|--|
| | | | |
| | | | |
| | | | |
| | | | |
| | | | |
| | | | |
| | | | |
| | | | |
| | | | |
| | | | |
| | | | |
| | | | |
| | | | |
| | | | |
| | | | |
| | | | |
| | | | |
| | | | |
| GAYLORD | | | PRINTED IN U.S.A. |

# The Right

# Mr. Wrong

*Also by Karen Sandler*
*in Large Print:*

Eternity
Just My Imagination
Table for Two

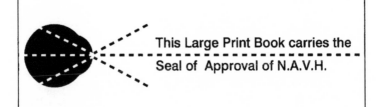

# The Right
# Mr. Wrong

## Karen Sandler

**Thorndike Press • Waterville, Maine**

All characters in this book have no existence outside the imagination of the author, and have no relation whatever to anyone bearing the same name or names. These characters are not even distantly inspired by any individual known or unknown to the author, and all incidents are pure invention.

Published in 2005 by arrangement with Karen Sandler.

Thorndike Press® Large Print Romance.

The tree indicium is a trademark of Thorndike Press.

The text of this Large Print edition is unabridged.
Other aspects of the book may vary from the original edition.

Set in 16 pt. Plantin by Al Chase.

Printed in the United States on permanent paper.

---

**Library of Congress Cataloging-in-Publication Data**

Sandler, Karen.
    The right Mr. Wrong / Karen Sandler.
        p. cm.
    ISBN 0-7862-6995-2 (lg. print : hc : alk. paper)
    1. Private investigators — Fiction.   2. Card dealers —
Fiction.   3. California — Fiction.   4. Nevada — Fiction.
5. Large type books.   I. Title.
PS3619.A54R54 2004
813′.6—dc22                                    2004057983

To Pauline Tenhoff,
my blue-haired grandma,
who's probably playing nickel slots
right now up in heaven.

As the Founder/CEO of NAVH, the only national health agency solely devoted to those who, although not totally blind, have an eye disease which could lead to serious visual impairment, I am pleased to recognize Thorndike Press* as one of the leading publishers in the large print field.

Founded in 1954 in San Francisco to prepare large print textbooks for partially seeing children, NAVH became the pioneer and standard setting agency in the preparation of large type.

Today, those publishers who meet our standards carry the prestigious "Seal of Approval" indicating high quality large print. We are delighted that Thorndike Press is one of the publishers whose titles meet these standards. We are also pleased to recognize the significant contribution Thorndike Press is making in this important and growing field.

Lorraine H. Marchi, L.H.D.
Founder/CEO
NAVH

* Thorndike Press encompasses the following imprints: Thorndike, Wheeler, Walker and Large Print Press.

# *Chapter 1*

Casey Madison veered her little red compact into the Starlight Casino's parking lot, taking a quick glance at her hair in the rear view mirror. Yuck. Bad hair day. She made a face at herself in the mirror, then sneaked a peek at her car's clock.

Ten after eight. The pit boss would read her the riot act.

She jounced over a speed bump, then swerved into an empty parking space, tires squealing. Eyes still on the mirror, she finger-combed her short honey-blonde hair back from her brow. The silky strands crackled with static from the dry-as-dust Reno air. Very bad hair day.

Shifting to climb from the car, she dragged her voluminous canvas bag across the console. It snagged on the brake handle, spilled some of its load of loose change on the floor. Pick it up? Leave it there? She was already late. She untwisted the bag's handle from the brake, straightened and banged her head on the doorjamb. Turning out to be a bad car day, too. Extricating herself from the compact, she slammed the door, then had to give it a shove with her hip when it wouldn't latch. A smear of dirt marked her black pleated slacks.

She slapped away the mess as she serpentined through the parking lot toward the casino entrance. The early morning October air chilled her, seeping through the thin fabric of her white dress shirt. Despite the coolness, a brilliant blue sky arched overhead. It was a day to spend outside, not cooped up in a noisy, smoky casino dealing blackjack.

With a sigh, Casey licked her thumb and tried again to blot out the beer stain a customer had spilled on her sleeve last night, but the splash of Bud Lite seemed to have found a home there. Next time she'd cut the guy off one drink sooner.

Casey greeted several Starlight regulars as she strode through the parking lot toward the casino. As she grasped the handle to the heavy glass entrance door, she caught sight of a man standing twenty yards away, just beyond the newspaper stands. The familiarity of the man's face registered first, and she brought one hand up reflexively to wave.

Her hand froze when she recognized Phil Zucher's grin. Fear scrambled up her spine as she jerked the casino door open. Slipping inside, she ducked behind a dollar slot machine.

*Lord, what was he doing here? He was supposed to be in jail!*

Casey dragged in a deep breath to calm herself. She'd be safe as long as she stayed inside the casino. Zucher wouldn't dare enter. She glanced over at the pit boss, Tommy, who was arguing with a dealer in the blackjack pit. Tommy was the last person she wanted to ask for help, but with Zucher here, she didn't have a choice. Trying to ignore the feel of Zucher's gaze on her, Casey turned and headed for the pit in the center of the casino floor.

"Tommy!" she called out to the beefy man.

Tommy took a moment out from his harangue to snarl at Casey, "You're late, Madison."

"Hung up in traffic." She slipped between two blackjack tables into the pit. Zucher's leer seemed to drill into her back. "Listen, Tommy, there's a problem."

The pit boss rounded on her. "Damn right there's a problem. Third time this week you been late."

Casey tamped down her impatience. "Tommy, it's Zucher. He's here."

"What? Where?" Tommy spun, his mouth set in a mean line as he searched the casino floor.

"There." Casey pointed. "He —"

He was gone. Casey leaned around Tommy, scanned the stretch of plate glass windows that fronted the casino. Not a sign of the card cheater.

Tommy jabbed at her with a thick finger. "What're you trying to pull, Madison?"

"Nothing, I . . ." Zucher's absence gave her more of a chill than his presence. "Never mind." She edged out of the blackjack pit and headed for the employee locker room. "Be right back."

The bing-bing-clang of slot machines drowned out Tommy's mean-tempered response. Casey escaped into the employee lounge.

It hadn't been traffic that had held her up today, but her neighbor, Mrs. Nesbitt. The elderly woman suffered from Alzheimer's and had locked herself out of her apartment again. Casey had stayed with her until the woman's daughter returned from a quick trip to the corner store.

Casey rooted through her canvas bag and came up with her black pumps, then lowered herself to a chair. As she tugged off her sneakers, the image of Phil Zucher's sneering face wormed its way into her consciousness.

Casey shuddered. The card cheater's phone calls had been bad enough. Zucher's menacing voice asking for her, then the quiet rasp of his breathing. His unspoken threats implicit in the silence.

But she could always hang up a phone. What would she do now that the card cheater was turning up at the Starlight?

She paused in the act of slipping on her left pump as another man's face floated into her mind's eye. The roughly handsome image teased her, set off a twinge in her heart. Jeff Haley could protect her, could shield her from Zucher.

But contacting Jeff Haley again would be a big mistake. She'd dodged heartache six months ago by keeping their contact strictly business. A more personal relationship would surely have ended in disaster. Just as it had with Roger, with Steve, with Tom and Ian.

Casey sighed as she drew on her other shoe. She had to face facts — she had a knack for picking Mr. Wrongs. Why add Jeff Haley to the list?

Casey allowed herself another moment's pleasure contemplating the lines of his face, then boxed Jeff Haley away in her mind.

Intent on forgetting him, Casey left the lounge, turning her focus toward tossing out cards to hopeful gamblers.

Jeff Haley stared up at the Starlight Casino, watching the glittery, garish pattern of lights chase itself across the tall facade. He'd just as soon turn around and head back to the office, in fact he'd just as soon spend a couple hours trapped in downtown Reno rush hour traffic than walk into that casino and face Casey Madison.

Damn that ditsy clerk at the one-hour photo counter. If he'd been keeping his eye on the automated photo machine instead of his girlfriend's chest, he might have noticed that Jeff's negatives got dumped in with someone else's.

A thorough search of the dozen or so numbered envelopes processed before and after his order came up empty. Two packets in that batch had been picked up already, one by a Mr. Fleming who, when called, told the clerk he had no extra negatives in his envelope. The other packet — damn his lousy luck — was Casey Madison's.

Jeff shoved his hands into his slacks and rocked back on the heels of his dress shoes. Out of Reno's hundred thousand plus population, his very incriminating shots of

Nevada State Assemblyman Bender frolicking with his mistress had apparently gone home in Casey Madison's photo packet. And since he'd only had the negatives developed — he hadn't wanted to risk making prints — he now had no choice. He'd have to contact the one woman he would gladly have never seen again.

He ran an impatient hand over his close-cropped hair. Lord save him from incompetent photo clerks and diminutive honey blondes. When he'd finished his business with Casey six months ago, he'd made it a point to avoid the Starlight. He'd even turned down a lucrative security contract the manager had offered his company, Discreet Investigations, on the off chance he might cross paths with Casey Madison again.

If he never saw the woman, it was easier to ignore the ache in his chest thoughts of her always generated. He could convince himself the yearning he felt for her was lust, pure and simple, not mythical feelings he refused to believe in.

He'd just make this a brief, businesslike encounter, he told himself as he strode toward the entrance. A thirty-one-year-old man ought to have at least that much self-control. He'd get his negatives, say his good-byes and get the hell out.

*Zucher was back.*

Casey tried to look over her shoulder without actually turning her head toward the casino's side door. She flipped another card onto the table for Mrs. Tenhoff, a Starlight regular. While the elderly woman considered the new addition to her hand, Casey chanced a quick glance outside.

"Hit," Mrs. Tenhoff muttered around her dangling cigarette. Blue smoke wreathed her head, a perfect match for her puff of hair.

Casey slid another card from the card shoe, squinting through the smoke to give a sidelong look at the door. He was lurking there, wearing something dark as he leaned against the casino entrance.

She returned her attention to Mrs. Tenhoff, who shook her head and tucked her cards under her bet. The sole player at her table, Mrs. Tenhoff fixed her sharp eyes on Casey as she picked up the queen of spades topping the dealer's hand. Just as she had been trained, Casey used the edge of the queen to flip over her hole card.

She unearthed the king of diamonds with an apologetic look at Mrs. Tenhoff. The old woman's sour expression informed Casey that her twenty beat Mrs. Tenhoff's hand.

Casey exposed the player's hole cards, counting them up rapidly in her head. Mrs. Tenhoff came up short with nineteen.

"Sorry about that," Casey told the old woman as she scooped up her bet.

Mrs. Tenhoff didn't reply, just stacked another three chips in the center of the white betting circle. Casey quickly dealt out another four cards onto the green felt table top.

A motion from outside caught her attention and her heart clenched. While Mrs. Tenhoff pondered her newest hand, Casey turned her head to get a full on view of the door. Zucher flashed her a sinister grin. Casey looked away, frantically searching the pit for Tommy. The pit boss was busy scratching his behind several tables down. Far enough away she'd have to scream for him to hear her in the noisy casino.

"You gonna deal or daydream?" Mrs. Tenhoff's query brought Casey's focus back to the old woman. Mrs. Tenhoff gave her an impatient glare as she scraped the table with the side of her hole cards, signaling she wanted a hit. Her hands shaking, Casey tossed out a card to the cranky Mrs. Tenhoff.

"Sometimes, dear," Mrs. Tenhoff spat out with the bit of tobacco that had clung to her tongue, "I get the impression you don't like dealing cards."

"Not much," Casey admitted readily. "But where else would I have the opportunity to meet a sweetheart like you?"

Mrs. Tenhoff cackled in delight, then dragged in a lungful of smoke. Casey gave the side door another quick, sidelong glance.

*He was gone.* No point in calling Tommy now. Chewing on her lip, she pulled the remaining cards from the shoe. She began to shuffle the four decks, one set at a time.

"I'd just as soon move on, dear," Mrs. Tenhoff said as she gathered up her chips. "That looks like an unlucky shuffle."

"Take care, Mrs. Tenhoff," Casey called out as the woman walked off toward the quarter slot machines.

Casey set the shuffled cards back in the shoe, then slipped out of her pumps. Sighing with relief, she scrunched her toes against the carpet and leaned against her table. Tommy scowled and marched over to her.

"You do that at break time, Madison," he barked at her.

"My feet are killing me, Tommy," she said. "Have a heart."

But Tommy wasn't in a sympathetic mood. "Put 'em back on," he growled. "And keep your eyes on the game, not on the door."

As if to punctuate his command, Tommy threw a look toward the door himself. His eyes fixed there a moment, then his face darkened in anger. "What the hell is he doing in here?" Tommy muttered.

Alarm burst full force inside Casey and the urge to flee washed over her. Zucher couldn't have actually come inside, he wouldn't dare —

The thought cut off when she saw whose arrival had ticked off Tommy. Although he stood backlit just inside the casino door, an indistinct silhouette, she knew this wasn't the man who'd lurked outside the casino earlier.

As he turned in Casey's direction and arrowed over to her, she began to tremble, but not with the fear the other man engendered in her. She shook with excitement, with joy, despite her frantic attempts to crush her response. She just barely managed a neutral expression on her face when he reached her table.

"Hello, Jeff," she said, not quite suppressing a smile.

He nodded. "Casey."

Her gaze swept over him, from the pale gray polo shirt stretched across his chest to the neat charcoal slacks that hung impeccably on his hips. Lord, he looked so good. She'd be panting in another second.

*Another Mr. Wrong, Casey Madison!* she told herself firmly. "So, what's up?"

Before he could answer, Tommy shoved his face toward Jeff's. "You on a job, Haley? Nobody told me."

Jeff eyed Tommy as if he was a particularly unpleasant bug. "Considering how close you came to screwing up the last case, I'd say keeping you in the dark is a good idea."

Tommy's angry sneer faded under Jeff's implacable stare. The pit boss looked away. "I got better things to do," Tommy grumbled as he crossed the pit to harass another dealer.

Jeff lowered himself onto a stool at Casey's table. "I need to talk to you."

Casey's ever-hopeful heart fluttered at the suggestion in the words, even as her spoil-sport mind told her he'd meant nothing personal by them. She made a face at Tommy, who was still casting them the evil eye. "I don't get a break for another two hours."

"You're not exactly swamped." He gestured at the empty seats at her blackjack table, the sparse weekday casino crowd.

She nodded her head toward the pit boss. "Tommy's got it in for me today."

Jeff's mouth tightened, bringing his high

cheekbones into sharp relief. No one could call his face pretty, Casey realized, with his short-clipped, nearly military haircut and black, black eyes. Yet when she gazed at the harsh lines of his face, she wanted nothing more than to stroke them into softness, to see a rare smile flash there.

Knock it off, Madison! Or you'll be headed straight for trouble.

Tugging a twenty dollar bill from his wallet, he dropped it on the table. "Then we'll talk here." He watched as Casey counted out two five dollar chips and ten ones, then picked up the stack. "So, how've you been?" he asked as he laid three dollar chips in the betting circle.

"Fine." She tried not to interpret the question as anything more than idle curiosity. She dealt the two hands, with an ace up for her. "Insurance?" she asked, prompting him for the side bet he'd need if she had a twenty-one.

He shook his head. "Any more problems with cheaters?"

She remembered Zucher lurking outside the casino and her stomach squeezed with anxiety. For an instant, she considered telling Jeff, turning the problem over to him. But getting Jeff involved in her life again was a bad idea.

"Not that I know of." She checked her hole card; it was a three, not a ten or face card.

Tucking his cards under his bet, he waved off a hit. "Tommy still giving you hell for helping me?"

Jeff couldn't possibly care. He was just making idle conversation, taking his own sweet time coming to the point. This was exactly how she always got herself into trouble with men — misinterpreting what they said, convincing herself they cared when they didn't. Enough wishful thinking, and she'd have Jeff madly in love with her.

Casey forced herself to keep her gaze steady on her cards and not on Jeff. She flipped her three of hearts, then laid a two next to it. "I can handle Tommy."

She could feel Jeff's eyes focused on her, burning her as palpably as a laser. It was all she could do not to look up at him. "Is he bothering you?"

A funny little sweetness filled her heart at his protective tone. Oh, God, she was doing it again. "No," she said, quickly quashing the feeling.

She returned her attention to her dealing, flipping another three next to her two. His penetrating gaze made her feel even smaller than her five-foot-one. She began rooting around with her left foot for her pumps, feeling a sudden need for those extra two inches.

"Because if he is, I can talk to Godwin —"

"No!" The last thing she needed was to have him intercede with the casino owner. "What was it you wanted?"

Bobbing a little as she searched for her shoes, she chanced a glance up at Jeff. His considering look sent a shiver down her spine.

He turned over his cards, exposing two face cards. "I need my negatives."

Puzzling out his request, her toe skimmed the heel of one shoe, knocked it out of reach. "Your negatives," Casey repeated, as she paid Jeff his winnings.

"The ones you picked up yesterday," he said as he stacked his chips together for his next bet.

No wonder she always misinterpreted the things men said. They never made any sense. Switching the shoe quest to her right foot, she said, "I didn't pick up your negatives yesterday."

The lines of his face sharpened, from stress, from annoyance, she didn't know. "You did. You just didn't know it."

She dealt the next hand, turning up an ace for herself. "Insurance?" She extended her toes again. "The only pictures I picked up yesterday were my own."

Her right foot managed to hook a shoe, and she focused on reeling it in. She planted a hand on the insurance line for balance, just as Jeff dropped two chips for his insurance bet. His fingers brushed hers, the contact rocketing up her arm. She jolted back, kicking the shoe out of reach.

"Damn," she breathed, for losing the shoe, in reaction to his touch, she didn't know. Then she made the mistake of looking into his eyes. The smoldering heat in his gaze nearly brought her to her knees.

Fingers trembling, she checked her hand. "Twenty-one," she said unnecessarily as she flipped up both cards. Avoiding his hands where they rested on the table, she scooped up his insurance bet and the cards, leaving his original bet intact.

"My negatives were with your pictures," he said as she tossed out another set of cards.

"That can't be," she said. "Those were my reunion pictures. Yours weren't on the same roll."

Confusion furrowed his brow. "Of course not." He blinked, as if trying to unscramble his thoughts.

She could understand his puzzlement. She hadn't the slightest idea what he was talking about. "I looked all through those photos. It's just me and my sisters."

His gaze sharpened on her. "You looked at the negatives?"

"No, not the negatives," she said, making another arc with her foot. "At least not before I —"

Her toes brushed the cuff of his pants. She shouldn't have felt his heat, couldn't have. But her skillful imagination filled in the details, sent her heart to racing.

A flicker of reaction, then he bent his head to his cards. He glanced at the jack she had showing, then signaled for a hit. "Then you haven't looked through them?"

"No." She dropped a card on the table for him, a king.

He frowned, then turned his hole cards up to show he'd busted. She took his bet, dropping it into her till, then reached for the cards. His hand covered hers, stopping her.

"I can pay for them if you have them," he said, his eyes steady on hers.

She tried to tug her hand free. "Have what?"

He didn't release her. "No questions asked, Casey."

Snatching her hand from his, she checked for the mark that his heat surely left. Her hand looked the same. She rubbed lightly at the spot. "I don't know what you're talking about."

He scrutinized her a moment more, as if seeking a lie in her face, then he shrugged. "There was a mix-up at the one-hour photo. My negatives ended up in someone else's packet. And they're pretty certain that someone was you."

She rearranged the chips in her till, her hand still tingling from the remnants of his touch. "Are they pictures from a case?"

He nodded, sliding a bet into the white circle. "A rather sensitive case. Pictures that could prove . . . lucrative to someone shrewd enough to use them."

"Lucrative . . ." Understanding hit, and her cheeks grew hot with indignation. "For blackmail you mean? And you figured I'd be underhanded enough to —"

"You wouldn't be the first woman to be duplicitous."

She gripped the plastic top of the card shoe until she could feel the edges bite into her hand. She'd like nothing more than to wrench it up and dump the contents onto his head.

"As if men aren't sneaky and under-handed?"

He shifted in his seat. "I'm not saying men don't do the wrong thing. But they're usually more up front about it."

"Like Phil Zucher?"

"Zucher doesn't count," Jeff said. "He's a louse, not a man."

He pointedly looked back down at his hand. Leave it to a man to forgive the male gender by dismissing the bad apples as anomalies. Casey's fists clenched, and she entertained a satisfying fantasy of landing a roundhouse punch on Jeff's jaw. Another image followed close on the heels of that vision — a soothing caress along his jaw, across his chin, his lips —

He scraped his hole cards across the table, drawing her attention back to blackjack. She tossed him a card.

"The only negatives in my envelope were of my sisters and me at Lake Tahoe," she said. "If you've lost yours, I'm sorry, but I have no idea . . . Oh!"

Her voice trailed off as a sudden thought occurred to her. Jeff, darn him, didn't miss a beat, his gaze coming up sharply to hers at the hesitation.

"What?" he demanded.

She swept her gaze up at him. "The negatives."

"What about them?" He bit out each word.

She gave a nervous chuckle. "I might have them after all."

25

With a hiss of air, he turned away from her on the stool, then faced her again. "And where might they be?"

His steady gaze rattled her, tossing her thoughts up like popcorn. "I mean, I may not. I remember thinking I had an awful lot of negatives for the number of pictures I had. But I figured some must have been bad, so they hadn't printed them. Of course I don't remember the roll being that long either, so I . . ." Her voice trailed off at his dark look. "What?"

He took a long breath as if grasping for patience. "So where are they now, Casey?"

"At my apartment," she said. "That is, if the mail hasn't come yet."

"The mail," he parroted. "What does the mail have to do with it?"

"Well, you see —" Movement beyond Jeff caught her eye and the words froze in her throat.

*Zucher was back.* The fear she'd stuffed away came bubbling up and Casey knew she had to get out. She needed some space, she needed safety . . .

The kind of safety Jeff Haley could provide. "I'll tell you on the way," she blurted.

"On your way where?"

"To my place," she said. "To get the negatives."

"On your break?" he asked. "Do you have enough time?"

"I can take my lunch now." She flagged down Tommy. "That'll give me an hour."

When she told Tommy she was breaking early for lunch, he looked eager to tear into her. But Jeff kept his dark, dangerous gaze on the pit boss until he backed off his usual verbal abuse.

"Damn well better get back in time," Tommy snarled at her as she ducked under the table to retrieve her pumps.

She waved her shoes at Tommy in response, then headed for the locker room. Over the clamor of the casino floor, she called out to Jeff, "I'll meet you out front."

She grabbed her purse from her locker, tossing the pumps in with a clatter. As she stuffed her feet into her sneakers, she gave herself a stern lecture on the foolishness of letting her emotions rule her life. She reminded herself that Jeff Haley had not the least smidgen of interest in her. And even if he did, he would eventually prove to be just as wrong for her as had every other man she'd fallen for.

Lecture delivered, Casey slung her purse over her shoulder and hurried out of the employee lounge. But despite her best efforts, she couldn't quite still the lightness in her feet, the spark of joy in her heart.

# Chapter 2

Jeff watched Casey approach, her sleek cap of honey-blonde hair bouncing, her compact body swinging with the motion of her legs, and felt the familiar tug somewhere south of his navel. He could see the innocence in her soft brown eyes from here, even through the smoke and the crowd of people.

He'd known enough two-timing women in his life to mistrust that seeming innocence. Behind Casey's ingenuous, heart-shaped face, within her small but curvy body were no doubt any number of devious bones. His own ex-wife had the look of a guileless innocent — and an unbroken string of infidelities during their marriage. Not to mention the dozens of women whose husbands hired him to follow — inevitably, they were up to no good. It just seemed to be built into the gender.

Yeah, Phil Zucher cheated — or tried to. Not bright enough to discreetly count cards, the crossroader's attempt to thumbnail the deck was clumsy enough that even a relative novice like Casey took notice. But Zucher's failed attempt to cheat arose more out of a stupid man's greed than native sneakiness.

Casey Madison was a hazard, pure and simple. Now if he could only convince his libido of that, that wickedly creative part of him that so easily imagined the petite honey-blonde in his arms, in his bed . . .

He slapped away that thought as she reached his side. He nearly needed to slap his hand away as well when he almost brought it up to stroke the honey silk of her hair that bobbed shoulder high to him. At six-foot even, he wasn't particularly tall, but there was something about their difference in heights that made him want to protect her.

"So where's your car?" She flashed white even teeth at him.

Distracted by the hint of cinnamon that drifted from her, it took a moment for the sense of her question to sink in. "My car," he said inanely, then remembered. "Damn! It's at the shop. I took a cab over here."

Her grin widened, and he realized her teeth weren't perfect. Her left eyetooth was turned a little bit sideways and he couldn't help wondering what that irregularity would feel like against his tongue. He thrust the image aside.

"No problem." She led the way out the door. "We can take my car."

He followed her out into the October glare and down the long line of autos and RVs. Flyers had been tucked under each windshield wiper, the fluttering white sheets advertising a car wash. Casey stopped at a battered red compact of uncertain parentage.

"Does that shoebox actually run?" He eyed the car doubtfully.

"Better than yours, apparently." She grinned. "At least it's not in the shop."

He mumbled an acknowledgment of her logic as she pulled the flyer from under her wiper blade. Still smiling, she flipped the sheet over and Jeff caught a glimpse of a handwritten scrawl on the back.

The color drained from her face. Eyes wide, she swiftly scanned the parking lot. Then she crumpled the sheet into a tight ball.

"What is it?" he asked.

"Nothing." She stuffed the wad into her voluminous shoulder bag. "Junk mail."

She wouldn't meet his gaze. He took a quick look around the lot himself, but if there was any menace out there, it wasn't apparent. He felt an urgency to press her for an answer. But hell, it wasn't any of his business, was it?

"You have to get in on the driver's side," she said, drawing his attention back to her. "The passenger door doesn't open."

She banged the driver door once with her small fist, then opened it with a loud clunk. He gazed down at the minuscule confines of the compact, wondering how he would fold his body into it.

"Watch out for the gearshift," she warned as he dropped into the driver's seat.

"Concerned for my anatomy?" He enjoyed the deep blush that rose in her cheeks.

"More concerned for the gearshift," she bit out tartly.

After a dicey moment straddling the hand brake, he managed to settle himself into the passenger seat. That he'd have to climb out the same way wasn't a comforting prospect.

That she'd be so close to him as they drove was even more disturbing, he realized as she climbed in. Her slender frame rested only inches from his broad shoulders and her hand when she reached for the brake was startlingly close to his thigh.

Remarkably, the car's engine roared to life with the first turn of the key. Casey shifted into reverse, her fingers tantalizingly close to his knee as she did so.

"I guess you've been busy," she said as they

pulled to a stop at the parking lot exit. With a screech of tires, she crossed two lanes of traffic and inserted herself into the flow of cars. "Catching bad guys and such."

Casey glanced into her rear view mirror as they slowed at a red light, her face relaxing as her attention returned to the road. Her nearness making him edgy, Jeff shifted in his seat. He reached for the radio to turn up the volume.

Just as Casey did. Their fingers tangled a moment, then lay frozen against the radio's controls. Her warmth burned against the back of Jeff's hand before she snatched her fingers away.

She shoved the car into gear when the light turned green. Forgetting what he'd intended to do with the radio, Jeff locked his hands into his lap. The memory of her searing heat settled in his mind.

"Business has been good," he muttered.

She eyed her rear view mirror again. "I heard Mr. Godwin mention your name once or twice," she said absently, then jerked the wheel to the left, cutting off a behemoth Cadillac. The driver of the Caddy laid on his horn, but beyond a tensing of her shoulders, Casey seemed unconcerned. "Thought you might be doing some more work for the casino."

She wrenched the wheel again, this time wedging them in front of a semi. The trucker bore down on them, waving a fist in agitation.

Jeff checked the fit of his seat belt. "Do you always drive like a lunatic?"

A swath of color warmed her cheeks. "I have to hurry, don't I? I only have an hour for lunch."

"I'd like to make it there alive," he muttered, then sucked in a breath when she cut through two lanes of traffic to turn left at a green — no, yellow — left turn arrow.

One last look in her rear view mirror and her tense shoulders relaxed. She puttered along at a more sedate pace, easing her little red compact onto Interstate 80 without one squeal of her tires. The late morning sun arched overhead, casting a harsh glare on the sere brown hills on either side. Crowded in close to the interstate, the casinos looked tawdry in the unforgiving light.

That same light seemed to touch Casey's creamy skin with a luminescent glow. Jeff imagined stroking her delicate features, running his fingertips along her cheekbones, trailing along the line of her jaw. He could feel the warm satin under his palm.

The whiny beep of the compact's horn

startled him out of his erotic fantasy. Casey jammed the horn a second time. "God, I hate it when people drive on my rear bumper." She glanced at him, at his hand that hung in the air between them. "What?"

Dumbly, he stared down at his hand, then snatched it back in his lap. "Nothing. Where the hell are we going?"

She flicked him what he could swear was a guilty look. "I, uh . . ." She looked around her, as if searching for an answer. "My apartment, of course."

"You're taking a damned roundabout route," he said, then wanted to bite his tongue.

Of course, she caught the slip. She narrowed her gaze on him. "How would you know? You've never been to my place."

The small space of the car suddenly seemed even tighter. He should have known his moment of weakness six months ago would come back to nip him on the behind.

Jeff shifted uneasily, settling his back against the passenger door. "I haven't." Not exactly a lie.

Her lips creased into a smile. "For all you know, I could be sleeping in the back seat of my car."

He flicked a glance into the back, his gaze running over the narrow bench seat. A sudden, vivid image sprang to mind — the two of them wedged there, his arms locked around her, her legs tight around his hips.

He ran a hand over his face to wipe away the image. "I looked up your address," he finally admitted. And drove to her apartment. But only once. And he'd stayed in the car.

"Oh," she said, pleasure in her tone. "But why?"

He shifted irritably in his seat. "I thought it might be good to know, in case I needed you."

Her soft intake of breath teased his ears, a sweet, appealing sound. When he glanced at her, the longing he surprised in her eyes worked its way inside his chest, scraped against his heart.

"But I didn't," he said flatly. He waited until the longing died in her face, replaced by a trace of hurt. He felt like the worst kind of monster for hurting her.

Looking away, he ruthlessly thrust the guilt aside. His ex-wife had been a master at that wounded look, usually when she was the one at fault. He crossed his arms over his chest and settled more firmly against the door, eyes fixed out the front windshield.

"So I know you're going the wrong damn way."

She laughed, the sound false. "You're

right. I think in the back of my mind, I was headed for Pearl's house. She's my Little Sister."

She eased her car toward the turnoff for Highway 395, then took the first exit. "It's a great program, Big Sisters. And Pearl's such a love. I guess she was on my mind and I just started to drive . . ."

As her voice trailed off, she glanced at him again, and he realized she was lying. Rather badly, since the flush in her cheeks gave her away. Again, Jeff burned to know why.

She pulled back on 395, this time going north, and positioned herself in the rightmost lane. Cars closed in fast on their rear, then zoomed around them at what seemed twice their speed.

Jeff checked the slim gold watch on his wrist. Nearly half her lunch hour was gone. "Can't you drive this shoebox any faster?"

"My car takes life at her own pace," Casey said primly as she pulled back onto Interstate 80.

Of course, the damn car was a she. Everything, from the empty soda cans rolling on the floor to the french fry bags jammed into the ashtray, seemed an extension of the woman herself. Although Casey herself was a damn sight prettier than her snail of a car.

Jeff kicked aside a Big Mac box and tried to ease the cramping in his long legs. "Do you have them somewhere safe?"

She nodded absently, driving in silence. Suddenly, she shot him a glance. "What did you say?"

"The negatives. Are they safe?"

"Sure," she answered, although she sounded anything but. She took the Keystone exit, then rolled up to the stop. She kept her eyes on the road as she waited for an opening in the traffic.

"Where are they?" he persisted as she turned right onto Keystone.

"At my house." She slanted him another quick look. "Except . . ."

"Except?"

Her fingers on the steering wheel raced through a rapid tattoo. "Shouldn't be a problem though."

He gripped her shoulder and shook it. "What shouldn't be a problem?"

"The mail," she informed him. "It never comes before noon."

In spite of himself, he glanced at his watch. Eleven-fifteen. "What," he managed, "does the mail have to do with anything?"

She flicked a glance at him. "The negatives," she stated the obvious, "shouldn't have gone out in the mail yet."

He couldn't have heard her right. "The negatives are in the mail?"

"In my mailbox actually. I left them out for the mailman."

Jeff struggled to understand. "You gave my negatives to the mailman?"

"Well, he wouldn't have them yet since the mail never comes until after twelve."

Jeff took a breath, wondering if next she'd be telling him Who was on first. "Let's start over . . . you left the negatives out for the mailman."

"And the reunion pictures. I packaged them all up to send to my sister Deb." She faced him. "I'm sure I told you that."

Jeff's jaw began to ache from gritting his teeth so tightly. "No, you did not."

She shrugged. "Whatever. I wouldn't worry about it. I'm sure they're still there."

Casey maintained a leisurely pace down Keystone. Jeff, eyes riveted on his Timex, watched the minutes pass. "Can't this damn car go any faster?"

Unperturbed, Casey eased into the left lane. "I'm going the speed limit."

His right foot tensed as if it were pressed to the accelerator, trying to urge more speed from the reluctant car. She flashed him a smile, its provocative message adding arousal to the stew of emotions surging through him.

"Mellow out, Jeff. It's only twenty-five after. The mail never comes before noon."

She turned away too quickly to catch his glare. Figuring he'd better follow her advice before he put his fist through the windshield, he leaned back in the seat and closed his eyes. But with his eyes shut, he dragged in her cinnamon scent with each breath, until he ached to trace down its source with his tongue.

They finally pulled up to her apartment at a quarter to twelve. She fussed with the gearshift and hand brake, then opened her door. When she turned and planted her feet on the pavement, Jeff slung one leg over the console to follow her out of the car.

He was half on her seat before he realized she hadn't vacated it. She was bent over, groping in the back for her purse. In his awkward position, his hip molded against her tempting behind and his arm rested against her slender back.

She stilled in her search for her purse. In the back of his mind, Jeff wondered what effect the gearshift would have on his growing arousal. At the forefront of his Casey-addled brain, his libido urged him to pull the rest of himself into the driver's seat and settle Casey into his lap.

She solved the dilemma for him by leaping out of the car. He followed more slowly, his erection adding challenge to the process.

By the time he'd extricated himself from the car, she was buried elbow deep in her purse. "What are you looking for?"

"My mailbox key," she told him.

He edged past her to pull open the lobby door. "You don't keep your mailbox key with your car key?"

As she moved through the door, she dived farther into her bag. "I don't want to lose it."

Following her inside, Jeff sought for reason in what she'd said. He came up empty. "Come again?"

"I lose my car keys a lot." She sank down onto the bottom step of the staircase, still digging. "If I keep all my keys separate, I can't lose them all at once."

Of course. Perfectly logical. "Which box is yours?"

Her purse seemed to have swallowed her head as she pawed away at its bottom. "Two-thirteen," she replied, her voice muffled.

Pacing over to the bank of mailboxes, Jeff squinted at the little window in Casey's box. He could see a white envelope inside.

"What color was the envelope —"

"Found it!" she called out, holding the key up like a beacon. She nudged him aside, and he leaped back at the contact.

"Is it there?" he asked as she swung open the box.

"Oh!" she cried, staring down into the box. "That's right."

Leaving the white envelope in the box, she swung the door shut again and locked it. "The mail hasn't come yet."

"Then why didn't you get it out?" Jeff pointed to the white envelope in the box.

She looked puzzled a moment, then her honey eyes widened in understanding. "Your negatives aren't in that envelope."

Scrubbing at his face, he struggled out of the rabbit hole. "They aren't?"

"Of course not." She dropped her key into the depths of her bottomless purse. "Why would I put them in with my phone bill?"

Jeff counted to ten. "Then you didn't leave them for the mailman?"

"Oh, no," Casey assured him, and hope unfurled within Jeff. She squelched it a moment later when she added, "I mailed them at the post office — Express Mail."

That particular shade of red on Jeff's face

41

couldn't be healthy, Casey thought.

"Sorry, I forgot." She smiled more broadly, hoping to placate him. "I'd started to put them in the mailbox, then I remembered I'd be passing the post office on my way to work. I saw the sign for Express Mail, so I . . ."

Jeff's color hadn't improved. Casey bit back the stream of words that seemed to want to tumble from her tongue whenever she tried to explain herself to Jeff. It happened every time — she'd fall for a man and immediately her IQ shrank to Neanderthal levels.

But she hadn't fallen for Jeff. She couldn't. She wouldn't. She just had to pull herself together.

"I guess your negatives are on their way to my sister's," she finished lamely, whooshing her hand in imitation of a plane.

Jeff didn't seem to find the humor in that. "Where," he ground out, "does your sister live?"

His dark eyes looked dangerous. In spite of herself, Casey took a step back. "San Diego," she squeaked.

Jeff passed a hand over his face. "San Diego," he repeated. He stared off down the street, seemed to grope for composure. "Could we go upstairs, please?"

Casey shrank back at his deadly calm tone. She had a fleeting image of him strangling her out of sight of witnesses in her apartment. "Why?"

"I need to use your phone. To call the post office."

She let out a breath she didn't know she'd held. "Sure. Just let me find my —"

"— key," he finished for her, his tone resigned.

For once she found it quickly, wedged in the bristles of her hairbrush. She led the way up the stairs, a shiver running up her spine at the thought of Jeff in her apartment. As she reached the second floor landing, she allowed herself a moment's fantasy of him sweeping her into his arms and kissing her with mad abandon.

*Stop it, stop it, stop it!*

Pushing the door open and stepping inside, she gestured toward the kitchen. "Phone's on the counter. Excuse me." She tossed her purse on the sofa, then headed for her bedroom, intent on escape.

Once in her room, she sank to her narrow twin bed and dropped her face in her hands. Good grief, what was she doing? A woman with such a lousy track record with men ought have better sense!

Roger alone should have proven to her

she was an awful judge of character the day he cleaned out her checking account. And Steve before him, who downed a case of Bud every weekend. Then, Tom — or was it Ian? — who'd tried to sell her car out from under her while she was at work.

Thank God she'd never let any of them move in. And double thanks that the skunks had shown their stripes before she became intimate with them. But by the time she'd discovered she'd been badly used, it had already been too late for her heart.

Casey flopped back on her bed and stared at the ceiling. She'd done so well the past six months. After her near miss with Jeff, she'd managed to protect her heart. But it only took seeing Jeff's face and she was ready and willing to stumble into the same old trap.

Yeah, he looked like a pretty straight-up guy — hadn't they all? But given time, reality would rear its ugly head and Jeff's warts would show, just like the others.

Casey rose from her bed, her head pounding. It was just this business with Phil Zucher that had thrown her off balance. Seeing him outside the Starlight, lurking with his evil grin, leaving threatening notes on her car, waiting to . . . to. . . .

Well, she didn't know what he was waiting

to do, but it sure wasn't to invite her out to coffee.

Any woman under that kind of stress would fall prey to a pair of broad shoulders like Jeff's and dark, intense eyes that seemed to delve soul-deep.

She dug the aspirin bottle from the bottom of her night stand drawer and swallowed dry the one whole pill and the collection of fragments still left inside. Wincing at the acrid taste, she finger-combed her hair as she stepped back into the living room.

Jeff had removed the stack of magazines from one of the kitchen stools and sat with his back to her, phone tucked against his ear. The taut gray knit of his polo shirt snugged against his ramrod straight back, tempting her to touch him. She shoved her hands into the pockets of her slacks.

She waited until he hung up the phone. "Any luck?" she asked, crossing the room toward him.

He scrubbed at his face with his hand. "Your package already went out. The post office isn't supposed to be so damned efficient."

She hovered near him, wishing she could curve her arm around him. She clenched her hands in the pockets of her pleated black slacks instead. "What now?"

"I call my client." Jeff tugged out his wallet and slipped a card from it. He punched out a phone number as Casey gathered the stack of magazines from the second stool and dumped them onto the floor.

Casey eased herself onto the stool, her knees accidentally brushing his. He hesitated, then turned away from her, tucking his legs under the counter.

"It's Haley," he said into the phone, then listened. "At an apartment in Reno." He spared a quick glance at Casey. "Nobody. Just someone I know."

He turned at Casey's indignant gasp. He shrugged at her as if in apology, then returned his focus to the phone. "I don't have them, exactly." A squawk of anger from the receiver had him pulling it away from his ear. He held the phone close again. "I know. I *know*."

Another round of complaints sifted from the receiver and Jeff's expression hardened. "I said you'd have the damn negatives by Monday and you will." Casey shivered at his dangerous tone, making her glad she wasn't the target of his anger. "If I don't deliver, don't pay me. But I'll deliver." He listened another moment, then barked out a good-bye before hanging up.

Casey waited until he seemed to have his

ire in check. "Should we call Deb?" At his curt nod, she reached for the phone. "I'll ask her to send them back when she gets them."

He rubbed at the furrows between his brows. "Post office said they should get there by Friday," he told her as she dialed. "Have her Express Mail them back."

Casey waved a hand at him as Deb's answering machine picked up. A Humphrey Bogart sound-alike implored her to leave a message or she'd regret it — maybe not today, maybe not tomorrow —

A squealing beep cut the pseudo-Bogart off in mid-sentence. She waited for the beep to end, but it went on, and on, and —

"What?" he asked her. "What's happening? Did she answer?"

Casey shook her head, wincing as the beep burrowed into her ear. "Answering machine," Casey told him. "It doesn't seem to be working."

"Give me that." He reached for the receiver, held it to his ear and frowned, then hung up the phone. "Dial again."

She hit the re-dial button. Humphrey got to the word "today" in his imprecation before the endless beep kicked in. Casey held the receiver out to Jeff so he could hear.

With a growl, Jeff snatched the phone from

her and pressed re-dial. She could see the expectation in his eyes as the answering machine message played, then his scowl when the beep started up. He sat listening to it for a good long minute, as if he could bully it into proper operation from six hundred miles away.

He set the receiver down so carefully, he seemed perfectly calm — except for the white skin stretched across his knuckles. He narrowed his gaze on her. "When does she get home?"

Chewing on her lower lip, she checked the clock. A quarter past twelve. "Four on a Wednesday — I think."

Jeff rose from his stool and towered over her. "You think?"

Casey sat up straight, trying to add inches to her diminutive stature. "She's a nurse. Sometimes she works odd hours. But I'm pretty sure that on Wednesday . . . Oh!"

Jeff's eyes widened. A peculiar mixture of caution and dread played in their dark depths. "What?" he ground out.

She tried a grin, but at his black look, she faltered. "She's working double shifts this week."

He dragged in a long, slow breath. "Meaning?"

Casey locked her fingers together in her

lap. "Meaning she might be home at midnight."

His grip tightened until Casey wondered if he'd crush the Formica. "Or?" he grated out.

The words came out in a rush. "Or she might spend the night at the hospital."

Wary relief crept into Jeff's face. He settled back onto his stool. "Then we call her at the hospital."

"Great idea," Casey agreed, "call her at the hospital."

He picked up the receiver and cradled it between his shoulder and his ear. Casey admired the way his muscles rippled beneath the gray knit of his shirt as they tensed to hold the receiver in place.

"Well?" he drawled, his gaze expectant.

She tugged her eyes from the muscles of his shoulder. "What?"

He flicked down the phone's disconnect button as the dial tone changed to an annoying staccato. "The number of the hospital?"

She blinked. "I don't know the number."

A knot tightened in his jaw. "Then the name? I can get the number from information."

"I don't know the name either."

His eyes widened and she thought he

would rise up and swallow her whole. He replaced the receiver with a clatter. "Why," he spat out, "not?"

Casey's first response was to cringe, then anger flared up, burning away her intimidation. "She's a contractor. She works for a service. I can't keep track of where she'll be on a given day."

He studied at his toes and seemed to be counting the stitches in his leather shoes. "I don't suppose you know the number of the service?"

Casey hopped off her stool. "Of course I do. It's in my address book."

Jeff peered over her shoulder as she rooted through the teetering pile of magazines and junk mail on the counter. His nearness made her want to lean back into him, to curve herself against his broad chest. She sighed at the impossible, digging deeper for her quarry.

Finally she unearthed the little red book, releasing a shower of Post-Its and shards of paper when she plucked it free of the stack.

She flipped through the pages. "Now, did I write it under 'D' for Deb, 'N' for Nurse, or . . ."

Jeff reached around her. "Let me see."

"I'll find it," Casey said crossly, turning to keep it from him. "Here it is, under 'W' for 'Work Numbers'." She slapped the address book triumphantly on the counter.

He glanced at the number. "Where's the area code?"

She looked down at the page. "Here," she said, pointing to the "D" scrawled next to the number.

"That's not an area code."

"Sure it is," she said loftily. " 'D' stands for Deb, which means San Diego, and the area code for San Diego —"

"I know what it is," he said. "Why don't you just write it out?"

"Because it's easier this way."

He laughed, not nicely. "Easier?"

"It is for me."

He reached past her for a pencil. "Humor me." He wrote the area code next to Deb's work number with emphatic strokes.

Then he picked up the phone and dialed. She watched his face as he waited for someone to answer, the distant focus of his eyes softening their usual sharpness. He tipped his head down a little when he finally got a response on the other end of the line and Casey wondered how his close-cropped dark hair would feel under her fingertips.

His face tightened as he listened, his impatience back. His irritation seemed to grow as Casey discerned from his lengthening silence that he'd gotten a recording rather than a real person.

"Is it the voice mail?" she asked him. "If you press nine, you can get the operator —"

He slammed down the phone. "They're closed."

She checked the clock on the microwave. "It's not even one o'clock. How can they be closed?"

Pushing off his stool, he began to pace in the confines of her small breakfast nook. "Some kind of off-site workshop. They won't be back until Friday morning."

Casey followed his restless prowl, fascinated by his leashed tension. "Then we'll have to keep trying Deb's. Or wait until Friday."

Whirling at the dinette table, he reversed direction. "I have to have the negatives by Monday."

"That shouldn't be a problem," Casey said soothingly. "If Deb's busy working, she won't have time to send them on, either. So as long as we get a hold of her by say, Friday . . ."

Her voice trailed off when she realized he'd halted his pacing and stood staring at her. "What do you mean," he said, his expression growing thunderous, " 'send them on'?" And step by careful step, he drew closer.

# Chapter 3

Jeff felt like a damn yo-yo, and Casey Madison held the string. "Send them on to who?" he asked, moving dangerously closer to her.

Casey's wide eyes trained on him, their sweetness an ache inside him. "To my sister Liz."

Jeff dropped a wall of ice between himself and those beguiling eyes even as he neared her. "Why would Deb send them to Liz?"

Casey pressed back against the kitchen counter, her breasts lifting with the motion. "Because she's next in line."

His thighs brushing her knees, he halted. "Next in line for what?"

She caught her lower lip in her teeth, eyes angled up at his. "For reprints."

She continued to worry her lip as she kept her gaze on him. He wanted to replace her teeth with his own, to nibble gently at her tender lip, then move his mouth along her jaw line, to her ear, down her throat. . . .

He backed away a pace, folding his arms across his chest. "Explain." Then he added with bare courtesy, "Please."

She eyed him warily as the words began to tumble out. "Liz shot the pictures actually, but I said I'd get them printed, since Liz never has the time. Of course, I always forget, so it took me forever to take them in. Anyway, we'd agreed we'd send them round-robin to all the sisters so they could get their reprints made of the shots they wanted . . ."

Jeff passed a hand over his face. "Let me get this straight. After Deb's through with the pictures, she'll send them to Liz . . ."

"Right." Casey nodded. "In Phoenix. That's in Arizona," she supplied helpfully.

He zeroed his gaze on her. "I know where Phoenix is. And when Liz is done with them?"

"She'll ship them off to Shar." He shot her a questioning look, and she added, "At Mono Lake."

"Hey, only a hundred-fifty miles south of here." He laughed harshly. "I suppose I should be glad they're coming back in this direction. And after that? Any more sisters?"

"Not that I know of," she said. "Shar'll return them to me for safekeeping."

Jeff's gaze roamed her cluttered kitchen, passing over the piles of debris on the dinette table. "Safekeeping? I'm surprised you didn't lose them in the short time you had them."

She tipped her chin up. "I may look disorganized, but I know right where everything is."

He had his doubts about that. "You're sure Deb won't send the pictures off before Friday?"

"Positive," Casey told him. "Absolutely. I mean, Christmas cards don't mean everything, do they?"

"Christmas cards," he parroted, scrambling for her logic. "What do Christmas cards have to do with anything?"

"Just because she gets those out every year right on time —" She halted her flow of words, her expression thoughtful. "Okay, there's the birthday cards, too. And that loan Shar made her, I guess she paid that like clockwork, but she can't be efficient at everything, can she?"

Uneasiness settled in Jeff's belly. "Are you saying she might send the pictures out before Friday?"

Casey shrugged. "I know *I* wouldn't."

"But you damn well got mine out right away," Jeff growled at her.

"Only because Deb made up the envelope for me," she said. "She addressed it, put the postage on it."

Jeff closed his eyes. This Deb sounded as

diabolically efficient as Casey was not. He fixed his gaze on her again. "I can't take the chance."

"With what?"

"I need her address."

"Whose?"

"Deb's," he said, exasperated. "Your sister's."

She eyed him with mistrust. "Why?"

"I'm going down personally to get the negatives."

She looked mulishly stubborn for a moment, then a speculative light flashed in her eyes. "I can't do that."

The thought fleeted into his mind that if he strangled her, he'd never find Deb's address in the hodgepodge of Casey's little red book. He dragged in a breath, begging for patience. "Why not?"

She crossed her arms over her chest, a smile playing on her face. "I can't send a total stranger to my sister's house."

There was something suspicious about that smile. "I'm not exactly a total stranger."

Her honey-brown eyes widened with innocence. "But how well do I know you, really? You could be an ax murderer."

He gaped in astonishment. "You know damn well I'm not an ax murderer."

"Probably not." She tilted her head,

looking up at him sidelong. "But you can never be too sure."

Hands fisted, he looked down at the patchy avocado green carpet, at the wall with its crookedly hanging pictures, at the chipped light fixture on the ceiling. Then he fixed his gaze on Casey. "I am not an ax murderer, Casey Madison. You can trust me with your sister's address."

"I'm sure I could," she assured him.

The tension knotting the back of Jeff's neck eased when he realized she would be reasonable after all. He plucked a mostly blank scrap of paper from under an empty Orange Crush can. "Just write it here —"

"But to be on the safe side," she continued, "I'll be coming with you."

Jeff fumbled the pencil he'd been about to hold out to her and it clattered to the floor. "You're what?"

"Coming with you. Down to San Diego. That way I can be sure of your intentions."

"My intention," he enunciated slowly in an attempt to keep a lid on his temper, "is to get my negatives. I have no interest in your sister whatsoever."

"So you say," she said, wagging her index finger at him, "but this is my baby sister, Jeff. I have to protect her."

"But there's nothing to protect her from!"

he exploded. "I'm one of the good guys, Madison! I *catch* the bad guys!"

"Nevertheless," she said primly, arms linked across her chest again, "I'm going with you."

This was too much! This was more than a man could take. There was no possible way he would fly all the way to San Diego with Casey Madison. If he didn't kill her first he'd bed her, and that was a can of worms he had better sense than to open.

Jeff stared down at her, at the tumble of sleek honey-blonde hair, at her breasts framed by her slender arms and knew he had to do something to dissuade her. Without thinking, he cupped her shoulders with his hands, maybe to set her down on the stool to have a talk with her, maybe to shake some sense into her.

He realized his mistake with the first warm contact against his palms. Her flesh seared him as if the white cotton of her shirt weren't there, and the soft flexing muscles of her upper arm seemed to stroke his skin. Eyes fixed on his, her arms relaxed from their tight hold on her body.

He felt the weight of her hands against his chest and thought his heart would rocket across the room. "Casey," he whispered, a warning, a plea.

"Oh," she murmured, the soft exclamation curling inside him.

He moved his gaze down to her lips and studied them, traced their line, imagined their silky feel. Her lips parted and he wanted to explore the cleft with his tongue.

Arousal, hot and sharp, lanced through him. He shouldn't kiss her, he wouldn't — he lowered his head, moving closer. Her breathing quickened, matching the pace of his own, and he saw excitement, and what almost looked like terror in her eyes. He drew nearer, could nearly taste the honey of her mouth.

The phone rang, its shrilling biting into his ear. He stilled, flicking his eyes to the source of the sound, damning it to hell. When the phone jangled a second time, he ignored it, tipped his head to angle his mouth closer.

Dimly he heard Casey's answering machine click in, heard its message rattle out. He barely registered the snarling voice that cut in after the beep; he was too busy relishing the warmth of Casey's breath.

"Madison? Madison! If you're there, you damn well better pick up. This is Tommy, Madison —"

She jerked away from Jeff, stepped quickly around him to snatch up the phone.

"Tommy?" she gasped.

Jeff backed away, putting more distance between them. He was trembling, by God, was weak in the knees like a damn teenager.

"At home, Tommy," Casey said into the phone. "You called me here, remember?" She listened a moment, then said, "Something came up with Jeff."

Something damn well did, Jeff thought with grim humor. That particular part of his anatomy was still standing at attention.

Casey winced at something Tommy said and began worrying her lip. Irritated at listening to half a conversation, Jeff considered putting his ear close to hers so that he could hear. But that would just be asking for trouble.

"No, Tommy," Casey said placatingly, fingers threading into her hair. "Yes, Tommy. I'll make up the time, I promise."

Jeff's restless gaze fell on the speaker button on the phone, and he itched to activate the speaker. He had no real justification for hearing what Tommy, the worm, had to say. It was just Jeff's natural curiosity chewing at him.

Suddenly a dark flush rose in Casey's cheeks and her eyes flashed with anger. "What did you say?" she asked, her voice barely above a whisper.

Pushing past Casey, Jeff slapped the speaker button. "— quit rolling around in bed with Haley," Tommy's voice boomed on the speaker, "and get your ass back to work —"

In one motion, Jeff punched the speaker button again and grabbed the receiver from Casey. "This is Haley," he barked into the phone.

The silence at the other end of the line stretched for long seconds. When Tommy spoke again, he was full of bluster. "You tell Casey if she wants to keep her job —"

"She's working with me for the moment." Jeff glanced over at Casey. Anger had turned to mortification, and she wouldn't meet his gaze.

Tommy's voice turned mean. "I know what 'work' she's doing for you."

"Get your filthy mind out of the toilet," Jeff growled. He tried to ignore the fact that given another few minutes he and Casey would have been engaged in exactly the activity the lecherous pit boss had accused them of.

Tommy laughed. "I just wouldn't mind a little of that kind of action myself."

Rage bubbled inside Jeff at the thought of Tommy's crude hands on Casey. He wanted to pull the damn phone from the wall, wrap the cord around Tommy's throat. Jeff forced a calm he didn't feel into his tone. "Where's Godwin?"

"In his office."

"Put me through," Jeff demanded.

Tommy's bluster gave way to surliness. "He's busy."

Jeff's ire distilled down to one, dangerous word. "Now."

Even Tommy recognized the peril. He blurted out, "Just a minute," and clicked the phone on hold.

Casey glared at him. "I don't need you to defend me. I can handle Tommy."

Before he could respond, Henry Godwin came on the phone, claiming his attention. "Henry, I have a favor to ask."

"Calling in one of the hundred-odd I owe you, eh?" the Starlight's owner boomed.

"It's about Casey Madison," Jeff told him as the object of his discussion gave him dirty looks over her shoulder.

"The blackjack dealer," Godwin recalled immediately. "What about her?"

Jeff racked his brain for a plausible excuse for keeping Casey all afternoon, something that would absolve her of fault. Then he could leave her here and go to San Diego with a clear conscience.

But then Casey whirled back to him,

arms wrapped under her breasts, anxious honey-brown eyes on him. As she stepped closer, his thoughts started chasing one another, then froze, mid-synapse, when a drift of cinnamon reached his nose.

"I need to borrow her for a few days," his mouth said, to his utter shock. "To help me on a case."

"Something to do with the Starlight?" Concern filled Godwin's voice.

"Unrelated," Jeff assured him. Jeff caught sight of Casey's sweet, upturned face and had to battle a ripple of excitement running through him. "I have to take her to San Diego with me."

I can handle this, Casey told herself. Yes, he was a man, a gender she had a particular weakness for. And yes, she needed his protection for the moment. But surely she had enough willpower to spend time with Jeff without falling in love with him.

Of course, it would be easier if she didn't have to look at him. She passed her gaze over his tantalizing chest one more time, then turned toward her bedroom. "I'd better go change."

"I'll call the airlines," Jeff said. "This is going to be damned expensive flying on such short notice."

Just as she stepped inside her bedroom, the word "flying" caught at her ears and pulled her to a halt. She turned to face him. "Fly? Where?"

He stared at her as if she were crazy. "To San Diego."

The familiar fear clenched at her insides. "I can't fly."

He let the phone he'd picked up slide back into its cradle. "What?"

"I can't fly."

Pushing off from the kitchen counter, he shoved his hands into his pockets, head bent as if begging for patience. "Why not?"

"I can't." Panic crawled up her spine; she batted it away. "I won't get on an airplane."

She could see him struggle to understand. "You're afraid of flying?"

"No," she said slowly. "I just can't be on a plane. It's too small."

One brow arched in understanding. "You're claustrophobic?"

"I guess that's what it is." She shuddered. "It's pretty scary even thinking about it."

"Have you ever tried it?"

Something tightened in her chest at the memory. "Once. Reno to San Francisco. It was . . . very bad."

His gaze fixed on her, its darkness burning into her. "Yet you can ride in a car."

"A car's different." She tipped up her chin, feeling the need to explain. "I'm more in control. You can stop a car any time."

She could see the skepticism in the set of his face. *He was going to leave her behind.* He probably thought it was pretty ridiculous for a grown woman to let her fears control her. No doubt Jeff figured she could damn well get on a plane if she wanted to.

*If Jeff left her behind she'd have no one to protect her from Zucher.* A battle waged inside her, twin fears — confinement in an airplane or being left to Zucher's mercies.

Jeff dragged in a breath, as if to tamp down irritation. "Then we drive. Get your things together. We'll stop off at my place first, then we'll pick up my car at the dealer's."

At first she thought she hadn't heard him right, then her relief exploded in a grin. "Great. Sure. Just give me a minute."

She hurried to her bedroom before he could change his mind. She wriggled out of her black slacks and white dress shirt, then threw on a pair of soft, snug jeans and garnet v-neck sweater. She grabbed handfuls of panties and T-shirts from her dresser drawers, barely taking note of what she tossed into her gym bag. She snatched another pair of jeans from the closet, a handful of toiletries, her jacket and a two-week-old copy of the *Reno Gazette* she hadn't read yet. The zipper stuck twice before she managed to close it over the mess and race back out to Jeff.

He looked as if he were having second thoughts already. Casey breezed past him, gym bag slung over her left shoulder, purse suspended from her right. "Let's go," she said.

"The phone was busy at the dealer's," Jeff said, following her to the door.

Casey only listened with half an ear. What had she forgotten to do?

"But my car should be ready by the time —"

Casey jolted to a stop, whirling as she remembered one last chore. Her hands landed, flat-palmed against Jeff's chest. She looked up at him, at once thrilled and uneasy at their proximity.

Something hot and intensely sensual flared in his eyes. Her brain screamed warning signals.

She slipped past him, trembling all over. "One more quick phone call."

"I'll wait outside." His voice was tight with something that sounded like anger. She worried that he wouldn't wait, but would be gone when she'd finished her call.

But she couldn't leave before calling Pearl Whitemountain. She always let her Little Sister know when she had to cancel their weekly meeting.

Ten-year-old Pearl answered the phone on the first ring. "What time are you coming tonight?"

Casey chewed at her lip, hating to disappoint her. "I can't make it, sweetheart. I'm going away for a couple of days."

"But my soccer game!" Pearl protested. "You'll miss it!"

"I'll call tomorrow, sweetie," Casey told her. "You can tell me all about it then."

After assuring Pearl six times they'd meet next week as usual, Casey hung up and peeked out the front door. Jeff leaned against the stair rail, impatience in every line of his body.

He quirked an eyebrow at her. "How'd he take it?" he asked as she quickly locked the door.

She headed for the stairs. "Who?"

"Your boyfriend," he said, following behind her. "I assumed that's who you were calling."

"I don't have a boyfriend," she said as she descended.

He put out a hand to stop her, one step above her. "Why do I find that hard to believe?" He flicked a glance at her mouth, his expression briefly distracted.

His hot and cold attraction for her confused Casey, roused a jumble of hope and alarm within her.

"Believe it, Haley." She tipped up her chin. "Men are far more trouble than they're worth." Then she whirled and continued down the stairs, her heart pounding.

She took care to keep her distance while he struggled into her car, waiting until she was certain he'd settled himself. Tossing her purse and the gym bag into the back seat she slid into the red compact. The car rumbled to life crankily and only complained a little when she shoved it into first.

She risked a quick glance at him and fumbled second gear when she realized he was staring at her. "What?" she asked as the compact's gears screamed in outrage.

He covered her hand with his and popped the shift lever expertly into second. Before her breath could so much as catch at the warmth of his hand, he'd pulled it back.

His gaze hooded, he asked, "Will you be okay riding in my car all the way to San Diego?"

"Should be." She upshifted, keeping her attention on the road. "I might need to drive sometimes. Stop occasionally to stretch my legs."

Pulling onto Mayberry, she fitted the compact neatly between a Harley and a Buick. She waved her thanks to the Buick as its driver flashed its lights on and off and nearly kissed her back bumper.

Jeff sucked in a breath. "I don't think he intended to let you in."

"He should have." She caught the bare yellow end of the light at Keystone, and tagged along behind the Harley. She whipped over another lane, pleased that only one car honked at her.

She felt Jeff staring at her again. She spared him a quick look as she slowed to dodge a pedestrian. "What?"

His eyes narrowed. "Where are you going?"

Was this a trick question? "To your place."

"You know where I live?"

"Of course not. But I assume you do."

"I do." Waning patience edged his tone. "But you haven't asked me, and you're going the wrong way."

Heat rose in her cheeks and she tipped up her chin. "You should have told me."

"I'm telling you now."

"You should have told me earlier, before I came this far."

A strangled sound seemed to catch in Jeff's throat. She slanted him a wary look. "You shouldn't grind your teeth like that."

"Just turn around, Madison," he grated out, "and head back to McCarran."

She cut across another lane of traffic, then angled into the left turn lane and caught the green arrow before it changed. Her U-turn cleared the far curb with inches to spare.

Jeff's long sigh sifted into her ears. "What?" she asked as she goosed the accelerator.

"Did you see the sign?"

"What sign?"

"The 'No U-turn' sign."

"No. Where was it?"

"Where you made the U-turn."

The car came to a shuddering stop at the light and Casey turned to Jeff. "Do you want to get to your place or not?"

He made a sound, like a snarl of frustration, of explosive energy barely contained. One look at his tensing hands and she knew he wanted to grab her and shake her. The thrill trembling up her spine at thought of his hands on her raced neck and neck with her fear of the danger burning in his eyes.

"What?" she asked, this time the word a mere whisper.

His eyes grew impossibly darker, then dropped to her mouth. A thread seemed to grow taut between them. Despite herself, Casey leaned closer.

Abruptly he faced forward and hunkered down with his arms folded across his chest. "The light's green," he growled. "Drive."

She released a breath she hadn't even known she'd held and pulled into the intersection. As she drove, he barked out the turns, as if he wanted to minimize his conversation with her, as if he were angry at something she'd done.

"It isn't my fault I don't know where you live," she said in a low, tight voice.

"Left," he said, pointing to a small side street. "No, it isn't."

She slowed as they pulled into a residential area of ranch-style tract homes. "Then why are you mad at me?"

"I'm not angry," he said, his harsh tone making a lie of the words. "It's the blue one on the end there."

"You are," Casey stated.

"Pull in the driveway," he said as she reached the blue house. "I'm just irritated."

The car squeaked a little as she jounced up the driveway. "With me?"

"No," he snapped out. "Come on, I feel like a sardine in here."

Scrambling out, she stood back to give him room. Once he'd unfolded himself from the car, he retrieved his keys from his front pants pocket and strode to the neat white front door.

Casey followed him up the concrete walk. "Your grass is so green. How do you get such a green lawn in October?"

He slipped his key into the lock and jerked it to the right. "I water it."

She stayed close behind him as he went inside. "You're still irritated with me, aren't you?"

He rounded on her. "I'm not —" He cut off the shouted words. He seemed to tower over her, his broad chest millimeters from her. "I'm not irritated with you, Casey," he said in a more reasonable tone. "Just with the situation."

Yet she could see the tightness around his mouth when she gazed up at him, the narrowing of his eyes. Without considering why she did it, Casey raised her hand to his cheek and stroked it gently with her fingertips. She supposed she wanted to relax him, to soothe away the tension.

His hand shot up and his fingers closed around her wrist. "Don't."

Her tightly curled fingers dug into her palms. "I'm sorry."

He released her, his anger dissipated, a look of confusion in its place. He stepped back away from her. "I'd better pack." He turned on his heel and hurried from the room.

Casey trembled, although she wasn't sure why. She closed the front door, then turned to survey Jeff's home. She stepped down from the cream-colored tile entryway to the rich blue-gray carpet of the living room. A mission-style sofa and side chair with thick navy cushions dominated one side of the room. The pellet-burning stove and hi-tech stereo system filled the opposite wall.

No knickknacks, no artwork on the walls, not even a magazine on the mission-style coffee table. Vacuum cleaner tracks marked the carpet and lemon furniture polish scented the air. Even the glimpse of the kitchen Casey could see revealed gleaming countertops and an immaculate floor.

What would his bedroom look like? Would she be able to spot just a bit of muss, something to show the man actually lived here? An open book on his bedside table, maybe, or a dab of toothpaste on his bathroom sink.

Sinking onto the sofa, she snuggled into the surprisingly soft cushions. Feet propped on the coffee table, she tried to imagine his bed. Hospital corners, no doubt, and his bedspread a precise two inches from the floor on each side. White sheets and a pale blue chenille spread, she decided.

"Madison, get your feet off my coffee table."

She plopped her feet to the floor. He'd changed into crisp blue jeans and a long-sleeve striped T-shirt pushed up to the elbows. A garment bag hung from one hand and a jacket from the other. The muscles in his arm flexed as he readjusted the garment bag.

Casey tore her gaze from the play of muscles. "What color are your sheets?"

Good Lord, what had made her say that? His eyes narrowed and she saw the hint of annoyance in his face. "Black. Why do you ask?"

She looked away from him, at the tidiness of his living room, at the stark, spare furnishings. Unbidden, the image of him waiting for her in a nest of tangled black sheets sprang to mind. She could see him leaning on one elbow, beckoning to her, his long, powerful legs stretching across the bed, his bare chest rippling as he reached for her.

"Never mind," she said as she hopped to her feet. She sidestepped the coffee table away from him, then headed for the door.

He watched her, not moving, as if still waiting for an explanation. She grabbed the front door knob, opened the door. "Let's go."

He only hesitated another moment before striding toward her to follow her to the car.

# Chapter 4

"Your car's not ready, Mr. Haley," the service writer said as he tossed a set of car keys at a mechanic.

Taking a tighter grip on his temper, Jeff glared down at the slight, balding man. "What do you mean, it's not ready?"

The service writer scribbled on his clipboard, then tucked his pen behind his ear. "It's still on the lift."

Casey Madison already had him tied up in knots, Jeff damn well didn't need this further aggravation. "They told me this morning it'd be ready by noon."

Throwing his clipboard on the counter with a clatter, the service writer grabbed another set of keys. "After the mechanics fixed the ignition switch, they discovered two of your fuel injectors were leaking."

"And they didn't repair them because . . ." Jeff prompted.

"Because we needed your authorization —"

"You have it," Jeff snapped. "Fix it. Now."

"— and because we don't have the injectors. We have to send to Sacramento for them," the man said as he trotted around a white mini-van and climbed inside.

Jeff pulled open the passenger side door. "When will you get them?"

"Monday, Tuesday at the latest," the service writer told him.

The van's engine roared to life. Jeff leaned into the vehicle to keep the service writer from pulling out. "Then I'll just drive it as is."

The man shook his head. "I wouldn't recommend it. You risk a fire if you drive it any distance."

"Would anyone else have the parts?"

"Not likely." The service writer shoved the van into gear. "They're striking back East. Half our parts are on backorder."

Jeff slammed shut the van's door in frustration and dragged in a lungful of gasoline scented air as the vehicle headed for the mechanics' bay. At least exhaust smelled nothing like cinnamon. Turning on his heel, he headed back to where Casey waited in her little red shoebox.

She sat sideways in the driver's seat, legs out the open car door, sneakered toes tapping a rhythm on the asphalt. When he got close enough to see past the door, he saw a tattered *Reno Gazette* resting in her lap.

He leaned against the roof of the compact. "We have to rent a car."

She tossed the newspaper into the back. "Why?"

"My car's not ready." The enticing shadow at the vee of her sweater drew his gaze; he forced himself to look away. "I have an account with one of the rental agencies at the airport —"

"You don't need to rent a car." She rose, crowding him, and he backed away. "We can drive down in mine."

Eyeing the ramshackle red compact, he laughed. "Drive six hundred miles in this?"

"She's slow, but she's steady." Casey patted the roof of the car. "And there's plenty of oil in the back seat."

Jeff watched her wipe the smudge of dirt from the palm of her hand on the seat of her jeans. How would it feel if he stroked her there, ran his hand along the curve of her bottom?

Then her words sank in. "Oil? In the back seat?"

"Just a half-case or so." Casey tucked her hands into her back pockets so that the garnet knit of her sweater hugged her breasts. "She burns a bit more oil than the average car."

Jeff stared at the white cans piled on the floor. "Where'd you manage to find oil in cans?"

"The flea market." She grinned. "It was super cheap."

Considering how old the oil probably was, it should have been free. "I appreciate the offer, but I'd prefer more reliable transportation."

"My car *is* reliable." She looked up at him, her lower lip thrust out slightly in a pout. Between that full lower lip and the breathtaking lines of her body in the vivid red sweater, Jeff's thinking processes fizzled into static. Then she leaned over the open car door, her breasts brushing against the window. His mental static spiked into lust.

Irritated at his out-of-control libido, he flapped an impatient hand at her to move aside. "Humor me. I'll feel a lot better in a rental."

She stepped back far enough to allow him to climb in, then dropped into the car beside him. Thank God she hadn't taken the key out of the ignition, or she'd be digging through her purse for it. But she didn't reach for the key, just sat with a wondering look on her face.

"Oh!" she said softly, then bent her head to peer through the steering wheel at the dash.

"What?" he asked her. "Why aren't you starting the car?"

One finger on the odometer, she seemed to be counting under her breath. "I'm trying to find out if we need gas."

He stared at her as she continued her near-silent counting. "Why don't you just look at the gas gauge?"

"Be quiet," she scolded, "or you'll make me lose count."

He looked where her finger pointed at the odometer. "Of what?"

"I told you," she said crossly, "I'm trying to figure out if we need gas."

He grabbed her arm and pulled it away from the dash. "Please explain to me what the odometer has to do with whether you need gas."

She sighed with impatience. "I have to calculate the number of miles I've traveled since I last got gas."

His palm heated against the soft skin of her inner wrist, the warmth tempting him to stroke its silkiness. He snatched his hand back, tried to shake her heat from his palm. "Why don't you just look at the gas gauge?"

Honey-brown eyes wide, she gazed at him a moment before returning to her scrutiny of the odometer. "It's broken." She took up her count again. "I wish I could remember if those last four digits were six-four-one-two or four-six-one-two . . ."

"You mean you get gas based on the number of miles you've driven?"

She threw him an annoyed glance, as if he were being terribly dense. "I know what my gas mileage is. Depending on what kind of driving I'm doing, a tank of gas takes me between two hundred and three hundred miles —"

"That's a difference of a hundred miles!"

"— so I just subtract my previous odometer reading from the current one to see if it's time to get gas."

"And I suppose you never run out of gas."

"Haven't yet. Except sometimes I don't remember my last odometer reading." She snagged her lower lip with her teeth. "Like now."

Jeff rubbed at the tension building between his eyes. "You don't write down the reading."

"Well, I would," she said as she worried her lower lip, "except if I did, I'd probably —"

"Lose it," he finished for her. "Look, we're only going to the airport. Even if you're low, surely you have enough gas to get that far."

"Oh, I'm sure I do." She smiled at him, revealing that one little out of place tooth that teased his imagination.

He blotted out the image. "Then let's get going. You can fill up with gas while I get the rental."

"Well," she said, hands restless in her lap, "well, that would be a good idea, except . . ."

What now? Jeff thought. "Except?"

"I think my battery's gone dead," she said in a rush. "I tried to start her a few minutes ago, when you were checking on your car, because I wanted to move her, you see, out of the way, and park her on the other side." She took a breath. "But when I turned the key, the car just made a noise, kind of an uh-uh-uh, then a click-click-click, then she didn't make any noise at . . ."

Her voice trailed off under the weight of his glare. Jeff considered shaking her to release some of the pent-up frustration she kept generating in him, but he knew it wouldn't help matters. If he touched her, he might not let go.

Instead he growled, "Why didn't you tell me before I got in the damn car?"

She tipped her chin up, her expression prim. "You didn't ask."

His exasperation mounted into the danger zone. He would have liked to storm out of the car at that point, but of course his only way out was through the window or over

Casey. The window was too damn tight a fit. And if he slipped across Casey's lap it would be his jeans that would be too tight.

"Get up and let me out, please, Casey," he said with a self-control that amazed even him.

She didn't argue, leaping out to comply. Stepping back, she gave him plenty of room. But between his rising temper and the temptation of her slender body, Jeff felt as though he'd burst by the time he got out of the car.

Jeff tracked down the service writer, who obligingly scared up a battery tester, which revealed that the battery had indeed expired. The parts department located a replacement that only cost twice as much as it would have at an auto supply store and one of the mechanics lent Jeff the tools to install it himself.

New battery in place, the red shoebox started up without a hitch. They'd nearly pulled out of the dealership before Jeff remembered his cell phone in the trunk of his car, then wasted another five minutes waiting for one of the mechanics to lower the gray sedan from the lift.

When they finally pulled up at the car rental, the time had stretched past three. "Hell," Jeff muttered as he pried himself from the compact.

Casey dove into the back seat for the canvas duffel bag she called a purse, her rear an appealing sight. "What's the matter?" she asked as she emerged, hair mussed, tempting him to smooth it back.

Jeff slammed the car door, needing something to distract him from her soft silky hair. "It's damn late. We have at least ten hours of driving ahead of us. We'll have to go all night to get to San Diego by morning."

Wriggling a little, she resettled her bag on her shoulder. "Can you do that? Go all night?"

Jeff narrowed his gaze on her sweet, innocent-seeming face. "Is that an invitation?"

Color rose in her cheeks and Jeff had the sudden, startling realization she hadn't a clue how suggestive her question had been. "I meant — I just — I didn't —" She shut her mouth, hurried past him into the rental car lobby.

As he watched her go, Jeff couldn't hold back a smile. Maddening as Casey was, she was damned fun to rile.

Jeff followed her inside, saw her staring intently at the soda machine off in the corner, no doubt doing her best to ignore him. An irate man in a rumpled business suit stood before the sole clerk behind the counter, jawing away. The clerk, a young woman who acknowledged Jeff with a smile, listened patiently to the businessman's complaints.

As Jeff stood waiting, Casey started digging in her bottomless canvas bag. After close to a minute of excavation, she pulled her arm back out, a look of disappointment on her face.

"This could take a while," Jeff called out to her. "Go gas up your car. I'll meet you at your apartment."

"At my apartment?"

"You'll need to leave your car somewhere."

"Oh. Right." She shoved up the sleeves of her red sweater. "So you think I shouldn't worry about the break-ins?"

Jeff stepped up to the counter as the florid-faced businessman finally stalked off. "What break-ins?"

She did that little wriggle thing again to reposition her bag on her shoulder. "Someone's been smashing car windows in my neighborhood. Stealing radios, CDs."

Jeff tossed his credit card at the clerk. "Then we need some place safer."

"How about the Starlight?" She wandered toward him, arms crossed over her middle. The sweater's vee gapped slightly. When he caught himself trying to look down her sweater, he realized it was going to be a damned long trip.

"Fine." He turned away from her. "The Starlight. See you there."

Even after she left, a hint of cinnamon drifted in the air. It seemed to follow him to the four-door gray sedan in the rental lot, curling around him as he drove to the exit. Just before he pulled out, he remembered Casey standing before the soda machine. Damned if he didn't detour to the lobby and park outside. He wanted a soda anyway, he told himself. He hadn't stopped just for her.

He didn't believe a word of it.

He spotted her outside the front entrance to the Starlight, her gym bag beside her, her shoulders taut with tension. When he pulled up, she took a step back, a look of fear on her face. Then she smiled with relief and tossed her bag and purse in the back of the car.

"Mind if I drive?" she asked before shutting the back door.

"Damn right I do. You're a maniac behind the wheel."

She gave him an offended look. "I've never had an accident."

"Yet."

She stared at him a long moment, before her self-righteousness faded. "Please? I'm more comfortable driving than riding." She shrugged. "That claustrophobia thing."

Hell, how could he say no? Juggling the soda cans, he climbed from the car, passed her in front of the hood. Once they'd settled inside again, he held out the can of Orange Crush.

A smile of pleasure lit her face. "Thanks." She popped open the top and saluted him with the can. "You remembered."

It hit him then. When they'd worked together, all those months ago, mapping out strategies to catch the card cheater, she always drank Orange Crush. She'd even cajoled him into buying one for her one night when she was trapped at the blackjack table.

And he'd remembered. Without even thinking about it, he'd remembered.

She flashed him another smile, then took a long drink before setting the soda into the cup holder between them. His eyes fixed on that bright orange can, the image of her smile teasing at his heart.

As Casey turned onto Virginia Street, Jeff realized he could drive straight to hell and it wouldn't save him. Because she was already under his skin and burrowing deeper all the time. His only hope was finishing this misbegotten exercise quickly so he could get as far away from Casey Madison as humanly possible.

Casey turned away from the clamor of Virginia Street, heading for Interstate 80. As they waited at a stoplight, she took another long drink, the motion of her slender throat as she swallowed transfixing Jeff.

He turned away from her with an effort and reclined his seat a notch. "I'm going to try to catch a little shuteye. Let me know when you need a break."

"Sure," she said.

The softly spoken word worked its way inside him. He closed his eyes against it, resolutely shutting her out. But Casey, all unknowing, wouldn't let him be.

"Jeff?"

"Yeah?" he said gruffly.

"Thank you."

The genuine gratitude in her voice forced his eyes open. "For what? The soda?"

She looked confused a moment, glancing down at the can beside her. "No," she said at first, then followed her denial with a hasty, "yes. Thanks again for the soda."

Not what she'd intended to say, he was certain of it. But that vulnerable expression on her face threatened the barricades he'd built around his emotions, and if he was smart, he wouldn't pursue it.

He closed his eyes again and leaned back in his seat. "You're welcome."

As they pulled onto Interstate 80 and the car settled into the steady thrum of the highway, Jeff reminded himself that he'd damned well better be careful. If he wasn't, this infuriating woman — damn her sweetness — was quite capable of battering past his defenses. And if she made it past those barriers, there'd be nothing to keep her from his heart, and the well-guarded secret that he had nothing there to give.

They'd just passed Truckee when Casey first realized Zucher was following her again. She'd been admiring the vivid green of the pines and firs on either side of Interstate 80, marveling at the verdant contrast to the near desert-like conditions near Reno, when she caught a glimpse of the navy blue Ford S350 in her rear view mirror.

Lord, how had he managed to find her? When she'd left the Starlight this morning with Jeff, she'd been sure her evasive maneuvers had shaken the card cheater. Then she'd been all over town — surely she would have noticed Zucher on her tail.

Then it hit her — when they'd stopped for the light after leaving the Starlight, right before they'd pulled onto 80. On the periphery of her vision, she'd seen the blue pickup, but it hadn't registered at the time as *his* car.

God, he must have been at the casino the whole time. Could have grabbed her while she'd been waiting for Jeff.

She couldn't seem to take her eyes from the rear view mirror, the giant blue truck a menacing constant. Distracted, she turned into the highway's curve a little too tightly. The rattle of her tires striking the warning bumps snapped her attention back to the road.

Jeff roused from his nap. "Are you okay?"

"Fine," she said a little breathlessly.

"Are you tired?" he persisted. "Do you want me to drive?"

She shook her head. "It hasn't even been an hour. I can keep going."

Sitting up, he rolled his shoulders against the constraining seat belt and pulled the seat upright. "Where are we?"

Casey flicked a glance into the mirror again, wishing she could make the truck disappear. "Almost to Donner Summit."

Maybe they should have met at her apartment, break-ins or not. Then Zucher would never have known they'd switched to a rental car. She glanced over at Jeff. If she didn't figure out a way to shake Zucher, she'd have to tell Jeff the card cheater was following them. Not a pleasant prospect.

Jeff shifted, as if trying to shape the long lines of his body into the confining space. "Have you always been claustrophobic?"

*Maybe if you ignore it, the truck will go away.* "Sure," she said absently, attention back on the blue truck.

"Even when you were a kid?"

"What?" She tore her gaze from her mirror and her brain belatedly relayed Jeff's original question. "Yes, as long as I can remember."

"Was there something that caused it? When you were young maybe?"

"Not that I know of. I've just never liked being confined." Trying to take her mind off her pursuer, she slanted Jeff a quick look. "How about you? Any deep, dark secrets? Any personality quirks?"

"Yeah." He raised one brow arrogantly. "I don't like nosy questions."

She laughed, refusing to take offense at his stonewalling. "You never were one to reveal much. All those nights we worked together, you never told me a thing about your personal life."

"There's nothing to tell."

"There's always something." Was the Ford driving farther back now? Maybe it was someone else's blue pickup. "Have you

91

ever been married?"

He scowled at her. "Once."

"What happened?" she prodded. The Ford had definitely drifted back. It had to be someone else.

"We split."

She waited for him to add something further, but he just shifted his long legs and stared out the window. "Were you married long?"

"Too long." He leaned over and began to grope for something on the floor.

"What are you looking for?"

"Seat control. I need more leg room."

She pointed in the general direction of the floor at his feet. "Try that little doohickey there."

He bent to look between his legs. "Where?"

"There." When he still didn't find it, she reached down to show him.

"Wait!" he called out. "Let me!"

She kept her eyes just above the dash. "I can do it." She would have, too, if the road hadn't chosen that moment to turn left.

"Watch it!" he shouted, grabbing for the steering wheel. Which threw his shoulder into Casey's line-of-sight, blocking her only view of the road.

"Hey!" she yelled, finally sitting up

straight to reclaim the wheel. Dirt gritted under the tires as they edged along the sheer cliff face that towered above the right-hand side of the road.

Her sharp tug on the steering wheel overcompensated, and the gray sedan swerved into the left-hand lane. A sleek white sports car, gunning past them on the left, just cleared their front bumper as the sedan merged into the lane. The sports car roared on, oblivious to the near highway disaster.

"I need to pull over," Casey squeaked out. She eased into the first available turnout, high above Donner Lake. Once she pulled the hand brake, she let herself dissolve into a puddle of reaction.

Head down, eyes closed, she heard Jeff's voice rumble in her ear. "Are you okay?"

Gasping in a breath, she swivelled her head to see him leaning close to her. Her slowing heart picked up its rapid beat again, sending a different kind of lassitude into her limbs.

"Fine," she answered softly, then gasped in another breath. "You should have let me do it."

"Do it?" He looked confused. "Oh, the seat. But you were about to smear us on that hillside."

She slung an arm over the steering wheel for support. "It wasn't my fault the road turned left."

A ghost of a smile curved his lips. "I suppose not, but it is your responsibility to watch for things like that."

What would his mouth feel like along the pad of her thumb? She reached for her soda can, busying her itchy fingers in lifting it to her mouth. She drank down the last of the sticky sweetness and tossed the empty into the back.

"I'm ready to go now," she said.

He took his last swallow of soda, then neatly flattened his can. He placed it on the floor at his feet. "Do you want me to drive?"

"No, I'm fine."

He shifted in his seat, again trying to fit his long legs into the cramped space. The flex and pull of his muscles in the stiff blue denim captivated her. Obviously on its own wavelength, her hand reached out for just a taste of that fascinating length of deep blue.

Just in time, she re-routed her hand's trajectory. "Let me fix the seat," she said as if that had been her intention all along. Her left hand gripped the dash for support as her right hand reached for the seat adjustment.

Somehow his knee ended up nestled against her throat, his calf against the inside of her arm. It would take very little effort to wrap her arm around his legs, to press her face against the rough denim encasing them, to make her slow way up their length.

She grasped for the seat latch and missed, leaning with greater pressure into his legs. She heard the sharp intake of his breath, felt the tension in his legs as if he held them very still. She squeezed her eyes shut, wondering how she would ever keep herself from touching him, not in this accidental way, but intentionally, exploring him as she longed to do.

Then her fingers closed on the latch, and she tugged it to one side. As the seat moved back, she jolted backward with it and lost her grip on the dash. Only clutching at Jeff's lower legs kept her from sprawling on the floor.

She straightened hastily. "Found it."

Extending his legs into the newfound space, Jeff shifted in his seat as if not quite comfortable. "Still not roomy enough?" she asked him.

Then her eyes focused on the placket of his jeans and with sudden, breath-stealing insight, she understood his discomfort. Her gaze rose to his face and the heat in his dark eyes lanced straight down her spine to her very center.

She dragged her attention to the windshield. "Let's go," she gasped, then slapped the car into gear.

She guided the sedan back into the flow of traffic, gulping air. Maybe counting pine trees would work, she thought, or keeping a tally of the number of cars that passed them on the road.

When she passed the next big turnout, she barely noticed the big blue pickup waiting there. It was only when it pulled in behind her did she realize it was following her again.

# Chapter 5

By the time they'd passed Auburn and he'd run out of pine trees to count, Jeff realized that no amount of distraction would ease the torture of sharing this small space with Casey Madison. He'd thought the four-door sedan would be big enough for the two of them. But the memory of her body pressed against his legs while she groped for the seat latch still haunted him. As they'd descended from the mountains, the image would pop up at odd moments, its clarity sending a wave of sensation through him.

He'd given up readjusting his jeans each time his body reacted predictably to that taunting memory. He just bore the discomfort in silence, counting the trees alongside the road, or the number of breaths the woman beside him took.

They hit downtown Sacramento right at rush hour, their progress slowing to a crawl as too many cars tried to cram into too small a space on the freeway. Perversely, the traffic jam seemed to relax Casey; her fixation with her rear view mirror eased up and she stopped worrying her lower lip. The latter certainly relieved Jeff, since every time she nibbled on her lip, that one crooked tooth drew him, its smooth white surface tempting him to test its texture.

He slouched in his seat, covering his face with his hands. When did his imagination get so damned vivid? He scrubbed at his face and cast about for a distraction.

He sat up again. "Are you taking Highway 99 or Interstate 5?"

She squeaked into a gap between two cars, then turned to him as horns blared. "What do you think? Which is faster?"

"There aren't as many towns along Interstate 5, so there are fewer slowdowns."

"So I-5 is faster." Her gaze strayed to the rear view mirror again. Probably checking to see if the driver she'd cut off had pulled out a gun. One glance in the mirror and the tension returned to her face.

Jeff looked out through the scummy back window, just in time to see the driver behind them award him with a one-finger salute. Jeff turned back to Casey, puzzling over her anxiety. "I-5's probably a little faster, but 99 has more places to stop for gas or food."

"Mmm . . ." she responded, eyes looking left and right, as if for an escape. She gunned the engine, going for a minuscule opening between a semi and a Saturn, but before she could switch, the space closed up.

She slammed on her brakes, jerking to a stop as traffic came to a standstill. Jeff pried his fingers from the door handle as they started up again.

He leaned over, trying to see the gas gauge, but he couldn't without getting too close to her. "How are we doing on gas? Are we due for a fill . . . ?"

Without even looking, Casey shook her head. "Not yet. Let's try to get past all this traffic."

As she drove, all her concentration on the stop and go of cars, Jeff watched her. The creamy sweep of skin on her cheek was unblemished, and her honey-blonde hair fell in the tousled cap of a girl.

Why was it so damn easy to imagine the flesh along her cheekbones stained by passion, to see her eyes half-lidded by ecstasy? He'd never been with her that way, and yet he could so effortlessly conjure up the image of her beneath him, moving restlessly, wrapping her legs around him to pull him even closer, more tightly inside her —

He clenched his jaw, cutting off the too vivid picture. Yet on its heels followed another — Casey in the aftermath of love, her face soft and tender, her fingertips brushing his face. He could see the glow in her warm brown eyes, the light there only for him. . . .

Jeff squeezed his eyes shut, as if the image hung before him rather than in his mind. He damn well didn't want to examine the gentle warmth that suffused his heart. What the hell was he thinking? He'd better stick to erotic fantasies — they were a hell of a lot less dangerous.

The traffic eased somewhat as they cleared downtown Sacramento. Casey elbowed her car across three lanes of traffic to the Highway 99 exit. Jeff used the thrill of fear that Casey's driving gave him to dispel the last of his perilous fantasies.

"Can we make it to Manteca before stopping for gas?"

She settled into the slow lane, then checked the rear view mirror. A smile of satisfaction lit her face. "I guess so."

"Are you sure?" He angled his head, trying to see the odometer. "That's another sixty miles."

Another peek in the mirror, then she relaxed back against the seat. "Another sixty miles to where?"

"To Manteca." His exasperation mounted again. "Why is it half the time you're not listening to what I say?"

"I have a lot on my mind."

He laughed harshly. "You never struck me as much of a deep thinker."

She shot him a dark look. "There's a great deal you don't know about me, Jeff Haley. And you a private detective."

*I know you smell like cinnamon. That your hair shimmers like gold silk in the sun. That the curves of your body seem made to fit my hand.*

Aloud, he said, "I know you have three sisters."

"Which you just found out today. From me."

"That you deal blackjack."

She tilted her head toward him. "That's a no-brainer."

"That you've never been married."

She hesitated, just a breath. "That's true. I never have."

He damn well didn't like it when people pried into his personal life, so he didn't know what possessed him to ask, "Why not?"

She busied herself with veering around a car that was moving slower than her own. It struck him that her wild driving seemed almost self-defense against nerves.

When she finally spoke, he nearly didn't hear her over the drone of the engine. "Lousy judgment."

Despite his own good sense, he leaned closer to her to hear. "What do you mean?"

She sat up straighter, chin lifted. "I have lousy judgment when it comes to men."

"How so?"

She hesitated, flicking him a quick glance. "I only fall in love with rats."

"Rats?" he echoed.

"Bums. Cads. Bounders." Her humor seemed forced. "They all start out as perfectly charming princes, then turn into perfectly nasty frogs."

His gaze narrowed on her in the dimming light. "Just how nasty are we talking here? Abusive?" Outrage filled him that there were men out there that might have hit her, hurt her.

"Nothing like that," she assured him as she whipped back into the right lane, nearly clipping an aging Econoline. She hunched her shoulders against the obligatory horn honk. "Just your garden variety good-for-nothing males."

He cocked a brow at her. "You say that as if you place all men into that class."

"No, not really." She sighed, her gaze fixed out the windshield, on the slow crawl of traffic. "It's just that all the good ones . . ." She flicked him a glance and there it was again, that yearning.

"What, Casey?" he asked softly.

Brakes squealed, pulling Casey's focus back on her driving. She slammed on her brake pedal, and the sedan stopped a hair's breadth away from the car in front of them.

"So how about you?" she asked, a brisk changing-the-subject tone in her voice. "You were married once?"

He despised discussing his ex-wife, would have rather chewed railroad ties. He ought to tell Casey to mind her own business. But that would probably just encourage her to prod more deeply.

"She was the ex-wife-from-hell," he said succinctly, then cast about for a graceful way to terminate the conversation. "Should we have dinner in Manteca?"

"If you like," she said, then zeroed in on his unlamented marriage. "How long were you married?"

He sighed, surrendering to the inevitable. "Two years, six months and some number of days."

"No kids?"

"No, thank God." Jeff nudged aside his soda can with his foot. "Lily didn't want to ruin her figure."

Casey shook her head. "I wouldn't care if I got big as a house, as long as I could have kids. Lots of kids . . ."

Something tightened in his chest at the dreamy look in her eyes. He'd never wanted children, had been secretly relieved when Lily refused to bear him a son or daughter. But Casey Madison seemed to open a whole new window for him, a window of possibilities.

A voice seemed to whisper through that window — this is what it could be like, this is the secret the rest of the world knows. She turned to smile at him and he felt a growing softness start within him.

Then her gaze drifted to the rear view mirror and the dreamy look vanished. "Oh, damn," she moaned.

He clamped a lid on his wayward emotions. "What?"

"Nothing." She swerved into the next lane, squeaking behind a gold Lexus. "Nothing at all."

"It's damn well not nothing." Jeff turned in his seat, gaze sweeping the growing dark around them. Traffic had lightened, leaving space between their car and the ones around it. "Tell me what's wrong."

She worried her lower lip, fingers tight on the steering wheel. Another look in the rear view mirror. "Oh, Jeff," she said apologetically.

He didn't like the sound of that. "Casey,"

he said sternly. "What — ?"

Before he could squeeze more than the one word out, a truck dropped in behind them, headlights glaring into the rear window. The truck's engine roared, as if the driver were gunning it to catch up. The headlights grew nearer, ten feet away, five feet, now nearly kissing the bumper.

"Who the hell is that?" Jeff squinted into the brightness.

"Phil Zucher," Casey moaned.

"The card cheater?" Jeff tried to see out the rear window. He could just make out the lines of a monster truck. "What the hell's he doing?"

Casey cried out at the first scrape of metal against metal. "Following me," she gasped.

The car lurched as the vehicle behind pushed it. "What's he doing out of prison?"

"They only gave him six months in honor camp." She flicked him a glance. "You didn't know?"

"I didn't attend the sentencing hearing."

"He showed up at the Starlight this —" The words attenuated into a scream as the sedan shuddered with the impact from the pickup. "Oh God, Jeff, what do I do?"

Jeff swore, damning the fact that he wasn't behind the wheel. "Can't you go any faster?"

The lines of her body tightened as she

stomped on the accelerator. The sedan's speed increased infinitesimally. "This is as fast as I can go in this traffic."

Jeff craned his neck to see their pursuer; he clung like a tick to their bumper. "Watch for an opening to your left. When I say go, veer into the next lane."

"Okay," Casey said softly, a wealth of trust in the one word.

Jeff sensed the touch of the other car, the vibration in the sedan each time the pickup crowded closer. He could also feel the occasional loss of contact when the pickup backed away slightly.

He had to encourage Zucher to ease off that fraction of an inch. "Tap your brakes."

Casey turned to him, face white. "What?"

"Tap your brakes, then be ready to gun it into the next lane."

She swallowed and nodded, fingers locking around the steering wheel. She didn't move for a moment, as if gathering courage. One last look at him, then he felt the hesitation of Casey's foot on the brake.

In the instant after Casey slowed, Zucher reacted, backing off from the bumper. "Floor it! Now!"

Casey acted before he'd finished the command, juicing the accelerator at the same time she jerked the steering wheel to the left. But as dull-witted as Zucher was, his reaction time was sharp enough. He zipped in behind them again before Jeff could as much as take a breath.

"What now?" Casey gasped out as the pickup's headlights flared inside the sedan.

"I suppose going faster is out of the question."

"Any faster and I'll ram that VW in front of us." She threw a quick look his way. "Don't you have a gun or something?"

"I don't use a gun." He faced her, shading his eyes against the headlights' glare. "What would you have me do? Blast out the back window?"

"God, I don't know," she moaned. "Fire a warning shot or something."

"And risk killing someone else on the freeway?"

The bang of bumper against bumper cut off whatever she might have said in response. "Turn the wheel!" Jeff shouted. "Side to side, try to shake him off!"

She did as he told her, giving the wheel short sharp jerks that brought the car rattling over the warning bumps on either side of the lane. The ploy worked, Zucher braked, backing away.

"Change lanes," Jeff ordered, "to the right!"

She veered into the next lane and he knew from the engine's whine that Casey had floored it. Zucher moved up even with them, his face a mask of shadows.

"Oh my God!" Casey cried out, her car swerving as she stared at Zucher. "He's got a gun!"

"Hit the brakes!" Jeff shouted. He hadn't seen a weapon, but he damn well wasn't hanging around to find out. The momentum of the braking car jammed him forward against the seat belt. "Take the next exit!"

Casey whipped across the last lane of traffic to the exit. For once Jeff was glad she'd had so much training as a lousy driver. Zucher saw them pull off — Jeff saw the red of his tail lights when he braked — but the cheater had already passed the exit. It would take time for Zucher to make his way back to them, time Jeff planned to use to be long gone.

"Pull in there." He indicated a driveway into a darkened parking lot.

She slowed, but she didn't turn. "Shouldn't we keep going?"

"Damn right," he said, "but I'm taking over the driving."

She entered the parking lot, easing the car behind a thicket of oleander. She didn't climb from the car though, just sat rigid, fingers clenching the steering wheel.

"Casey," he said softly. She turned to him, eyes wide and shining with fear. "I can't drive unless you get out."

She swallowed, the sound audible over the rumble of the engine. "I know," she whispered.

But still she sat, and the urgency of their situation sent impatience shooting through Jeff. But he sensed how fragile she was right now, that she needed gentle handling. If he started barking orders at her, he'd have to pry her out of the car with a crow bar.

"Casey." He brought his hand up to her cheek, stroked her with the backs of his fingers. Her breath released in a sigh. "We're safe for the moment, but he'll find us as soon as he retraces our path." He curved his hand around the back of her neck, burying his fingers in her hair. "We have to go."

The warmth of her skin, the silk of her hair, the adrenaline rushing through him from their encounter with Zucher, all sent a shaft of arousal through Jeff so near pain he gasped in reaction. Time pressing on him all the while, he leaned toward Casey, turning her toward him as he did so. He closed his eyes, wanting to breathe in her scent, to dive into all the sensations of her.

He pressed his lips to hers. His heart stuttered, then pounded madly at just the satiny feel of her mouth against his. He pulled back, then tasted again, felt her soften with each brief contact. Her hands released the steering wheel and reached up to grip his shoulders. He could feel her body straining closer and it was all he could do to keep from dragging her across the car into his lap.

He backed away, letting go of her. "Get out," he said, the words harsher than he'd intended. "Please," he added, although he could see from the narrowing of her eyes that the courtesy came too late.

But she opened her door and slid out of the car. Jeff held himself still a moment, then wrenched the door open. She kept well away from him as he stepped from the car, waiting until he'd rounded the front before she slipped back inside.

Deep breaths of the chill night air didn't have much effect on his libido, but it seemed to calm his heart somewhat. He swung into the car beside her and used the slamming of the door to release some of his pent-up frustration.

But as he shoved the car into gear and pulled out of the parking lot, he knew his frustration would only get worse. Because all his fantasies, vivid though they'd been, would now torture him with an added touch of realism. Because he'd kissed her. And damn it all to hell, it'd been better than he could have possibly imagined.

Casey sensed Jeff's tension as a palpable thing, thickening the air between them. She knew he regretted kissing her, knew it without asking. She herself wished it hadn't happened, because now she couldn't think of anything else. Even Zucher had paled to insignificance.

She chanced a quick look at Jeff. His face could have been set in stone. "Where are we going?" she asked him.

"Over to Interstate 5." He turned to the left onto a dark street. Almost immediately, he turned right again. "Did you really see a gun?"

Scrubbing at her face with her hands, she tried to remember. "I thought I did. It was hard to tell in the dark."

They hit a dead end, the orange reflectors of a barrier glaring in the dark. Jeff swore, then backed out of the cul de sac. "Hand me my cell phone," he said when they'd gotten back on a through road. "It's in the glove box . . ."

She turned the phone on for him, then handed it over. From his no-nonsense conversation, Casey figured he'd called 911.

At one point he turned to her. "Did you happen to get his license plate number?"

She shook her head. "No plates. I think it was a new truck."

Jeff relayed the information to the 911 operator, then handed back the phone. She switched it off and returned it to the glove box.

"They'll do what they can," he said as they pulled onto the freeway. "Hard to track without a license plate."

He drummed a staccato on the steering wheel with his thumbs. "A gun doesn't seem to fit Zucher's personality," Jeff said thoughtfully. "But we'll have to assume he has one. I'd rather err on the side of caution." He glanced at her. "Tell me about Zucher."

"What do you want to know?"

"How long has he been after you?"

She tugged at the sleeves of her sweater, pulling them back down over her wrists. "I'm not sure. It was just calls at first. He'd leave these nasty messages on my answering machine, about how he was going to get me . . ." She sucked in a lungful of air, remembering the terror of the first call. "I thought he was still in jail . . . calling me from there. I didn't take him seriously."

"Did you report the calls to the police?"

She plucked Jeff's flattened can from the floor, turned it around and around in her hands. "I thought he'd lose interest and leave me alone after a while."

"But he didn't," Jeff said grimly.

She dropped the can into the back seat, leaned over to fidget with the glove box latch. "Actually, he stopped calling." Casey ran her fingers along the bumpy texture of the vinyl dash. "Then today, he showed up at the casino."

"Typical Zucher stupidity. They catch him anywhere near the Starlight and they'll slap him back into custody. Prison, not honor camp."

Casey propped her elbow on her knees, chin in hand. "Why is he after me, Jeff? Why not you? You're as much to blame for putting him away as me."

He cast a quick look at her, dark eyes blacker than the night outside. "Because you're a woman."

He said it as if it were a personal failing. "Meaning?" She encapsulated all her irritation in the word.

"Even a stupid man has an ego, Madison," he said. "And to have a woman point out his failure —"

"So it's my fault that Zucher's got it in

for me?" Outrage flooded her. "I should let him pound me because I caught him marking a deck?"

"No! Of course not." Jeff resumed his thumb-tapping on the wheel, agitation clear in the rap-rap-rap. "It's just that a man's ego . . . I mean, when a woman . . . Ah, hell." He gripped the wheel as if intent on morphing its shape. "You're a bad influence on me, Madison," he muttered.

Chin tipped up, she turned to face him. "Because I wound your fragile male ego?"

The heat in his dark gaze sent a cautionary thrill up her spine. "Because I can't think when I'm with you."

His profile might have been set in stone. A jumble of questions rolled through Casey's brain, foremost among them, *Why?*

She wasn't sure she wanted to know the answer. She returned her attention to the more pressing matter of Zucher. "What do we do if he does have a gun?"

"We call the police again."

"But he probably won't find us anyway, will he?" she asked, almost pleading. "I mean, we lost him, right?"

Jeff shrugged. "There's a hell of a lot of open road between here and San Diego. He could still catch up to us."

"Oh," she said, the sound whispery with fear.

His warm hand settled on her shoulder, squeezing gently. "Don't worry, Madison. I'll take care of you."

Now guilt swamped her, guilt that she'd brought danger to Jeff by insisting she go with him. She wished she could just make it all go away — Phil Zucher's pursuit, the chase for the negatives, her own dangerous, ill-fated attraction for a certain private investigator. In fact, while she was at it, she should wish she'd never met Jeff Haley, that her heart had never crossed paths with his.

A dull ache centered inside her at the thought. She shifted so that Jeff's hand fell from her shoulder. "Is it time to stop for gas?"

He checked the gas gauge. "Looks like it. We don't dare stop for dinner, but you can go grab something for us while I'm filling up."

She nodded, arms around her middle hugging away her anxiety. Jeff eased off the freeway and pulled into a well-lit gas station and mini-mart. He stopped at a pump, then reached down to pop the hood.

"I'm checking the oil, too." He climbed out, then leaned over to look at her. "Do you have money?"

"I'm not sure." She grabbed for her purse, started pawing through it. "I might have a few dollars."

He sighed, then came around to her side. He opened the door for her. "Here," he said as she climbed out. He held out a twenty.

She hesitated. "It doesn't seem right that you should pay."

"Take it," he growled, waving the bill at her. "It's my case, my negatives we're going after."

She plucked the twenty from his hand and headed into the mini-mart. Although she hadn't seen the blue pickup outside, she quickly scanned the room to be certain Zucher hadn't overtaken them.

Satisfied that he wasn't here, she strolled the food-crammed aisles, searching for something edible. She grabbed a couple boxes of crackers and a can of peanuts, then a Coke and a Crush from the refrigerator case. Dumping her booty on the front counter, she went back for some frozen burritos. She'd just finished microwaving the third one when Jeff came inside.

"Hold on to the twenty," he said. "I'm going to put it all on my card."

She stuffed Jeff's money into her jeans pocket, then followed him to the register. Juggling the hot burritos, she held them out to him. "Beef and chilies. I got you two."

He gave her a pained look. "I'm sure they'll be fine." He took the burritos from her, saving her from scorched fingers. He dumped them on the counter with the rest of their stash, then added a couple apples from the basket by the register.

Between the high-priced gas and the astronomic cost of their munchies, the total took Casey's breath away. Jeff accepted it stoically, tossing his credit card onto the counter without a word.

"Thank you," she said as she hurried to keep up with his long-legged pace.

He didn't even look at her, just made a bee-line for the car. "For what?"

She gestured with the redolent bag of burritos. "Dinner."

"Such as it is." He moved to her side of the car, opened the door for her while gripping the bag of goodies in his free arm. "Let's go."

In the car, she dropped the bag of burritos between her feet. She waited until he'd gotten in and started the engine. "Are you angry with me?"

"No," he snapped.

The tires squealed as he peeled rubber out of the service station. She waited until they'd reached top speed on I-5 again. "You're certainly acting angry."

His jaw was rigid, as if he clenched his teeth. "I'm not."

"I think I deserve to know if you're mad at me," she prodded.

She could swear she heard the sound of teeth grinding. "I'm just hungry, Casey." He held out his hand. "Give me one of those things."

Tearing the paper from one end of a warm burrito, she plopped it into his hand. He bit off a corner and gave it a cursory chew before he swallowed it.

Casey took a healthy bite of her burrito, chewing with gusto. "These are great. Just the right amount of grease."

"I just hope I can get it into my stomach without my tongue thinking about what it tastes like."

She made a face at him, then took another mouthful. "We could have gotten something else."

"I doubt there was anything much better." He ate the burrito down to the torn edge of the wrapper, then tried to remove the rest of the paper while keeping both hands on the wheel.

"Here," Casey said, taking the burrito from him and unwrapping it the rest of the way.

He finished the burrito in three bites, then

accepted the napkin Casey handed him with a nod.

"Do you want the other one?"

"I suppose. And the Coke."

As if to get it over with, he dispatched the second burrito more quickly than the first, then washed it down with a long swallow of Coke. Casey ate hers down to the last quarter the microwave had made shoe leather out of. She gathered all the trash into the bag and tossed it into the back.

She reached for the bag he'd placed on the back seat, her awkward position thrusting her breasts toward him. If she leaned toward him just a little, she could brush them against him . . .

"What are you doing?" he asked, his voice tight.

"Just getting the crackers." She snatched the bag and straightened. "Would you like some?"

He seemed to edge away from her. "No, thank you."

"An apple? Some peanuts?" She pulled out the can and shook it.

"Nothing, thank you."

"I can cut the apple up," she offered. "I have a Swiss army knife somewhere in my bag." She started to lean into the back again, going for her purse this time.

"No!" His hand shot out to stop her, then dropped just as quickly. "I don't want anything, just some peace and quiet. Can you manage that for five minutes?"

"Are you saying I talk too much?" she asked. He didn't say a word, just looked at her a silent moment. "Well, okay, I do chatter a bit, but only when I'm nervous."

His dark laugh quelled her prattle. Casey wrapped her arms around her and settled back in the seat. "I think I'll try to take a nap."

He muttered something that sounded suspiciously like, "Probably talks in her sleep."

"What was that?" she asked, tugging the sleeves of her sweater down for more warmth.

"Never mind." He looked at her huddling there. "Do you want my jacket?"

She tried to hold back a shiver. "There's one in my gym bag."

"No point digging through the bag for it." He groped in the back, his left hand steady on the wheel. "Just use mine."

He spread the satin baseball jacket over her, and a cozy warmth filled Casey. "Thank you," she murmured, already sleepy. His musky scent impregnated the jacket, so that she felt enfolded by him.

"You're welcome," he said.

For several long moments, she drifted in the twilight between awareness and sleep. The thrumming of the tires, Jeff's steady breathing wove themselves into snatches of dreams.

His softly spoken words seemed to surface from a great depth. "What am I going to do with you, Casey Madison?"

The tenderness in his voice plucked at her heart, roused her back toward wakefulness. She struggled to open her eyes. "What did you say?"

Silence, then he cleared his throat. "Nothing. Go back to sleep."

She did, but she carried him with her into her dreams.

# Chapter 6

If he thought a sleeping Casey was less hazardous than a wakeful one, he was sorely mistaken. Each sighing breath beckoned him, carrying the sweet scent of her warm body. As he drove, a series of fantasies played out in his mind of pulling over to the side of the road and dragging her into his arms.

He kept his hands firmly on the wheel, his foot pressed to the accelerator. With Zucher out there somewhere, Jeff couldn't let his libido place them in further peril. As long as there existed the possibility that Zucher was armed, Jeff had to assume that he was. And there was nothing more dangerous than a stupid man with a gun.

He stole another look at her curled up under his jacket. Her head had relaxed to one side and she leaned like a child against the seat belt strap. The shell of one delicate ear lay exposed where her hair had fallen away. Her lips had parted just slightly, and Jeff ached to taste the hidden depths of her mouth.

*What am I going to do with you, Casey Madison?*

He hadn't realized he'd said the words out loud until she'd spoken. He hadn't even known what he'd meant by them. They'd just seemed to spill out, pushed from his lips by an amorphous longing.

Probably heartburn from those gut-busting burritos.

Even without trying, the woman was disaster on wheels. True, his negatives had landed in her hands by mistake, but she was the one who sent them six hundred miles away. And by refusing to allow the authorities to deal with Zucher, she'd placed them both in danger.

And yet . . . he couldn't stand the thought of Zucher getting his hands on her. If she was in peril, he felt a hell of a lot better knowing she was with him than on her own.

Which meant what? That he was a man who still possessed a modicum of integrity, even if the sleaziness of his clientele and the slime he pursued daily threatened to drive it out of him. He had enough pride to not take advantage of Casey when she was so vulnerable to him.

Pride, hell. It was sheer willpower that kept his hands off her, and that was dwindling fast. Especially with the taste of her still on his lips, the softness of her still burning his skin, her scent still driving itself into his brain . . .

With a growl, Jeff slammed the door on the memory of kissing Casey. Attention fixed on the road ahead of him, he checked the sparse traffic that approached and passed. That was where he needed to channel all his energy — into driving safely while watching for Zucher, so they would make it to San Diego in one piece.

Then, once he'd picked up his negatives, once they'd returned to Reno, he'd take Casey Madison straight to the Reno PD. No arguments, no discussion. Then he could disappear from her life as he had six months ago. Resume his life sans Casey Madison.

Why did that sound so damned depressing?

Casey was still asleep when the engine cut out.

One moment they were sailing along at sixty-five miles per hour, the next, Jeff had no power. He pressed his foot to the floor, but the accelerator was no earthly use with the engine turned off.

"Damn!"

Jeff's oath woke Casey. He repeated the pungent curse, then muttered a string of them under his breath to mask the sweet sighing sounds she made while waking up.

She sat up straight, and Jeff's jacket slipped to her lap. "What's wrong? Why did you turn off the car?"

"I didn't." Jeff busied himself with the wheel as he pulled over to the side of the deserted highway. "The engine just cut out."

Quiet darkness surrounded them, broken occasionally by the zoom of a passing car. Casey rested her hands on the maroon satin of his jacket, fingers locked together. "Can you start it again?"

Jeff tried, turning the key and giving the car some gas. He could feel the engine turn over, feel it start to catch — then it died.

"Damn," Jeff breathed. "Damn, damn, damn."

Casey leaned toward him to peek at the gas gauge, the honey-brown silk of her hair perilously close to his arm. "You don't suppose we're out of gas?"

"It's been less than seventy miles since we fueled up. Would you back off a little, please." He could see his shortness had hurt her feelings, but in their current situation, he damn well didn't care. "Give me my jacket."

She handed it over to him. "Do you think you can fix it?"

As soon as he had the jacket in his hands, he realized his mistake. Her cinnamon scent had permeated the fabric so he could barely resist burying his face in the rich satin. God, it was like holding her.

"What?" she asked softly. "What is it?"

He looked up at her. She was only a heartbeat away from him, all warm womanly satin even more tantalizing than the soft fabric in his hands. It would be so easy to pull her closer, to press his lips to hers, to plunge his tongue into her mouth. He'd had the barest taste of her, had just an inkling of what she'd be like. . . .

Damn his adolescent daydreams. He shifted to relieve the pressure in his jeans and bent over his jacket, digging through the pockets. "I'm going to call the rental agency. Hand me the phone."

She pulled out the phone for him while he dug through the pockets of his jacket for the rental receipt. Switching on the dome light, he dialed the number on the receipt, then spent a frustrating two minutes listening to static before a live person finally answered. His brief conversation didn't exactly soothe his frustration.

He hung up the phone and resisted the urge to fling it out the window. "They wouldn't be able to get a replacement car out to us until tomorrow. They've authorized me to get it repaired." He scanned the empty farmland on either side. "I'll have to call a tow service."

She gave him a smug look. "I guess I shouldn't say I told you so."

"I told you so what?"

"We should have taken my car." She crossed her arms over her chest. "We never would have broken down."

He pressed the pre-programmed number for his auto club. "If we'd taken your car, we would have never made it out of Nevada."

"Would too." She stuck her tongue out at him and Jeff was caught between amusement and lust at the thought of what that tongue could do.

Then a woman's voice came on the line, barely audible through the fizz of static. Before he could as much as say hello, they'd slapped him on hold. Biting back another curse, he tucked the phone between his shoulder and his ear, then dug in his hip pocket for his wallet.

"Did they answer?" Casey asked.

"I'm on hold."

Casey looked around them. "Where are we?"

"In the middle of nowhere." Jeff passed a hand over his face. "Damn, they'll need to know where we are."

"Aren't we still on I-5?"

Jeff looked up the highway, then down, straining to see a landmark in the dark. "Yeah, but I have to give them some point of reference."

"We're south of Manteca," Casey offered. "Tell them that."

"There's over eighty miles of highway between here and Manteca," he said. "They'll probably want us to be more specific."

A semi roared past them, the wind of its passing making the car shudder. Its headlights picked out the reflectors on a sign in the distance.

"I see a sign," Jeff said, relieved at the reprieve. "You stay put, I'll go check where we are." He handed her the phone and his auto club card. "Keep them on the line when they come back."

A burst of cold air blew into the car when he opened the door. Despite his better judgment, he pulled on his jacket before shutting the door behind him. He tried not to enjoy Casey's warm fragrance in the jacket as he jogged toward the distant sign.

The blustery wind tugged at him as he trotted along the roadside gravel. The cold briskness coupled with the exercise cleared his head somewhat, although not enough to drive Casey from his mind.

He couldn't quite help himself; he pulled his jacket more tightly around him, savoring her essence that clung to the maroon satin. He couldn't recall ever fixating on a woman's scent like he did with Casey. He sure didn't like the implications of his obsession.

The highway sign was affixed to the concrete pillar of a freeway overpass. Another car obligingly lit the sign's reflectors as Jeff neared it, so that he could read "Fresno County" in neat white lettering against a green background. He spun on his heel and headed back to the car.

He'd made it half-way when he saw oncoming headlights approaching the sedan, then the vehicle they were attached to pulling over to the side. His heart blasted into overdrive as the vehicle stopped just behind Casey's bumper and a door swung open.

He didn't remember picking up speed, couldn't even recall the sensation of his feet punishing the ground. He just knew he had to get to Casey before Zucher did, had to find a way to put himself between her and the gun. . . .

She had her door open and was about to

rise from the car. Why hadn't she stayed put, or tried to run away? Now Zucher towered over her, his gun no doubt ready, unafraid to kill her on this dark, deserted highway.

Jeff took in the tableau in an instant — Casey's eyes lifted to his, hair whipping across her face, Zucher dwarfing her with his lean, lanky body. . . .

But Zucher wasn't lean or lanky, nor was he seventy-some years old like this man looked. And he didn't own a Jeep Cherokee with an elderly lady inside.

Jeff managed to slow to a trot so that he didn't overrun the gray sedan and the Jeep. He pretended he'd intended to run until his lungs exploded in his chest; might as well keep his idiocy to himself.

"Jeff Haley." He offered his hand to the older man. "How're you doing?"

"Bob Stendt." He enclosed Jeff's hand in his firm grasp. "We're fine, but it looks like you folks are having a bit of trouble."

Jeff dragged in another lungful of the icy air. "We've got the auto club on the line, they'll be sending someone out —"

"No we don't," Casey told him.

"Don't what?" Then he noticed she no longer held the phone to her ear. "What happened? Why aren't you listening?"

"I was just telling Mr. Stendt." She thrust the phone out toward him. "There was all this static, then it said, 'signal lost'."

Jeff took the phone from her and scowled down at the displayed message. "Damn." He pressed the recall button to bring back his previously dialed number, but the call still wouldn't go through.

"Not too many cell towers out here," Mr. Stendt told him. "Sometimes you can't get through at all."

Jeff bent over the phone again and re-dialed the number. No response. Another try. Still no connection. While Casey and Mr. Stendt chatted softly beside him, he entertained a fantasy of pitching the phone into the fields beside the road.

"Would you like to go sit in my car while you wait?" Mr. Stendt asked Casey.

Casey turned to Jeff, as if — a preposterous notion — she were asking permission. "Go ahead. I'll come get you when the call goes through."

Hugging herself against the cold, Casey smiled up at Mr. Stendt. "That would be great."

She headed off with Mr. Stendt, a relief, an agony. Following her slim body with his eyes, he saw the shiver she couldn't quite hold back.

"Casey!" he called out, "let me get your jacket."

He opened the sedan's back door, then dug through her bag for something that resembled a jacket. The only thing that qualified was a voluminous hodgepodge of vivid patchwork, dangling with ribbons and tiny gold bells.

"Thank you," she said, reaching for it.

The wind must have shaken something loose in his brain, because instead of handing it over, he held it out for her to put on. She slipped her slim arms into the sleeves, her movements sending a waft of cinnamon into the air.

She tossed a throaty "Thank you" at him over her shoulder that sent a thrill jetting up his spine. His fingers itched to free the thick strands of her hair caught by the jacket's high rolled collar, but he resisted. Let her tug them free.

As she continued to the Jeep, he turned away, focusing on the closing of the car door as if it were crucial to world peace and the continuance of mankind. Casey's sweet voice faded on the wind as she and Mr. Stendt walked to the Jeep and climbed inside.

Jeff turned to see her talking animatedly with the woman he presumed was Mrs. Stendt. He could see Casey clearly in the illumination provided by the Jeep's dome light, but he suspected he would be able to track her even in the dark. Not a comforting thought.

Five tries later, he connected with his auto club. Miraculously, he didn't lose the signal in the time it took for them to return from leaving him on "ignore." He managed to bark out his membership number and their location before static overcame the line again.

Assured that the tow service would be out sometime before the next millennium, Jeff headed for the Stendts' plush Cherokee. Mr. Stendt rolled down his window as he approached.

"They're on their way," Jeff told him. "You folks might as well take off."

"As long as you're sure," Mr. Stendt said.

"No point in us keeping you. Thanks for your help."

Casey said her good-byes and slid out of the Jeep. The Stendts pulled out with a wave as Casey and Jeff made their way back to their car.

"When will the tow truck driver be here?" Casey asked, her arm bumping his as they walked along.

"Something short of forever," Jeff muttered in response, trying to edge away from her.

He crossed to the passenger side just as she did and they collided softly, her jacket's thick padding like a bumper. He held her away from him, his fingers wrapped briefly around her slender arms before he continued to the passenger side.

Hands still burning with the contact, he opened the door for her. Somehow the bulky jacket dwarfing her diminutive form was as sexy as hell. It was too damn easy to imagine her snuggled inside it with nothing underneath.

He slammed the door shut behind her. Pretty soon he'd slam one of the car doors off its hinges, she had him so rattled. He dragged in deep breaths as he circled to the driver's side, preparing himself for the long wait beside her in close quarters.

Folding himself inside the car, he dithered over the light for a moment — on or off? On, she would be all too visible in her riotous jacket, off and they'd be sitting in the suggestive darkness.

Opting to turn the light off, he immediately regretted it as her scent seemed to place caressing hands on his face. Arms crossed over his chest, he stared down the ribbon of highway, thinking of the civil engineering required to build a road, the amount of water needed to grow broccoli — anything but the infuriating, tantalizing woman beside him.

"Jeff."

She intruded on his libido-tempering thoughts. "What?" He hoped by snapping the word out he'd dissuade her.

No such luck. With a rustle of cloth and the merest tinkling of bells, she turned toward him. "You know how long the Stendts have been married?"

Not the last question he might have expected, but close to it. "No," he said eloquently.

"Fifty-three years," she said, breezing right past his shortness with her. "And you know what else?"

"Hmm," he said, beginning to count the white lines dividing the highway lanes.

Still her sweet voice intruded. "They still make love twice a week."

That dragged his attention to her. "He told you that?" The old lech! And he'd let her sit in the car with the pervert!

"No." She laughed, an intoxicating sound in the darkness. "His wife did. She was quite proud of it, but it embarrassed the heck out of him."

Now I've gone and done it, he realized as he faced her. I've let her in.

He couldn't see much of her, just her soft edges lit by a moon that had finally decided to show its face. But that dim image, paired with the spice of cinnamon and the sighing sound of her breathing, sent his heart rocketing in his chest.

There was no damn choice in it — he had to touch her. He'd cup his hands on her shoulders, he decided, knowing he wouldn't feel much through the thick jacket. He wouldn't have to move his hands, and he could relieve the itching in his palms just with the briefest of contact.

It all sounded very logical until he'd done it. Once his hands curved around her slender shoulders, they took over, running along her arms, then back up, past her collarbone, to her throat. If he'd had sense, he would have never dipped his fingers into the bulky rolled collar, but he was beyond sense into sensation, and clear thought was a ridiculous notion.

She breathed in sharply when his hands, still slightly cool from the night, wrapped around the slender column of her neck. But she didn't jump or pull away from the chill, she leaned into him, across the center console. She seemed to yearn toward him like a young plant toward the sun.

Interleaving his fingers in her hair, he ran his fingertips along her sensitive scalp. She moaned, the sound shooting straight to his groin. Her hands spread across his chest under his jacket, then moved to nestle on his shoulders. That nearly broke the last of his control, and he ached to pull her mouth to his, feeling as if he'd die in the next moment if he didn't.

But damn it, he wasn't going to kiss her anymore. It was too hazardous to his emotional well-being, his mental health. He didn't have to fall prey to her warm and teasing touch on his shoulders, the tempting cinnamon scent of her.

He leaned closer and her soft brown eyes widened. He heard a little hitch in her breathing, a tantalizing invitation. She wanted to kiss him, he wanted to kiss her — what was the problem?

Lights washed over her face and he dimly heard the crunch of tires on gravel. He ignored the sound. Her welcoming hands on his shoulders started pushing at him. She was trying to communicate something, but he was enjoying the feel of her under his hands far too much to listen. Then she pushed harder, fingers tightening on his shoulders in an unmistakable wake-up call.

Pulling away abruptly, he settled back into his own seat. He rubbed at his eyes, feeling as if he'd been snatched from a dream.

She gestured out the windshield with a

shaking hand. "The tow driver is here."

The truck was parked directly in front of them. "Right. I better go talk to him."

"Yes," she said, her voice higher than normal. "You should."

He turned back to her, his gaze taking in her wide brown eyes, her soft, parted lips. Heaven waited for him just one breath away.

He groped for the door handle, fumbled it open. "Gotta go talk to the driver." He climbed from the car, the cold, punishing wind returning him to sanity.

# Chapter 7

Saved by the tow truck driver.

Casey drew a trembling finger across her lips as Jeff strode toward the pot-bellied driver climbing from his truck. Jeff hadn't kissed her — why could she feel the imprint of his mouth? Why was her heart still hammering a million miles an hour?

Because she'd wanted him to so badly. She'd craved a repeat of that all too brief kiss she'd experienced earlier. It might be perilous, it might be foolhardy, but she'd wanted his lips against hers so very much, she could taste it.

God, she wanted to taste *him*.

No man had a right to come in such a tempting package. Men like him shouldn't be allowed out of the house without a warning label — *Caution! Not recommended for the weak-willed and heartache-prone.*

Casey sighed as she watched Jeff and the driver walk back to her car. It always started this way. Aching for a man's kiss, dreaming of his touch. Then bang, giving her heart and soul to a toad.

But dam it, she was going to do things differently this time. Yes, she was attracted to Jeff. Yes, another kiss would be yummy. But that didn't mean she had to fall in love with the man!

With new determination, Casey pushed open the door and climbed out. She just missed stepping on the tow driver who lay prone half-way under the car. "Freddy" his shirt said, the name stitched in white on a red pocket patch. Jeff stood nearby, angling a flashlight under the car.

"Every one 'a these damn things is different," Freddy announced from under the car. "And so full 'a plastic, man cain't hook a tow chain nowhere."

He scooted out from under the car and ambled over to the other side, tugging up his pants over a generous belly. Once he'd squirmed under the rental car, he called to Jeff, "Toss me that chain there, mister."

Jeff bent to one knee and fumbled under the car for the chain. He muttered a curse under his breath, then handed Casey the flashlight. "Hold this."

He stretched out prone at her feet, one arm sweeping under the car. "Bring it lower," he told her. She crouched so that the light shone directly under the car, Jeff's head so close she could have stroked his close-cropped hair. What would it feel like? she wondered. Harsh against her hand, or smooth, like —

"Tip that light back up," Jeff barked out. Casey jerked the flashlight back up and scooted out of reach of Jeff's hair. A moment later she heard the dull clanking of metal as Freddy dragged the chain into place.

Jeff remained full-length on the gravel and dirt, following Freddy's instructions as they wrapped the chain firmly on the sedan's chassis. Then both men rose and slapped the dust off their clothes.

Casey returned the flashlight to Jeff, who handed it over to Freddy. She studied the arrangement of chains dubiously. "Is this how you're going to tow it?"

"Nah," Freddy told her as he headed for the cab of his truck. "Goin' to pull 'er right up on the bed."

He climbed inside the cab and a moment later, the back end of the truck bed tilted to ground level. Freddy returned to the back of the truck and fixed the chains to a pulley arrangement on the bed. He activated the pulleys and the gray sedan climbed the bed of the truck like the Queen Mary pulling into dock.

After Freddy leveled the truck bed again, he fussed a bit more with securing the car, waving off Jeff's offer to help. "Got to do this part myself," he muttered as he checked all the linkages again.

"Done," Freddy finally called out. "Climb in."

Casey realized he meant the cab of the truck and the first tingling of alarm coursed up her spine. She followed Jeff around the back of the truck, then hung back when he gestured her inside before him.

"I'd rather sit by the window," she said.

He scrutinized her face. "Are you okay?"

"Yeah." She tried to laugh, but didn't quite pull it off. "Fine."

Jumping into the truck, he scooted close to Freddy to give her room. She was trembling now, despite her efforts to scold herself into calming down. *It's just the same as riding in the car,* she told herself. Yet when she swung the door shut, she had to close her eyes and drag in a deep breath.

"How far to the service station?" she asked, forcing an even tone.

"Fifteen miles to Willowood," Freddy told her as he pulled on the highway. "Won't take long."

*Twenty minutes, tops,* her logical side calculated. But another voice inside her screamed, *Twenty minutes that I can't move, twenty minutes trapped inside this truck.*

Without realizing it, she moaned. Jeff turned to her and asked softly, "What is it?"

"It's stupid." Her hands gripped the edge of the seat as the truck jounced along the highway.

"What?" he pressed, leaning closer. His nearness only kicked her panic into over-drive. "Tell me."

Of its own volition, her left hand grasped his. "I can't," was all she managed.

He squeezed her hand tightly in response, the contact a thread of comfort. "Can't what?"

"Can't ride in here." She tried to take a breath, but couldn't get enough air. "In the truck."

She glanced at him to gauge his response. He didn't seem impatient, only perplexed. "It's only another ten miles or so, don't you think you can —"

His reminder of the distance still to travel unwittingly turned up the magnitude of her irrational panic. She started panting, unable to fill her lungs with enough air.

"I've got to get out." She groped for the door handle. "I've got to get out, *now*."

Her fingers closed around the door latch and lifted it with a frantic jerk. She fumbled with the seat belt release, then tossed it aside when it gave way. She shifted so that her feet hung out the partly open door and watched the pavement blur beneath her.

In a dim, quiet part of her mind, she knew the truck was traveling too fast; if she jumped, she might die. But her claustrophobia drowned out reason, sent one message to her brain — get out, get out, get out, get out!

She nudged herself forward, urgency prodding her. But before she could move another inch, a powerful barrier snaked around her middle, holding her back. She tried to tug free, fingers scrabbling against Jeff's implacable grip, but her panic-induced strength was no match for the iron muscles in his arm.

"What's she doing?" Freddy yelled. "Close that door!"

"Pull over!" Jeff bellowed to the truck driver. "Pull over, now!"

She kept her eyes fixed on the asphalt under her feet, dizzy with the movement, until the pavement gave way to the dirt roadside. Jeff's arm remained like steel around her middle as the truck slowed and finally stopped. He let her go immediately when she pulled against him, let her slide down to stand, gasping, beside the truck.

"What's the matter with her?" Freddy called out over the rumble of the truck engine. "She crazy?"

"She's claustrophobic." Jeff stepped

down beside her. "She can't handle riding in the truck."

"It's so stupid," Casey said, feeling ashamed, "I feel so stupid."

"It's okay." His arms curved around her. "You're not stupid."

She leaned into his embrace, her heart slowing in the safety of his arms. "What are we going to do? How will we get to the service station?"

His fingers smoothed back her hair. "We'll think of something, sweetheart."

She rested her head against his chest, chagrined at the rapid thudding of his heart. She must have scared him to death.

"I'm sorry," she said.

"It's not your fault. We just have to figure out how to get to Willowood."

Hands resting on his chest, she felt its rise and fall. If only she could stay this way forever, secure, enfolded in Jeff's protection.

Freddy's voice intruded. "You kin ride up top in yer car."

Jeff pulled his arms away and stepped back from her. He looked up at the truck driver, who leaned over the seat toward them. "Is that safe?"

"Safe as ridin' up here," Freddy assured him.

Hands shoved in his jeans pockets, he

faced her. "Would that work? Would you feel better sitting up there?"

"I don't know." She rubbed her arms, feeling bereft without his touch. "It might be okay."

Passing a hand over his short-cropped hair, he stared out at the empty fields lining the roadside, then up at the rental car. He tucked his hands back in his pockets. "Would you feel better if I rode with you?"

Casey smiled in relief and joy. "Yes. That would be much better."

"Then let's get movin'." Freddy slid out of the passenger side. "Just step here, little lady." He pointed to a metal foothold just behind the cab.

She laughed, the weight of her panic dispersed. "This must be made for giants," she said, trying to lift her foot to the thigh-high step. She couldn't quite cock her leg high enough.

In the next moment, she felt hands close around her waist, and she knew immediately they weren't Freddy's. Jeff lifted her easily so that she didn't even have to use the step, but scrambled directly onto the bed. As she placed a hand on the car to steady herself, Jeff climbed up beside her.

"Which side do you want?" He stood close behind her.

"Driver side." She hesitated just a moment, absorbing his heat. "If you don't mind."

He moved to the passenger side. "Doesn't matter to me."

She climbed inside and shut the door. As the tow driver pulled out again, she had two realizations — one, that she was really quite comfortable here in the car and two, there was something blatantly intimate about riding up here out of sight of the casual observer.

The truck driver couldn't see them. The traffic was sparse enough that there were few passersby to even notice them. Only a trace of moonlight shone inside the car, silver against velvety black.

Casey laughed, the sound breathy. "It's very cozy in here."

Jeff grunted an answer, as if the tenderness he'd shown her a few moments ago had never happened. She glanced at him, and his brooding gaze ensnared her. There was no gentleness in his eyes, only a dark fire she didn't want to name . . .

A line grew taut between them, a connection that burned hotter by the minute. "Jeff," Casey murmured, not sure what she wanted to say, or if she even wanted to say anything at all. Still, he remained silent, as if a single word would drive him to do something he had no intention of doing.

She burned for him, ached for him. The rhythm of it pounded in her, a trembling excitement that seared past all her good intentions. And she had only to look into his face to know he felt the same for her. The power of it filled the car and pushed at them, prodded them.

"Jeff," she said again, knowing she had to do something, say something, to keep herself from that familiar peril. To keep her heart from doing something foolish. But if there was a magic word, she didn't know it. "Jeff," she whispered, a breath of sound.

She didn't even see him move; in the next heartbeat his mouth was on hers. His fingers locked behind her head, holding her against him while his tongue slipped inside her mouth, twisted and fought with hers. Her body sang with his touch, trembled with it.

If she had better sense, she would stop him now, before these powerful sensations took complete control of her. But she couldn't stop, not just yet, and with each moment of pleasure, she felt herself slipping further into the same heart-wrenching trap.

She drew back slightly, tipping her head away from him. He seemed to take it as an invitation to nuzzle her neck and his lips along her throat was nearly her undoing. But then he pulled away, and set her back into her own seat, his hands only lingering on her arms a moment before he let go.

He sighed, slumping down in his seat. "I wasn't going to do that."

"A really bad idea," she agreed, although it had felt like anything but.

He shifted restlessly, stretching out his long legs, then drawing them up. "You're driving me crazy, Casey Madison."

She gazed up at him. "I don't mean to."

"You do it without thinking." He reached out, tucked a strand of her hair behind her ear. Then he snatched his hand back, glaring at it as if it had momentarily escaped his control.

"You make me pretty nutty, too," she admitted.

"We don't have to give in to this, you know." He leaned back against the passenger side door as if to place more distance between them. "We're adults, not a couple of randy teenagers."

"Adults. Right." Her gaze followed the rough angles of his face, the powerful column of his throat. Then she raised her eyes to his. "What are we being adult about?"

"Sex," he said. "The attraction between us. That's what this is all about."

"Sex," she repeated.

"Right. We can admit that we want each other, without falling into bed."

"Of course," she agreed, although she found his matter-of-fact assessment rather irritating. "Since it's only sex."

He met her gaze, dark eyes intent. "What else would it be?"

What else indeed? The only other possibilities were certain disaster.

"Nothing at all," she muttered, hunkering down in her seat.

She could still feel his gaze boring into her. "I'm not built for commitment, Casey. I've walked that road, and it gave me nothing but trouble."

She tipped up her chin, trying for a haughty look. "Who said anything about commitment?"

A long silence sent prickles up Casey's spine. "Then we're agreed," he said finally. "We admit there's something between us. We just don't act on it."

Casey craned her neck to peer up at him. What was that question in his voice? Did he hope she'd contradict him? That she'd suggest they throw caution to the wind and hop into the back seat together, have a little commitment-free fling?

Not a chance. That was the last thing she

wanted. At least when she wasn't gazing into those fathomless black eyes, their heat a searing invitation.

She snapped her head forward again and stared out the windshield. "We're agreed," she said, her breathy whisper giving the lie to her determination.

Sensing him watching her, Casey fixed her eyes on the growing brightness of the lights of Willowood before her. Willpower, that was all it took. Willpower and a cast-iron chastity belt.

How the hell was he going to keep his hands off her?

Jeff fisted those guilty hands in his lap as the tow truck pulled into the dim-lit service station. Casey sat silent and prim beside him, face turned away. He wanted nothing more than to stroke that stiff spine, have her melt back against him.

He didn't completely understand his weakness for this woman. She kept him on edge, in a constant state of confusion. She wasn't frail and needy like some women were nor hard and shrill like his ex-wife. But capturing Casey's essence was like trapping a soap bubble. Just when he thought he'd gotten his hands around the puzzle, he found himself holding nothing but air.

And leaving him craving more, Jeff acknowledged as Casey slipped out of the car. He watched her carefully step to the tow truck bed, a steadying hand on the car's hood. His arrogant declaration that they could be adults about this, that they didn't have to fall prey to their baser urges, sizzled to dust with each graceful move of Casey's body.

She waited for him to climb from the car, then turned to face the tall blond man in gray coveralls who came out to meet them. The man's wide grin was way too friendly as he reached up to help Casey down. She laughed when the blond beefsteak's hands closed around her waist and clutched his shoulders as he swung her down.

Feet on the ground, she tipped down the mechanic's nametag, so she could see. "Thank you, Dave." She slanted a smile up at him.

Jeff felt something bite into his palm and looked down to see he'd wrenched some chrome from the truck's roof line. Why the hell should he care about Casey's interest in that seething mass of testosterone? He had no hold on her.

Refusing Dave's offer of a hand down, Jeff jumped to the pavement. "I don't suppose you can get to this tonight."

"Afraid not." The mechanic planted his hands on his hips, threatening to burst the seams of his grease-stained coverall. "I just hung around to get your keys."

Jeff dug for them in his pocket. "The engine just cut out, no warning."

"Could be the fuel pump." Dave ran an appraising eye over the car. "I probably have one that'll fit. I'll check first thing in the morning."

Why was he standing so damn close to Casey? "Thanks. I appreciate it." Jeff moved between them as if he needed to point something out to Dave. Casey stepped away from him. "Rental agency will take care of the bill." He held out the receipt with the phone number.

"I'll take care of it." The mechanic tipped his head toward the glow of a motel sign just up the road. "I'll help Freddy get this inside if you want to go check in. Tell the manager I sent you. You'll get a bit of a break on the price."

Planting a hand at the small of Casey's back, Jeff nudged her in the direction of the motel. She waved at the mechanic over her shoulder. "Thanks, Dave!"

Jeff had to resist the urge to give her a shove. "Do you come on to every man you see?" he hissed in her ear.

"What?" she gasped.

"You were all over him."

"I was not!"

He grabbed her shoulder as they reached the street, waiting while a car passed. "And he didn't seem to be able to keep his hands off you."

She shrugged away from him, and crossed the street in the wake of the car. "He only helped me down from the truck."

Jeff caught up, wrapped his fingers around her upper arm. "He damn well could have helped you without fondling you in the process."

"Fondling —" She stopped in her tracks and whacked him with the back of her hand. "For crying out loud, Jeff, the man is married."

He rubbed at the spot on his chest where she'd hit him. "How do you know?"

"I saw his ring, for heaven's sake."

"Then you were making moves on a married man?"

Shrieking her frustration, she stomped off toward the motel. Jeff let the distance between them lengthen, counting silently to ten, then to twenty before he followed. She'd slipped inside the motel's office door by the time he caught up.

"Your wife tells me you had a breakdown," the stocky man behind the counter said.

"She's not my wife," Jeff snarled, slapping down a credit card. "Two rooms please."

"I'm sorry," Casey said sweetly to the man behind the counter. "He isn't always this rude. He's just a little testy because of the car problem."

The manager beamed at Casey. "I understand completely."

Jeff plucked the credit card slip from him and scribbled his signature. He swallowed back a growl as the manager gave the keys to Casey and his hand lingered over hers. Jeff gripped Casey's shoulder and urged her to the door.

Casey wrenched herself away from Jeff as soon as they'd left the office. "Must you shove me around?"

"Just trying to save the poor guy from your wiles. What's the room numbers?"

"Ninety-one and eighty-one," she read off the key tags. "The only thing he needed saving from was your rudeness."

"Thirty-three, thirty-four," he read off the doors as they reached the end of the bank of rooms. "Where the hell is ninety-one?"

She peered at the tags again. "Upstairs maybe?"

"The motel's only one story. Let me

see." Jeff took the keys from Casey. "You read them upside down. We have rooms sixteen and eighteen." Jeff turned on his heel and strode back the other way.

"Anyone could have made that mistake," Casey insisted, dogging his steps.

Anyone named Casey. He was relieved the rooms weren't as far apart as Casey's misread numbers had led him to believe. He was also glad they were at least one room apart. He didn't like the idea of their having adjacent rooms. . . .

They rounded a corner and headed down an open corridor that fed a blast of air through it like a wind tunnel. He read the numbers on the left, twenty-six, twenty-four, twenty-two . . . He realized their rooms must be next to each other after all.

She skipped ahead of him. "Here's eighteen," she said.

And sixteen right next to it. With a sigh, Jeff handed her a key. "You go on in, I'll go back to the station and get our luggage."

Jeff jogged across the street, telling himself he should at least be grateful there would be a wall between them. Her scent wouldn't tease him, the soft sound of her breathing wouldn't torture him.

He retrieved their luggage from the car, sent the impatient Dave home to his wife, then trotted back to the motel. "No problem," he muttered to himself. "I can handle this."

And he was sure he could. Until he let himself into his room and found Casey sitting at the foot of his bed.

"How did you get in here?"

Casey leaped to her feet, the booming sound of Jeff's voice setting her heart to pounding. "You scared me! Do you have to come barreling in here like that?"

"It *is* my room," Jeff said as he dumped their luggage on the bed. "Tell me how you got in here." He tossed her purse perilously close to the edge of the bed.

"Through the connecting doors. Hey!" Casey grabbed for her purse as it sagged onto its side, half the contents spilling onto the floor.

"Those doors are kept locked," he persisted, towering over her as she knelt to gather up her things. "How did you get through to my side?"

"It wasn't locked," she informed him. "I wondered where these gardening shears got to." She dropped them back into her purse.

"I don't want you over here," he said. He was grinding his teeth again, she could tell from the sound of his words.

She returned the last item to the canvas

bag's generous maw, then rose. "My TV doesn't work, so I came over to watch yours."

"Then we'll switch rooms," he said, grabbing up his bag. "You can have this one."

He strode off through the connecting doors, pulling hers shut before locking his own with a decisive click. Casey watched as her door creaked open into the same position she'd found it in when she'd come through from the other room. Then she dropped her purse on the nightstand, and climbed up onto the bed.

She could finally let go of the tumult of emotions she'd been holding so tightly inside. She sat Indian-style on the bumpy chenille spread, feeling the confusion of fear and joy and anger expand and grow until it filled her. It overflowed her edges until it seemed even the universe couldn't contain it.

Lord, she didn't know whether to laugh or cry. Her adult life had always been a tumble of disorganization, full of unexpected surprises and small tragedies. After a childhood of rigid expectations, drilled into her by a mother who wanted more for her daughters than she'd had herself, flightiness had been Casey's rebellion.

This weakness for the wrong men was part

and parcel of her childish defiance. After seeing the mistakes her mother had made, after the endless lectures to take another path, her foolish heart seemed ready to march her into disaster.

And oh, how Jeff made her ache to surrender to those budding feelings. Despite his admission he wanted nothing but sex from her, that commitment was obviously not on his agenda, her wishful thinking had her dreaming impossible dreams.

Rising from the bed, she cast off her T-shirt and wriggled out of her jeans. Flinging bra and panties to the floor, she headed for the bathroom, intent on showering away her doom and gloom.

As she stood under the warm spray, letting rivulets of water wash away the grime of the road, she lectured herself out of her doldrums. It was time to accept reality — with her track record, it was far too hazardous to fall in love. She was bound to end up with a rotter like Steve or Tom. Or a man like Jeff, who would enjoy her in bed, but rejected a lasting relationship.

Her dreams of a houseful of children were harder to give up, but maybe she should just shift her focus to being a favorite aunt. Surely, at least one of her sisters would marry some day and she could save all her mothering for their offspring.

That will be enough, she told herself as she shut off the shower and grabbed a towel. You'll love them as much as you would have your own. And you have Pearl, too, to love.

Yet as she rubbed the moisture from her body, then vigorously toweled her hair, her heart wasn't really in her new resolution. Her heart, she realized, as she slung the towel around her shoulders and finger-combed her hair, might take a little more convincing.

Her heart might have had a fighting chance if she hadn't marched out of the bathroom stark naked and come face to face with Jeff in her room.

Jeff had never moved so fast.

He banged his behind on the door frame, scraped his arm as he scrambled back through the opening, jammed his finger shutting the door. He flipped the lock as an afterthought, although he was the one who needed locking out, not her.

Hell, why hadn't her door been shut? He passed his hand over his face, trying to wipe away the image of her slender body, sweetly scented from her shower. Her waist was narrower than he might have imagined, the flare of her hips more enticing, the triangle of curls at the apex of her legs —

God, he wasn't going to think about that. Or the rosy tips of her small breasts, perfectly shaped for caressing, or the line of her legs, from calf to knee to thigh to —

Stop it! He walked away from the door pacing from one end of the small room to the other, tempted to put a fist through the wall, a lamp through the window, to tear the covers from the bed —

To take her there. God, he wanted to drive himself into her, to bring her to climax over and over again. . . .

A light tap on the connecting door dragged him from his turbulent thoughts. He strode to the door and rested his ear against it. "What?" he growled.

"Was there something you wanted?" she asked, her voice faint through the door.

He could hear her embarrassment and he felt like an ass for causing it, however inadvertently. He took a breath, trying to clear the laser-sharp memory from his head. "I was going out for some ice," he said through the door, feeling like an idiot, "did you want anything?"

She hesitated, and he couldn't help but wonder if she was still naked, standing nude two inches from him. He damn well wouldn't even consider that.

"No, thank you," she said finally, her voice

stronger. "I'm going to bed now."

Come to bed with me, a little voice clamored in his head. "Fine," he said aloud. "I'll see you in the morning."

He supposed she moved away from the door then, maybe even now she was slipping that silky, trim body of hers between the sheets. He pressed his head against the door frame, pushing until the pain of the wood biting into his forehead shielded him from thoughts of her.

Then he headed for the bathroom and turned the cold water on in the shower, as high as it would go.

# Chapter 8

"How were your eggs?" Casey asked cheerfully, as if she hadn't spent half the restless night awake and thinking of him.

Jeff managed a monosyllabic grunt as he took a swallow of thick, black coffee.

"My pancakes are delicious." She pushed her fork through the syrup-laden stack. "Would you like a bite?"

He raised his hooded gaze to her, fixing his eyes to hers, as if the morsel he wanted to savor was something quite different from pancakes, something very, very bad for him. A flush rose on Casey's cheeks under the weight of his stare, and she thought she might melt on the spot.

Then he tore his gaze away and shoved his empty plate back. Turning in the booth, he shifted his gaze to the busy coffee shop. "No, thank you."

No thank you for what? Oh yes, pancakes. Or was there something else he was refusing?

She shivered and tried to blink the dryness from her eyes, the consequence of a night with too little sleep. When he'd called her at eight a.m., the ringing phone had startled her out of the only deep sleep of the night. She'd just gotten to the good part of a very sexy dream, starring her rough-voiced alarm clock.

"Forty-five minutes," he'd barked, "outside."

As she'd tried to rub the daze from her eyes, she wondered if he'd just leave her if she took too long. Probably, after she'd paraded herself in front of him last night. She knew it hadn't been her fault he'd burst into the room like that, but somehow she thought he'd find a way to blame her.

And from all appearances during breakfast, he did. In fact, he'd expressed nothing but displeasure from the moment he'd laid disapproving eyes on her hot pink Albert Einstein T-shirt and purple baseball cap. From then on, his conversation had consisted of brief commands ordering her here and there until he'd maneuvered her into the coffee shop. Then he'd limited his vocabulary to those words necessary to ask the waitress for eggs and bacon, rye toast, please.

She'd started counting his parsimonious words. By the time she slipped away to call her Little Sister, Pearl, on the coffee shop

164

pay phone, he was up to twenty-two. Assuming he hadn't spoken while she and Pearl enthused over the ten-year-old's two goals in yesterday's soccer game, his tally was now twenty-five.

Determined to enjoy her pancakes, she dipped an already syrup-soaked forkful into the syrup pot until half of them fell off the fork. Then she busied herself with fishing them out of the drink.

He caught her when he'd turned to slurp up more coffee. "How can you eat all that sugar?"

Thirty-two words. She smiled up at him. "It keeps me sweet."

His look was frankly dubious. She stretched her smile until it became downright saccharine, until his own lips twitched as if he resisted the humor of it. Then she dipped her fork into the syrup pot and sucked the sweetness off the tines, only meaning to add to the joke.

But when the tip of her tongue crept out to lick the last of the maple flavor from her lips, his gaze darkened again. His lips parted, just slightly, and his eyes fixed on the motion of her tongue. Then he seemed to grow angry again, glaring at her before he turned away to survey the broad backs of the truckers sitting at the counter.

Casey sighed and cut another careful bite of pancake. As she chewed the sticky mouthful, she gazed out at the freeway towering above them, watching the traffic roar by on Interstate 5. If only she could wish herself into one of those cars, she mused, and fly far away from here. Away from Jeff and his bad influence on her heart, away from pursuing card cheaters . . .

Her eyes widened as they tracked the progress of one particular vehicle above them on the interstate. She swallowed the last of her pancake, now dust in her mouth. Her fork clattered to her plate.

"Oh," she managed in a strangled gasp.

Jeff whirled to face her. "What?" he snapped.

"Oh," she moaned, as the navy blue pickup slowed as it crossed over the freeway bridge.

He dropped his hand over hers and squeezed. *"What?"*

Casey lifted her free hand and pointed a wavering finger in the direction of Interstate 5. "He's back."

Jeff turned in the direction she indicated just as the blue monster truck picked up speed again. He scrambled out of his seat, slapped the coffee shop door open with an impatient hand and hurried out to the sidewalk. Casey watched his head swivel as he followed the progress of the truck, now out of her sight.

When her eyes dropped to her pancakes, she thought she might lose them all, right here on the table. They sat heavily in her stomach, anxiety agitating them like socks in a washing machine. She took a long drink of her water, gulping ice and all, the chill shocking her stomach into obedience.

Jeff was back, tossing a ten dollar bill on the table. "Let's go. With any luck he didn't see our car in the garage."

"He must have," she said as she slid out of the booth and followed him from the restaurant. "He slowed down."

"Then we'd better hurry," Jeff said, his hand on the small of her back, "before he gets to the next exit and turns around."

Casey's heart fell when they reached the service station and saw the gray sedan still up on the lift. "He's not finished."

Jeff strode into the garage. "I'll see what's keeping him."

Casey chased him like a puppy dog, too unnerved by the reappearance of Zucher to care. She met Dave's friendly grin with a weak smile.

Scowling at her, Jeff turned to Dave. "Why aren't you done?"

Dave's smile faded. "I had a hard time finding a fuel pump that fit. I don't keep too many in stock."

"How long before you're finished?"

"Just about done now," the mechanic said. "I was about to bring her down again."

"Do it," Jeff said, "now."

Striding out of the garage to scan the freeway again, Jeff left Casey to soothe Dave's irritation. "He's like that in the mornings before his coffee kicks in." She patted the mechanic's arm just as Jeff peered back inside the bay.

Dave returned Jeff's glare. Casey gave Dave a placating look, then moved to Jeff's side. She grasped his arm and tugged him away from the garage. "Must you be so rude?" she hissed.

Jerking his arm free, he glowered down at her. "Zucher's breathing down our necks, you'll have to excuse me if my manners aren't up to snuff."

"Dave's doing what he can to get the car finished."

"And he'd do it quicker if you weren't flirting with him!"

She gasped, stifling the urge to haul off and slug him. "I was *not* flirting, I was just being — Oh my God!"

Jeff turned to where she stared, stunned,

at the freeway. It was almost too far to see, but . . . "Is that a blue pickup?" she asked, hoping she didn't really see Zucher's truck coming back their way on the interstate.

"Damn!" Jeff said, then added a few, even more pungent comments. "Dave!" he roared, striding back toward the garage.

"He's pulling off the freeway," Casey called out to Jeff. "He's coming down the exit."

Dave backed the sedan from the garage bay and pulled up beside her. She reached for the driver's side door. "I'm driving," Jeff said, putting out a hand to stop her. "Get in. I need to sign the work order."

She circled to the passenger side, still reluctant to give up the hope that Zucher had disappeared. She sneaked a peek at the access road alongside the service station and nearly sank to the pavement in despair.

"He's coming," she whispered, then she shrieked, "he's coming!"

Time suddenly jumped a track, altering its speed so that everything moved in slow motion. Jeff ran from the garage, but she could see every footfall raise and lower in excruciating detail. When she still stood staring at the blue pickup drawing ever nearer, even his shouted words, "Get in, damn it!" seemed drawn out, until she could hear only sounds and couldn't make sense of the words.

She felt the door thwack her on the thighs, and she realized Jeff had opened the door from inside. "Casey!" he shouted. "Get in!"

The sound of his voice finally broke her from her terror and she leapt into the car, slamming the door behind her. Jeff jammed the sedan into reverse, gunned the engine — and the car stalled.

"Oh God, oh God," Casey chanted as Zucher pulled into the station's driveway. The car whined and whined against the turn of the key.

The blue truck moved nearer and nearer and she watched like a gawker at an accident scene. Oh my Lord! Was that a gun in Zucher's hand?

Casey thought her heart would stop as Zucher waved that frightening black shape, his mouth gaping as he screamed at them. She'd die of fright, her life was over — the car's engine roared to life. Jeff goosed the car into reverse, leaving Casey's stomach behind, barely missing a line of parked cars. Casey looked over at Zucher; he was too close, they'd never make it. His pickup lurched forward. . . .

Jeff cut the wheel left, right, knocking over a row of metal trash containers.

Zucher's truck hit the first rolling barrel and it careened back toward them; Jeff barely managed to avoid hitting it. Zucher tried to imitate Jeff's trick, but the massive truck didn't respond as quickly. He missed the barrel, but crashed into the concrete block wall behind the station. Before Zucher could recover, Jeff blasted out of the service station and hightailed it to the interstate.

Time resumed its normal progress. Casey gulped in air. "That was close," she managed between gasps.

Jeff gripped the steering wheel. "Did he have the gun? I was too damn busy starting the car to see."

"I saw something black. He was waving it around."

Jeff's mouth set in a grim line. "I hope he doesn't give Dave any trouble."

The possibility settled like a lump of ice in Casey's chest. "God, I hope not." She laughed, an edgy sound. "I guess we should call the police again."

He took in a breath, let it out slowly. "Feel up to doing it?"

She rubbed at her arms, trying to shake off the last of her fear. "Sure." She pulled the cell phone from the glove box. She was proud of how calmly she reported Zucher's reappearance to the Fresno County Sheriff.

After she put the phone away, they lapsed into silence, the drone of the tires on the pavement filling the car. Casey's heart quieted, although she couldn't completely cast off her anxiety.

"Do you think he'll catch up?" she asked Jeff.

"Depends on how much damage he did to his truck," Jeff answered. "He didn't just drive off, I'm sure of that."

Despite herself, Casey turned to look behind them. "He'd be after us by now."

"Right." Jeff flicked a glance in the rear view mirror himself. "So we have to hope we've got an hour or more lead time."

Casey reached into the back seat and retrieved the two-week-old *Reno Gazette* from her gym bag. She held it in her lap, still folded. "Jeff?" she asked, looking up at him.

"Hmm?" He kept his attention on the road.

"Those negatives of yours," she said, one hand restlessly smoothing the paper, "what's in them?"

He glanced at her, his gaze falling to the newspaper in her lap. He tipped his head down toward the *Gazette*. "Him."

Casey looked down at the paper, at the front page photo of Assemblyman Will Bender shaking hands with the vice-president.

"You have pictures of the vice-president?"

"No." Jeff stabbed a finger at Assemblyman Bender. "Him."

"Oh." She studied the jovial face of the assemblyman, his grin wide as he gripped the vice-president's hand. "Why did Will Bender ask you to take pictures of him?"

Jeff laughed, not a pleasant sound. "Bender didn't ask me. His wife did."

"His wife —" Casey's eyes widened as she understood. "Oh!" Her eyes slid down to the *Gazette* in her lap. "Gosh, I've always liked him."

"As do thousands of female voters," he said dryly. "Most especially one particular female voter."

The full picture burst into Casey's mind. "You mean you snapped photos of Assemblyman Bender with . . . while he was . . ." She couldn't quite bring herself to say it.

"In the throes of passion, you might say," Jeff filled in.

"Oh," Casey said, crestfallen. She always had admired Will Bender, one of the few politicians who actually seemed to see himself as a servant of the people. "I suppose he does this sort of thing all the time."

"Well, no," Jeff admitted. "There wasn't a hint of scandal before Lola."

"Lola." Casey grimaced at the sultry name.

"What does Mrs. Bender plan to do with the photos?"

"Release them to the media."

"But the election's on Tuesday. If she publicizes those photos before then, that could change the outcome."

Jeff slanted her a look. "Oh," Casey said, feeling hopelessly naive. "That's what she intends."

Jeff seemed amused by her outrage. "I'm afraid so."

"But it isn't right!"

Jeff narrowed his gaze on her. "And his philandering is?"

"Of course not! But if Mr. and Mrs. Bender have problems, they should be working them out in private, not taking them to the media."

"I agree," Jeff said. "But it does prove my theory."

"Which is?"

"That men and women are inherently incompatible."

Casey shook her head. "I don't believe that. I may be a total loss at picking the right man and you and your wife may have been a bad match —"

"I suppose you could call it a bad match," Jeff said. "I believed in fidelity and she didn't."

"Oh," Casey said, not sure what else to say. "I'm sorry."

He shrugged off her apology. "Ancient history. So tell me how many happy couples you know."

She tried to think, running through her circle of friends. "Well . . ."

"Your sisters?" he prompted.

"Not married."

"Your parents?"

She sighed. "My father left my mom when we were just kids. She never remarried."

"There. You see?"

"I don't!" She turned in her seat to face him. "What about you? You must know someone who's happily married."

"My sister, Heather. But she's the exception that proves the rule." He stared out the front windshield. "My marriage taught me a valuable lesson, Casey. Steer clear of emotional entanglements. I always let a woman know up front. If she can't accept that . . ." He shrugged.

Casey almost believed him — the cold words, the nonchalant tone. Would have, if not for the rigid line of his jaw, the trace of pain in his dark eyes.

And every feminine instinct within her wanted her to soothe that hurt, to ease it.

Urged her to pull him into her arms and hold him, kiss him, love him. . . .

Stop it, stop it, stop it! Darn her lousy instincts, her weakness for wounded animals. This particular beast would probably gnaw off her hand rather than take comfort from her.

Casey tossed the newspaper into the back seat and stared at the endless fields of cotton stretching on either side of the highway. The midmorning sun backlit Jeff's face, outlining his sharp features, throwing them into shadow.

Something prodded her to say one more thing, to have the last word. He could chew off her arm to the elbow, but she was determined to make one last declaration.

"Jeff."

He glanced at her, then back to the road. "What?"

"I don't agree."

His brow furrowed. "With what?"

"Your theory . . . about men and women."

His mouth twisted into a sardonic smile. "Why not?"

"Because there's something you're forgetting. Something I very much believe in."

"And that is?"

"Love," she said quietly. "Even if I never

find it, even if it's not for me . . . I believe."

The silence that followed her statement seemed to pound in her ears. Jeff took a long slow breath, a finely drawn whisper of sound.

"I don't." Real regret filled his voice. "I can't anymore."

Casey sighed. What could she say to that? She sank lower in her seat, lassitude from last night's sleeplessness overcoming her. "How much longer?"

"Hours yet." He caught the yawn she couldn't quite hold back. "Take a nap. It'll make the time pass more quickly."

Grabbing her jacket from the back seat, she snuggled under it, relaxing within its warmth. As she drifted off, she could swear she felt a touch across her brow, as if Jeff's fingers had swept the silk of her hair from across her eyes. Then she slept, carrying the touch into her dreams.


*Love.*
The word burned in his mind, shimmered like the glitter of sun on water. It was just as brilliant. And just as ephemeral.

When had he stopped believing in love? After Lily's first lover? Her sixth? When he realized she'd never intended to keep to her marriage vows?

Or had he doubted that emotion even

before then? Had he lost faith in the middle of one of his parents' fights, when he and his sister holed up in the basement and played Crazy Eights, flinching with each shout that battered through the shut door?

Jeff swiped a hand over his face, trying to erase the memory. Why did Casey's quiet words make him want to believe again? She confused, enraged, and irritated him all in turns — that certainly wasn't love. She aroused him nearly beyond bearing — far more than any other woman had. But that was only lust.

He took another look in the rear view mirror, assuring himself that Zucher didn't trail them, then fixed his eyes on the pavement ahead. He had to get his mind off her sweet body, her tantalizing scent. A quick roll in the hay wouldn't be enough for Casey — she'd made it clear she wanted the whole enchilada. And since he couldn't give her that, he had to keep his rampant libido in line.

He had to just say no.

No matter how he ached for her, hour after torturous hour, dying for one touch, a hand curved along her waist, or a palm against her breast . . .

He shook himself free of those dangerous thoughts, refocusing his attention on the road. He checked the odometer, making a count of how many miles they could travel before stopping for gas. That sort of mental exercise had always served to distract him from wayward thoughts in high school math, but the steady sound of Casey's breathing kept dragging him from his calculations.

Two hours later, when he'd run out of sophomore algebra problems and the car looked ready for another drink of gas, Casey finally woke. She looked even more appealing newly awake, her cheeks slightly flushed, a crease from the seat belt across her cheek. Then she stretched, her jacket sliding away, her breasts pushing against her hot pink T-shirt as she arched her spine.

The rumble of the warning bumps under the tires jerked Jeff back to reality. "I'm about to stop for gas." He shifted in his seat, irritated at his errant thoughts. "Would you try your sister again? Phone's in the glove box."

"Sure." She rubbed sleep from her eyes as she reached for the phone. "Where are we?"

"Just north of Buttonwillow."

Jeff winced at the squeal from Deb's answering machine when Casey put the call through. "No go," she said, replacing the phone in the glove box.

"We'll try later."

The last mile to the service station passed

in companionable silence. When they stopped, Casey trotted into the mini-mart to nuke another stomach-punishing meal while Jeff re-supplied them with gas and oil. Then Casey took over the driving while Jeff slept oblivious to her highway near-misses, only occasionally wakened by the honking of an irate horn.

They hit Los Angeles in mid-afternoon, slowing to a crawl in a city where rush-hour was a twenty-four-hour proposition. It took two hours to poke along through the heart of the city, then they had to contend with the creep of cars headed down Interstate 5 for San Diego.

By the time they finally pulled up in front of Deb's small stucco house at eight-thirty, the silence they'd lapsed into was no longer companionable. Casey had become downright sullen after Jeff tore into her somewhere near San Onofre when she'd almost sideswiped a Chevy. He'd kept his opinions of her driving to himself after that, contenting himself with a growl each time she got close to another car.

When they parked at the curb, Deb was just climbing out of her VW Beetle, her body sagging with the weight of a full day on her feet, wisps of red hair escaping from her braid. She shrieked with excitement when she saw

Casey, throwing aside her backpack and her weariness to race over to her sister. Although just as slender, redheaded Deb was taller than Casey, dwarfing her when she pulled her into a rib-cracking hug.

"Why didn't you tell me you were coming?" Deb exclaimed when she finally pulled back, her blue eyes raking Jeff as he leaned against Casey's car.

"We tried," Casey said. "Your answering machine is broken."

"I'd wondered why I hadn't gotten any calls lately, but I've been on shift almost non-stop." Her attention settled on Jeff, frank interest coupled with suspicion in her eyes. "Who's your friend?" she asked lightly, ready to disapprove.

"Jeff Haley," Casey told her sister. "Jeff, this is my sister Deb. Let's go inside and I'll tell you everything."

Deb snaked an arm around Casey's waist, effectively closing Jeff off from their intimacy as she headed up the walk. "I have to warn you, the place is a mess."

Casey laughed. "Your messy is neater than my clean." She glanced over her shoulder at Jeff. "Would you bring my purse in for me, please?"

He turned on his heel and headed back for the car. He'd just as soon keep his distance from those two anyway, from their easy closeness that tugged at his heart. How long had it been since he'd seen his sister, Heather? Too damn long and no excuse for it when she only lived twenty minutes away from him in Sparks.

He dragged her purse from the back seat and heaved the canvas bag over his shoulder. He knew why he avoided visiting Heather. Ten minutes spent in the circle of her happiness, with the husband she loved dearly and their two-year-old son, and his own bleak life was thrown up in stark relief. Heather's joy renewed and depressed him all at once. He could only take it in small doses.

Jeff pushed open the front door of Deb's small tract home, and swung Casey's purse next to Deb's backpack under the small writing desk by the door. His gaze roamed what he could see of the house — the small, cozy living room lit by the yellow glow of a table lamp, the tiny dining room off of it with its glass-topped café table and chairs. Other than the towering stack of mail on the desk, the lone sock by the sofa and the folded, unread *Union Tribune* on the recliner, the house was impeccably clean.

Jeff blinked against the brightness of the dining room light as Deb switched it on. "Does it meet your approval?" She eyed him warily, just a trace of hostility in her tone.

He pasted a neutral expression on his face. "Just wondering if you were any more, ah, organized than Casey."

"Diplomatically put." Deb's face relaxed into a genuine smile. "Keeping a less than orderly house is a trait unique to Casey."

"My ears are burning," Casey said as she entered from a side door. She brushed past Jeff in a cloud of cinnamon, crouching to drag out her purse. She rooted through the bag a moment, then straightened with a hair brush in her hand. "Did Deb tell you?"

A warning tickled up Jeff's spine. "Tell me what?"

Casey pulled the brush through her honey-blonde hair, wincing when it caught on a tangle. "About the negatives."

The warning expanded into alarm. "What about the negatives?"

He turned at Deb's sigh, took in the apologetic look on her face. "I'm sorry," she said.

"What happened?" Jeff asked.

"She doesn't have them." Casey shook her newly brushed hair into its usual tumble.

Jeff tried to puzzle out what they were saying. "You mean she hasn't gotten them yet?"

Casey dove back into her purse. "Oh, she got them."

Jeff turned from Casey to Deb. "Then where are they?"

Deb chewed her lip, the gesture reminiscent of Casey. "They're on their way to Phoenix."

# Chapter 9

Casey watched the rise of Jeff's chest as he sucked in a long breath. "How could you have sent them out already?" he asked Deb.

Casey knew that look in her sister's eyes, the mix of fire and ice. Casey glanced at Jeff, his towering rage narrowing his eyes and tensing his jaw, and almost felt sorry for him.

"They came in this morning's mail." Deb spoke with deliberation, as if Jeff were mentally deficient and needed things explained slowly. "I went through the photos, picked out the ones I wanted, then dropped them off at a one-hour on the way to work. Then, when I got sent home early —"

"You dropped them in the mail," Jeff finished for her.

"I overnighted them," Deb corrected, her irritation seeping into her tone. "I wanted to make sure Liz got them before she leaves for a week-long photo shoot."

Jeff was grinding his teeth now; Casey could see his jaw working. Casey chewed on a thumbnail, mesmerized. "But the negatives," Jeff persisted, "you had to have looked through them."

Deb turned her back on Jeff and headed for the recliner; only an experienced sister could see from the set of her shoulders how angry she was. She sank into the chair and slipped off her shoes. "Just to match the photos with the frames I needed."

Casey decided some neutral intervention was needed. "The negatives have these little numbers on them," she supplied helpfully, "and you match the picture with the right number —"

"I know how it works," Jeff growled. He rounded on Deb, standing over her. "You never noticed some of those negatives weren't yours?"

Casey switched to another thumbnail as Deb's blue eyes grew colder. "I told you, I didn't look at all of them. I laid them on a light table, I picked out the ones I wanted and put the whole darn mess in the re-order envelope."

Jeff took a step closer, hands fisted. "But you had to have seen if mine were there!"

Deb sprang from her chair, fiery hair wisping around her face as she confronted him. "I did not look at every negative. There were a dozen or more on the bottom I never bothered with."

"How could you have not seen them?" Jeff roared.

"I was in a hurry! I was on my way to work!" She shot fire at him, then said tightly, "I do not have to explain myself to you. I never saw your damn negatives."

Jeff opened his mouth, and Casey was sure whatever he was about to say wouldn't improve relations with her sister. She leapt to her feet, wedging herself between them. That put her far too near Jeff, so that the only place for her hands was on his chest, but she ruthlessly ignored the heat jetting up her arms.

He retreated a step, taking him out of range of her touch. Casey tipped her head toward her sister with a placating smile. "Deb's got a bit of a problem with her temper."

"*I* do!" Like a bulldog, Deb closed on Jeff again. "What about him?"

Placing an arm around Deb, Casey eased her away from Jeff. "You've got to be exhausted. Why don't you sit down again?"

Deb shook off Casey's hand and stalked off toward her bedroom. "I have to go change."

Jeff glared at her retreating back. "Your sister is a pain in the butt," he ground out.

Casey padded back to the sofa and curled up on one end. "Actually, Deb's the sweet-tempered one of the family." She scrunched her toes between the velvety blue sofa cushions and leaned her head against the back.

Jeff turned to face her. "Is that right?"

Casey nodded. "And Liz is the smart sister, Shar the motherly one."

"What about you?" Jeff asked quietly. "Where do you fit in, Casey?"

The innocuous question dug deep, an old familiar thorn. If only she could answer, she might understand why real love always seemed to elude her grasp.

She could feel his gaze on her, could sense him waiting for her response. She pasted on a saucy grin and looked up at him sidelong. "I don't know — resident troublemaker?"

He didn't speak, didn't smile, just kept his dark, intense eyes on her. Why wasn't he agreeing with her assessment? Hadn't he already told her she was nothing but trouble?

He stared at her one long moment more, then he dropped down on the other end of the sofa. Slouching down with a sigh, he threw an arm over his eyes.

Casey dug her toes deeper into the cushions. "I'm sorry Deb sent the negatives on."

"Not your fault." He lowered his arm and looked at her. "If your sister wasn't so damned efficient —"

"Same to you, Haley," Deb said, returning from the bedroom. She'd pulled on a fuchsia running suit that should have clashed with her red hair, but didn't.

Deb flopped down next to Casey. "How about something to eat, Sis?"

Jeff edged away from Deb, shooting her a dark look. "We wouldn't want to put you out."

"Casey wouldn't be," Deb said. "You might."

Jeff sprang to his feet. "We ought to get going anyway."

"To where?" Casey asked.

"Phoenix," he said, pacing. "To get the negatives."

"Don't you think we ought to stay the night?" Casey asked. "Start fresh in the morning?"

Deb shifted, tucking her long legs under her. "Those pictures won't arrive until tomorrow afternoon, anyway. We'll call Liz, tell her to hold on to them for you."

Energy seemed to coil inside Jeff like a spring. He scrubbed at his face with his hands, then turned to Casey. "I suppose you're right. I'm dead on my feet anyway."

Deb brought Casey into a one-armed hug.

"You can sleep with me, Sis." She tipped her head toward Jeff. "He can sleep on the sofa."

"I wouldn't want to trouble you," Jeff said. "If you'll point me to a motel —"

"Oh, stow it. The sofa makes into a bed. You can sleep here." Deb unfolded herself from the sofa and put a hand out to Casey. "Come help me with dinner."

"Watch you make dinner, you mean." Casey followed Deb to the kitchen. "Unless we're having boiled water."

She heard the sound of the front door closing and assumed that Jeff had gone out to get their bags. "Where did you get that guy?" Deb asked as she pulled a jar of spaghetti sauce from the cupboard.

Casey dragged one of the café chairs into the kitchen. "Remember when I helped arrest that card cheater?"

"You mean Sleazeball?" Deb asked, recalling Casey's nickname for Zucher.

"And remember the hunky private eye I said I was working with?"

"Vaguely." Deb dumped the jar of sauce into a pot, then added a sprinkling of oregano. "I think I was in the middle of finals at the time."

Reaching behind her, Casey snagged a banana from the counter. "Anyway, Jeff's him."

Deb stripped the skin from an onion, then grabbed up a kitchen knife. "Wait a minute. Isn't he the one you had a mad crush on?"

Casey heard the scrape of the front door opening, heard the sound of Jeff dropping the bags to the floor. "Shh," she hissed as Jeff's footsteps approached. "I never said that."

"I'm sure you did." Deb cut the onion neatly in two, then proceeded to chop it. "I remember you moaning about it over the phone every time you called."

Jeff stood in the doorway, his bag over his shoulder. "Can I use your bathroom?"

Deb turned to him, gesturing with the long knife. "No, you'll have to go ask the neighbors," she said sarcastically. "Of course you can. Through there." She pointed with the knife.

Casey waited until she heard the bathroom door shut before she spoke again. "It was just a silly thing I was going through at the time."

Deb paused in her onion chopping and looked up at Casey. "That was right after Mom died, wasn't it?"

Casey nodded, the tightness in her throat catching her by surprise. "So if I started having those silly feelings toward —" She waggled the banana toward the bathroom door. "— it was only temporary. He really doesn't mean a thing to me, now."

Deb squeezed olive oil into a skillet, then dumped in the onions. "If you say so." She gave the skillet contents a stir. "Why don't you call Liz? Phone's right there."

Casey rose to reach for the phone, surprised to find a banana in her hand. She put the poor mangled fruit down on the counter and lifted Deb's portable phone. Deb's address book lay in plain sight, right next to the phone, and she had Liz's number listed under "M" for Madison.

"Takes all the adventure out of finding a phone number," Casey said as she dialed.

"What was that?" Deb asked as she scraped sautéed onions into the sauce.

"Never mind." Casey listened as the phone rang, waited for Liz to pick up. She heard a click, then Liz's recorded voice intoning, "This is Madison Industrial Photography. We're not in right now. At the tone —"

"Answering machine," Casey told Deb. She felt a pressure between her shoulder blades and knew without turning around that Jeff had returned.

"Tell her to hold on to the negatives," he said from the kitchen doorway.

Casey waved him off as Liz's machine beeped. "Liz, this is Casey. Guess what? I'm on my way to see you. Just a short surprise visit."

"The negatives," Jeff hissed from just behind her.

He smelled of soap and his own indefinable male scent; for a moment Casey forgot what she was about to say. She shrugged away from him, and persuaded her brain to remember the words. "Anyway," she continued into the portable tucked against her ear, "we should be there tomorrow."

Jeff loomed over her shoulder again, his heat now wreaking havoc with her senses. "The negatives, Casey."

Shooting him a dirty look, Casey turned away again. "Oh, and one more thing. You should be getting the reunion pictures tomorrow from Deb. I mean, they're originally from me, but then I sent them to Deb —"

Jeff slapped a hand across her mouth. "The negatives," he repeated, each syllable bitten out.

She jerked her mouth free of his hand. "So anyway, Liz, just make sure you hold on to the pictures, okay? And we'll see you —" A long beep signaled that she'd run out of message tape.

Circling around Jeff, she replaced the portable on the counter. "I didn't need you coaching my every word."

"I just wanted you to get to the point."

Casey started going through cupboards, looking for plates. "I was getting to the point, in my own way."

"Hah!" He reached past her, unerringly opening the cupboard that held the dinner plates. "You would have been telling her what you had for breakfast next."

"I would not!" Casey said.

"Pancakes," Deb said as she dropped a box of rigatoni into boiling water. "It was the first thing she told me."

"Deb!" Casey protested.

"Well, it was, Casey." Deb was unrepentant. "Just hand those plates over here, would you?"

Ignoring Jeff's smirk, Casey took the stack from him, judiciously avoiding contact. "I got around to the pictures, didn't I?"

Deb took the plates from her. "Silverware's over there, Jeff. Would you lay it out on the table?"

Casey and Jeff moved to the drawer at the same time, their hands colliding on the drawer pull. She heard his sharp intake of breath, felt the tension in his fingers when he pressed against hers. It took two sharp mental orders, but finally her rebellious fingers pulled away and gave him right-of-way.

He grabbed up handfuls of forks and

knives, and carried them into the dining room. Casey wiped her hands on her jeans, trying to brush away the heat.

"Casey," Deb said, and Casey nearly hopped out of her sneakers. "Would you nuke some of those rolls I have in the freezer?"

She tugged open the freezer door, its cold blast cooling her face. Rolls. She was looking for rolls. Somehow she'd forgotten what rolls looked like.

With a sigh, Deb reached around her, pulled out a plastic bag. "Here. Thirty seconds each in the microwave."

Casey posted herself in front of the microwave and followed Deb's instructions with precision. Every once in a while, she heard a clank from the dining room and wondered just how long it took to place three forks and three knives on a table. Maybe he was rearranging the chairs.

She was tempted to take a peek; she would only need to lean back a little in the small kitchen to look through the doorway. But maybe it was just as well he was out of sight. Somehow, even table setting seemed to have erotic possibilities when it was Jeff performing the task.

Casey only ruined one roll when she set the timer to three minutes by mistake, which wasn't bad considering her past disasters in the kitchen. And placing a roll on each plate next to the steaming rigatoni was easy enough. The real challenge would be handing the plates to Jeff so that he could place them on the table. If his fingers brushed hers during the transfer and she fumbled the plate. . . .

He *was* arranging chairs when she carried the first one into the dining room. He'd pulled one out of the way so that the remaining three could be placed equidistant from each other around the circular table.

"I thought we needed a little more room," he said in answer to her unasked question.

"Okay." She handed him the plate.

"The table's small," he added.

"That's fine." Casey turned to go back for the next plate. "I'm sure Deb won't mind."

Deb didn't even seem to notice when they all sat down to eat. She was too busy laughing at Jeff's funny stories about past clients, her earlier animosity dissolving in the face of his humor.

Poking at her rigatoni, Casey stewed. She didn't even know Jeff *had* a sense of humor. He'd certainly never used it around her. But now, sitting elbow to elbow with her baby sister, he was a regular comedian.

"So what finally happened to the dog?"

Deb asked as she mopped up sauce with a piece of her roll.

"Jim, in my office, adopted it." He forked up the last of his pasta. "He's always taking in strays."

"That was Casey, when we were kids," Deb said. "Remember that kitten you found in the storm drain?"

Casey felt sulky, not entirely willing to be brought into the conversation. "What kitten?"

"You remember, that little black one." Deb turned to Jeff, her smile displaying perfect teeth. "Casey was always bringing home strays."

Casey ran the tip of her tongue over her crooked tooth, hating the feel of it. She surprised a look of hot intensity on Jeff's face as he followed the movement of her tongue. She brought her hand up to cover her mouth, and Jeff's gaze grew even hotter.

Casey rose, needing to escape the trap of Jeff's dark eyes. She gathered up her nearly full plate and utensils.

"You hardly ate a thing," Deb said.

"I wasn't as hungry as I thought," she said brightly. "Can I get anyone anything else?"

Jeff lay his fork and knife on his plate. "I'm done."

Deb picked up Jeff's plate and stacked it on top of Casey's. "Casey said she helped you on a case."

She could feel Jeff watching her as she added Deb's plate to the stack. "She helped me set up a card cheater."

"She told me that," Deb said. "But what exactly did she do?"

Casey stood poised in the kitchen doorway, the dirty dishes clutched in her hands. Jeff's long fingers fascinated her, the way they lay stretched out against the table. She imagined tracing each one with her lips, her tongue.

Stop it, stop it, stop it! She turned on her heel and went into the kitchen, depositing the dishes on the counter. She heard the rumble of Jeff's voice as he explained how the two of them had trapped Phil Zucher.

"It was a sting operation," he said. "She played along with Zucher, pretended an interest in his scheme. Then when she had all the details, she tipped me off."

Even the sound of Jeff's voice sent a thrill up her spine. She suppressed a shiver of reaction as she set the dishes into the sink. Deb entered the kitchen, then Jeff appeared in the doorway and leaned his broad shoulder against the doorjamb.

Deb busied herself with the leftovers while

Casey ran water into the sink. "Was she ever in any danger?" Deb asked.

"I wouldn't have let her do it if it were dangerous," Jeff said.

Deb scraped the tomato sauce into an empty margarine tub. "Still, it worried me when she told me about it."

"I took care of her every step of the way," Jeff said.

The thought of Jeff taking care of her set off a spreading warmth in her middle. With trembling hands she shook the contents of her plate into the garbage disposal, then slipped the dish into the hot soapy water in the sink.

He crossed the kitchen to where she stood by the sink. She felt his fingers threading into her hair, brushing against the back of her neck. His whisper seeped into her very bones. "I wouldn't let anything happen to you."

Dimly she heard Deb behind her slapping the top onto the sauce and tossing the container into the refrigerator. She could hear each separate inhalation as Jeff leaned in close to her ear. She wondered what Deb must be thinking, seeing the two of them, so close, so intimate.

The burbling of the phone startled Casey and she backed away from Jeff. Deb grabbed up the portable. "Hello?" she said as she walked out of the kitchen with the phone.

Casey stared at Jeff, the sharp lines of his face, the sensuous line of his lower lip. Do something, she screamed at him inwardly. Do something now.

He shoved away from the counter, raking a hand over his close-cropped hair. He stood with his back to her a moment, then turned to face her.

He gestured at the dishes. "I'll dry."

Certainly, that wasn't what he meant to say, meant to do. Casey pushed aside a twinge of disappointment and returned to the sink. She swished the dishes in the soapy water, scrubbing them clean with a sponge. She set them into the empty side, then fished for the silverware.

She placed the remaining plates and the silverware into the sink with care, then dropped the empty sauce pot into the soapy water. She rinsed the soapy dishes and placed them in the drainer in front of Jeff.

Under different circumstances, it might have been rather cozy, the two of them standing side by side doing dishes. If it weren't for the heat that sizzled between them, threatening to set the dishwater to boiling.

Deb returned, setting down the phone

with a sigh. "That was the service," she said. "I have to go back into work."

"I told you where the blankets were, right?" Deb asked Jeff as she paused at the front door.

"Hall closet," he reassured her. "Pillows on top, sheets and blankets on the bottom."

She shot a worried look at Casey, who stood beside him, eyes downcast. Deb had to sense the tension between him and Casey. Hell, the air was thick with it, pulsing around them both like a live thing.

Deb's narrowed gaze slid to Jeff and he understood the silent question — what are you doing to my sister? He would have answered her — out loud even — if only he knew.

"You've got the number, in case you need to call," Deb said, for the third time.

She smoothed her pale peach uniform where it bunched at her hips, tugging it down a little. It surprised Jeff that he didn't react to the movements of Deb's admittedly attractive body. In fact, watching Deb only made him think of Casey, and how she would feel under his hands.

"I'm sorry our visit was cut short," Deb said to Casey.

Casey threw her arms around her sister.

"We'll see you in the morning, before we leave."

Deb held her at arm's length, but Casey wouldn't look at her. Deb gave her a kiss on the cheek. "Later, Sis," she said, then slipped out the door.

"I'll help you make your bed." Casey's eyes focused somewhere in the middle of his chest.

He followed her to the closet, and took the blanket and sheets she handed him. "We had an agreement, Casey."

"I don't know what you mean." She squeezed past him with the pillows.

He trailed after her, dumping the bed-clothes on the living room floor. "The attraction between us. We acknowledge it's there."

"Fine. It's there." Still avoiding his gaze, she tugged a cushion from the sofa and tossed it aside.

Jeff followed suit, set the other two on top of the first. Then he bent to help her open the convertible sofa. "We just don't have to follow through."

She gasped in a breath and he could swear he heard the thread of tears in the sound. But she'd turned away from him to pick up the sheets, so he wasn't certain.

"Who said I wanted to?" she asked as she snapped the bottom sheet onto the bed.

Jeff fitted the two corners on his side onto the mattress. "I didn't say you did. I just thought . . ." Had he misinterpreted what he'd seen in the kitchen, the passion in her eyes? Was he the only one who could feel the exquisite line of tension stretched between them?

She lifted her gaze to his, and he could see the flush across her cheeks. He knew then that she felt it too, that she burned just as he did.

Turning away, she snatched up the top sheet. "I'm tired, Jeff. I'm stressed." She shook the sheet out onto the bed, the sharp crack punctuating the taut silence. "It has nothing to do with your irresistible sex appeal."

Anger roiled in him that she would refute what was so obviously between them. "You want me," he said harshly. "I know you do."

Her eyes widened, desperation deep within them. "I don't."

Her continued denial goaded him. He rounded the bed and reached for her, his hand caressing her face. "Then what the hell is this?" He drew his fingers up along her cheek, stroking her until her eyes drifted shut. "What is this?"

She shook her head, whispered, "I don't know."

He dragged his thumb along her mouth so that a sigh escaped her lips. He leaned close to her ear. "Then I'll tell you what you're feeling, Casey. It's sex. It's lust."

She opened her eyes, tipped her head back so that she could gaze up at him. "Maybe I want more."

"There is no more."

"There is if I choose it."

He didn't like the light in her eyes, didn't like what it set off inside him — a hopeful ache, a longing for something beyond his reach. A wish that he could redeem dead emotions, feelings that died the night he first found Lily in the arms of another man.

He had to extinguish that light. "How would you know what to choose," he said harshly, "when every other choice you've made about men has been wrong."

Just as soon as he'd said the words, he wanted to cut himself open and drag them back inside. He'd never seen such stark pain as he saw on Casey's face.

"Casey," he rasped out. "I'm sorry. Casey," he said more loudly as she backed away from him, shaking her head.

Tears spilled from her eyes. "I suppose I deserved that."

"No, you didn't. I should never have said

it." He reached for her, but his hand closed on empty air.

She snatched up her riotous jacket from where it lay next to her purse. "I'm going for a walk," she said, shoving her arms into the jacket.

"But Casey," he said, trying to inject a shred of reason into a conversation gone out of control, "it's nearly eleven."

But she probably never heard the tail end of what he'd said. Because the slam of the door cut him off as neatly as a knife.

He stood staring at that blank white door like a man gazing upon the wreckage of his car, wondering when the hell he'd made the wrong turn.

# Chapter 10

As Casey reached the end of the walk, the late night chill crept up her sleeves, sneaked under the jacket's hem. It sent a cold message with each step — stupid, stupid, stupid.

She continued to the end of Deb's block, then dropped down off the curb to cross the street. Why couldn't her grand, dramatic gesture have sent her feet into Deb's bedroom instead of out the front door? Then she could have been snuggled in self-righteous misery in Deb's bed, and reached the same conclusion that she was an idiot, in warm comfort.

Jeff had only spoken the plain truth. She had no judgment when it came to men, so how would she know what she was feeling for him? And she'd lied anyway — she'd felt so hot for him, she'd feared she'd incinerate on the spot.

As she continued walking, even her feet seemed to have better sense than her — they slowed with each step across the pavement. They refused to lift high enough at the curb on the other side so that she nicked her toe and tripped, nearly stumbling to the ground. A sad day when her own feet turned against her.

She could see the glow up ahead of what looked like a mini-mart at the corner, heard the roar of traffic from a busy street. She'd go that far and turn around. She dipped into her pocket and found the twenty Jeff had given her. She'd buy herself a Crush, then dawdle along walking back in hopes that Jeff would have gone to sleep by the time she returned to Deb's.

Then she rounded the massive hedge of the last house on the block, and caught sight of a crowd of tattoos and chains clustered around the entrance of the mini-mart. One look, and her legs threw in with her feet, becoming quite sulky about moving her forward, her knees banging against each other as she crossed the parking lot. When the entire crowd of men detached themselves from their motorcycles and leered her way, her arms said, "To hell with it," and flopped against her behind in an attempt to escape the scene.

"Hey, baby!" the mountainous one with the skull earring called out. "You comin' to see me?"

She giggled, a breathy sound, and shook

her head. The pack of men seemed to close in on her and she had to sternly order her legs to move through them. As she did so, her feet kept up an endless complaint, "If you'd stayed at the house with Jeff, this never would have happened," but she just stamped them a little harder to quiet them.

Shaggy-haired Mountain Man stepped directly into her path as she reached the door, his grin creasing the dagger tattoo on his cheek. Her neck turned stiff with fright as she bent it way back to peer up at him. He raised a hammy fist to the door, blocking her way to it.

Then he tugged at the handle, and pulled the glass door open. "Allow me." He gave her a toothy smile and stepped aside to allow her passage.

She might have expected a pinch on the behind, or a pat at the least, but the only thing that banged her backside as she stepped inside was the door when she didn't move out of the way fast enough. She heard their laughter in response to her little startled jump, but she didn't dare look back. She walked directly to the rear of the store for her Crush, then to the register, where a frowzy woman waited behind the counter.

The clerk snatched the twenty from her without a word and held it up to the light, one suspicious eye on Casey. Apparently satisfied with its authenticity, the woman slapped it on the register and rang up the sale.

"Got nothin' but singles," the woman said around her cigarette, eyes narrowed against the smoke.

Casey squirmed under the woman's stare and nearly refused the nineteen dollars change. "That's okay," she said, holding out her hand.

She stuffed the wad of bills into her pocket, the bulk biting into her thigh. She turned to leave, girding herself to face the bikers again.

"Yer drink, girlie," the clerk called out.

"Yes, right," Casey said, spinning on her heel again. She grabbed up the cold drink, then headed for the door.

Mountain Man pulled open the door for her again, his grin so broad that the dagger disappeared entirely. "Thank you," Casey murmured, trying not to show her fear. Back ramrod straight, she squeezed through the leather jackets and she marched past the row of Harleys.

"Hey lady," Mountain Man called out. "Kinda dangerous out there. Want me to walk you home?"

She spun to face him, scraping her hip on

the back end of a pickup. From the corner of her eye, she saw a head pop up in the cab of the truck, as if the driver had been sleeping across the seat and she'd woken him.

She backed away across the parking lot, shaking her head. "No thank you," she said, her voice sounding high and insubstantial, "I only live a couple houses down."

*That's right, tell him where you live,* her brain sneered, fully in concert with her body's mutiny. *Jeff's there,* she told herself. *He'll protect you.*

If you make it that far, her feet retorted, sullenly clunking against each other as she reached the far end of the parking lot. She chanced a look over her shoulder, expecting to see Mountain Man towering over her. He stood in the middle of the parking lot, watching her, and she was surprised to see the concern in his expression.

She rounded the high hedge bordering the parking lot just as she heard an engine start up and worried that the massive biker was coming after her. But no, that sounded more like a car engine, not the gravelly roar of a motorcycle. She hurried her steps anyway, the soda can icy in her hand, jacket jingling with each footfall.

When she first saw the headlights in her periphery, she didn't even tense; she figured they were attached to some passing car. Then she realized the headlights weren't moving past, in fact were keeping pace with her. That was still okay, she told herself, since these were the two headlights of a car, not the single lamp on a motorcycle. She didn't need to turn and look.

What if it was two motorcycles? Oh, God, she'd better look.

Her feet obligingly kept moving; after all, she was finally doing what they wanted, going home. She forced her neck to swivel to the right, although it would just as soon not know what menace lay in the street beside her. Her eyes arrived last on the scene, stubbornly refusing to focus on and register the vehicle moving alongside her.

It was a navy blue pickup.

With Zucher inside it.

She tried to scream, but the sound fizzled from lack of air. Her feet, damn them, froze under the weight of Zucher's malign glare, gluing her to the sidewalk. It wasn't until the card cheater spread his mouth in a crooked, evil grin, that her body finally got the flight message and took off running.

She couldn't feel her feet against the concrete sidewalk, couldn't taste the air she dragged into her lungs, wasn't sure when she dropped the soda can. She couldn't even hear the sound of Zucher's engine, although the truck cruised along nearly at her elbow. Instead, the imagined rasp of Zucher's laughter overwhelmed her, fueled her terror, carried her along in a dim haze of panic.

Go to Deb's, go to Deb's, her brain chanted as it commanded her feet to comply. But what about Jeff? her heart replied. What if Zucher has his gun and he shoots Jeff instead of me?

With a little whimper, she turned away from Deb's house and headed down a darker street. She'd brought this all on herself; there was no point in endangering Jeff because of her own stupidity. She cast a look over her shoulder. Zucher's truck clung to her like a tick, tracing her every step. At least she'd drawn him away from Jeff.

Would Zucher shoot her through the truck window, she wondered, then leave her in the street? Or would he force her inside so that he could take her away to some isolated spot before he did her in?

She couldn't breathe anymore, she simply couldn't scrape another breath into her lungs. She pushed her feet on, her legs rubbery, her body alternately hot from the exertion and cold from fear. Then Zucher pulled his truck over and somehow she got a second wind. Her legs moved impossibly fast, she was flying along the sidewalk.

She had a chance now, she could escape him. She'd find a bush to hide herself in so that he wouldn't find her. God, she was going to make it after all.

Then she truly was flying, although it took her a moment to understand why. By the time she understood she'd tripped on a chunk of sidewalk buckled by a eucalyptus root, she'd already slammed into the concrete. Her palms and elbows took the brunt of the fall, the knees of her jeans giving way from the force. As she lay, dazed, her eyes on the tangle of eucalyptus branches above her, she experienced a moment of piercing grief that she'd never see Jeff again.

Zucher, standing over her and blocking her view of the eucalyptus, couldn't have been more delighted. "Heh, heh, heh," he cackled. "Got you at last."

Exhausted, Casey reserved all her energy for breathing. She considered closing her eyes and wishing for deliverance, but survival mode kicked in and told her she'd damn well better keep her eyes open.

Zucher thrust the toe of a booted foot into her ribs. "Get up." He cast a glance down the dark street, then back at her. "On your feet."

Casey rolled to hands and knees, wincing as the sidewalk dug into her flesh, then struggled up. She flicked her gaze down, looking for a gun. She swallowed twice before she asked as boldly as she could, "What are you going to do to me?"

For a moment, Zucher looked downright puzzled. Then he grasped her arm, his bony fingers viselike through her jacket's padded sleeve. "None of your business," he said, giving her a tug.

Casey stumbled along in his wake as he pulled her to the truck. "Yes it is," Casey protested. "It's me you're kidnapping."

About to open the passenger side of his truck, he jerked to a stop so that she bumped into him. She jumped back hastily, feeling slimy from the contact.

He pulled her nose to nose with him. "I'm not kidnapping you." Just a trace of uncertainty quivered in his tone.

"You are too!" she said.

"Am not!"

"Of course you are!" She tried to reclaim her arm, but he held fast. "You followed me, you're dragging me to your car."

"That's not kidnapping," he insisted with complete illogic. "I'm just getting my revenge." Then he opened the car door and hauled her around it.

The gun was on the seat. It lay partially concealed by a rumpled taco wrapper, but in the dim light she could see the square black grip, the long, skinny barrel. A little mew of alarm slipped from her lips and she groped for the truck's doorjamb with her free hand.

He shoved her up into the truck; her clutching fingers *sproinged* her out again. He pulled her arm straight out and then pushed her body with it as if it were a battering ram; she bounced in and out of the truck as she held firm with her other arm.

She wondered dimly why he didn't just hit her or reach around her for the gun. Instead, he brought his knee up for extra leverage, pushing it against her hip until her fingers lost their purchase on the door jamb. A moment later, she tumbled into the truck, her hand falling on the gun.

She snatched her hand back with a gasp, terrified she'd set it off just by touching it. She'd never felt a gun like that — in fact, she'd never held a gun in her life. It reminded her more of a cellular phone than a gun. But what better idea than to make a gun shaped like a cell phone? she thought whimsically. The police would never guess.

It must be because she was about to die, she thought, that such peculiar thoughts raced through her mind and such odd images fleeted before her eyes. Because there was Zucher, vanishing in mid-stride as he trotted around the hood of the truck. And there was Jeff, his face suffused with a rage that made her shiver although it wasn't aimed at her.

By the time the sounds of Harley engines filled her ears, Casey realized it wasn't near-death hallucinations she was experiencing, but reality. Her feet and hands were way ahead of her, her hands simultaneously grabbing for the gun and the door handle and her feet launching her from the truck.

Jeff had Zucher on the pavement, one knee on his chest, hands gripping Zucher's flannel shirt. Zucher's head lolled from side to side as Jeff shook him, shouting, cursing, his anger incandescent.

"I've got the gun!" Casey screamed, holding it out in front of her. "Jeff, I've got his gun!"

That pulled Jeff's attention from his mauling of Zucher, unfortunately long enough for the card cheater to plant a knee between Jeff's legs. With a groan, Jeff fell to one side, hands shielding himself from another blow. But Zucher wasn't letting any grass grow under his feet as he leapt up and raced for his truck.

He'd left his engine running, which was lucky for him, Casey reflected, since he was able to pull away quickly enough to avoid the ring of Harleys closing around him. He swerved around Jeff hunched over in the street and roared off into the night. Mountain Man and another biker peeled off in pursuit, Harleys growling, as lights flicked on in houses all down the block.

Casey released the gun from nerveless fingers; it clattered to the pavement as she rushed over to Jeff. She threw her arms around him, then lost her balance and fell into his lap.

"Oh, I was so scared," she cried, pulling him against her.

He sucked in a breath, his face tightening as if he were in pain. "Get up," he hissed. "Off my lap."

She drew back, irritated that he didn't appreciate her concern. "I was scared for you. I just wanted to make sure you were okay."

"Madison," he gasped, then winced again as she shifted on his legs. "You're about to finish what Zucher started."

She remembered what Zucher had done with his knee. "Oh, God, I'm sorry." Her hands fluttered over him and for a breathless moment, she almost rubbed him to help him feel better, then realized just what part of his body she'd be soothing.

Cheeks flaming, she scrambled to her feet

and put a hand out to help him up. "I'm sorry," she said again as he rose without her assistance.

"Not your fault." Jeff adjusted his jeans with a grimace.

The two motorcycles that had chased Zucher returned. "Couldn't find him, man," Mountain Man called out as he dismounted from his Harley and headed their way. "You alright, buddy? That guy got you good in the . . ." His voice trailed off as his gaze slid to Casey. ". . . crotch."

"I'm fine," Jeff said, although when Casey laid a hand on his arm, he stiffened. He shrugged away from her. "I appreciate the backup," he said to the biker.

"No problem," Mountain Man said. "We were a little worried about your woman here when we saw her walking alone. You ought to keep her on a tighter leash."

Casey glared at the massive biker, but before she could say so much as a word of protest, she heard the beeping of a pager. Mountain Man pulled the device from the pocket of his leather jacket and peered down at it.

"Damn," he said with a sheepish look. "It's the old lady. I'd better get."

He hurried back to his Harley and started up the engine with a guttural roar. He veered off back down the street, his compatriots close behind.

Casey and Jeff stood alone in the street. "Where's the gun?" he asked her.

"I dropped it," she said, "I think it fell into the gutter."

Jeff crossed to the curb, then plucked something out of the leaf trash from the eucalyptus tree. He straightened, his back to her, and Casey could swear his shoulders were shaking.

Worried, she moved to his side. "What is it?"

His face bright with suppressed laughter, he looked down on her. "I — you —" Then he couldn't go on as the laughter burst from him, his guffaws filling the silence of the late night street.

He was waving the gun around, waggling its barrel at her as he laughed. Casey batted at his hand. "Jeff! Stop that! You could hurt someone that way."

That only set him off again, his mirth growing so loud that lights began coming on in the houses again. *He's hysterical,* Casey thought. *I'd better take the gun.* She grabbed for the barrel.

The barrel bent. She snatched her hand back in surprise and it sprang back into shape. That made Jeff laugh all the harder and

Casey, becoming irritated now, plucked the gun from his hand.

Rather, she plucked the cell phone from his hand. She stared down at it, confused. "Where did the gun go?" she asked Jeff.

Wheezing, he stopped for air. "I doubt there ever was one," he gasped out.

Heat flooded Casey's face. She peered down at the cell phone with its black plastic case and long springy antenna. "Well, it looks a little like a gun," she insisted.

Another weak chortle slipped from his lips. "In the dark, maybe." Jeff wiped tears from his eyes, then laid a warm hand on her back. "Let's get back to the house."

A little miffed at his laughter, thoroughly embarrassed by her mistake, Casey nevertheless fell in beside him. When his arm slid around her shoulders, she leaned into him, and curved a tentative hand around his waist. She felt his muscles tense, then he sighed and pulled her more tightly against him.

They retraced the steps to Deb's house in silence, Jeff's hand firm on her shoulder the entire time. He guided her up the walk, but stopped her on the porch when she would have gone inside.

"Humor me," he said as he eased the door open. "I couldn't lock it. Let me make a quick check."

Casey shivered on the porch, listening to the sounds of him moving around inside. As she waited, it seemed to grow colder, because her body began to shudder, to quake, out-of-control motions that no amount of rubbing her arms or stamping her feet could chase. By the time Jeff returned, tears wet Casey's face as her body shook with great, awkward movements.

"Oh my God," Jeff said, immediately sweeping her in his arms and bringing her inside. He kicked the door shut behind him, then carried her to the sofa bed, settling her in his lap. He grabbed for the blanket still neatly folded on the floor and enfolded her in it.

She winced at the brightness of the table lamp next to the sofa, turning her head away. She felt him lean, heard the click as he turned the light off, softening the living room to a quiet dimness.

She snuggled deeper into the blanket as her teeth began to chatter. "Don't know — why I'm — so cold."

"Reaction," Jeff said, his arms snug around her, locking her inside the blanket. She didn't feel closed in though, just secure. "You must have been scared to death."

"No," she denied, tears shredding the word into a lie. "Yes," she whispered. "I was terrified."

221

Her face buried in his neck, sobs overwhelmed her. Jeff's hand at the back of her head held her firmly to him. She turned, struggling free of the blanket, felt an instant of panic before he quickly released her. She threw her arms around him, bringing his solid warmth as close to her as she could without pulling him inside her.

"You're safe now," he murmured, "you're with me."

Her shuddering eased as his heat, his nearness drenched her, soothed her. She began to feel hot, impatient with the weight of the blanket. Still keeping one arm around him, she tried to push the blanket away.

"I'm hot," she said to him, querulous as a child.

He hesitated, then tugged the blanket from her. Now the jacket was too much; why did she need that confining garment when she had Jeff as a source of heat? She slipped one arm from her sleeve, then shook the jacket to the floor.

She wriggled in close to him, eyes still shut, sighing at the bliss of being so near him. She felt encircled and protected by him, well-being seeping straight to her soul. She shifted in his lap, settling herself against him. And froze.

The hard ridge of him burned her hip.

Childish comfort seared from her, replaced by a surge of emotion, of sensation that pooled low in her body.

Jeff stilled, his arms wrapped around her but motionless, and he even seemed reluctant to breathe. Unable to resist her body's urging, Casey pushed against him, pressing her hip into his rigid flesh.

Jeff groaned and tightened his grip on her. Remembering what Zucher had done to him, Casey asked, "Am I hurting you?"

"No," he said, then a dry chuckle slipped from his throat. "Yes. But not the way you think."

A soft moan whispered from Casey as she understood his meaning. She turned, surely intending to climb from his lap. But instead of moving away from him, she bent one knee so that she could bring it around him. Then she faced him, crooking both legs around his back. She thrust forward her pelvis, so that the center of her lay against his erection.

Jeff growled, harsh and fierce, as his hand gripped her bottom, pulling her against him. His other hand twisted into her hair, tugging her face up to his. He covered her mouth with his, instantly pushing his tongue inside, the surprise of his sudden invasion shooting sensation straight to her core.

His hand moved up to her waist, grabbed up a handful of her T-shirt and wrenched it free of her jeans. At the first touch of his fingers on her bare skin, she gasped and threw her head back. As his hand drifted up her ribcage, leaving behind a trail of shivering delight, he brought his lips to her exposed throat. He sipped at her flesh, moving along her neck to her jaw line, to her ear.

He drew the sensitive lobe into his mouth, then lightly scraped with his teeth. Casey cried out, trembling as her blood turned molten in her veins. Then his hand found her bra and his fingertips brushed along its edges to her spine. He followed the path of her spine to her jeans, then back again, leaving her gasping and her heart pounding.

Both hands circled her waist as his mouth drifted kisses across her face. His fingers dipped under the front closure of her bra, but he didn't release it. He ran the backs of his hands under the elastic, his fingertips just whispering along the underside of her breasts. Finally, when Casey thought she would die waiting for him, he slipped the catch free.

She thought his hands would immediately enfold her breasts. But he only gave them the lightest of touches, his palms barely grazing her nipples. That was enough to leave her groaning and squirming in his lap, driving herself against him. He hesitated, mouth against her throat, his hands not quite touching her breasts, their heat warming her.

He dragged in a long, harsh breath. Then his hands covered her breasts, pressing their small weight fully against his palms. Casey pressed her hips closer to him, and her head lolled back. She reveled in the feel of him, gloried in the sensations.

She was drowning, drowning in ecstasy. Her heart seemed to carom from her chest, to expand to fill the room. It all felt so right, every touch, every sigh. So perfect, so right. She was sure of it, sure. . . .

Like with Ian. With Roger. With Tom. The names crowded in, a litany of errors in judgment, a manifesto of mistakes. How could she know, how could she possibly know if her feelings for Jeff were any different than what she felt before?

Reason washed over her in an icy flood, dousing the sweet passion. She pushed away from Jeff's embrace; he released her instantly.

Feet on the floor, she backed away from the bed. Jeff switched on the light and it stung her eyes, forcing her to squeeze them shut a moment. When she opened them again, Jeff stood by the bed, watching her warily.

"I think we have a problem here," he said roughly.

"I'm sorry," she said, wrapping her arms around her middle.

"You have to stop doing that," he said.

"What?"

"Apologizing for what isn't your fault." He scrubbed at his face, released a heavy sigh. "I'm the one who should apologize. You were scared and vulnerable and I took advantage of that."

Lord, why did he have to be such a good man? It strained her willpower beyond bearing to resist caring for him.

"I need . . ." She took a long breath, tried to order her thoughts. What she needed right now and what was best for her were light years apart. "I'm tired. I'll see you in the morning."

Stumbling over her feet, she escaped to Deb's bedroom. She shut the door and leaned against it, face buried in her hands.

His quiet footsteps approached. "Are you okay, Casey?" he asked through the door.

"Yes," she said, the word a bare whisper. She turned to face the door, pressing her palms against it. "I'm fine," she said more loudly. "It was just that business with

Zucher. I was scared. You were right, I shouldn't have — we shouldn't have —"

She couldn't bring herself to say more, just stood there praying that he'd leave. She pressed her ear to the thin door and heard his breathing, each long intake and release of air.

Then she heard the shifting of his feet. "Yeah," he said, his voice a low rumble. "We shouldn't have."

Her heart clenched at the dismissal in his tone. She took a breath to ease the pain. "I'm going to bed, now." Then, when he didn't respond, she said, "Goodnight."

When she heard his footsteps move away from the door, she opened it a crack to make sure he'd returned to the living room. She hurried to the bathroom to prepare for bed, then checked for his presence again before retreating to the bedroom. As she passed in the hall, she caught a glimpse of him stretched out on the sofa bed, his arm thrown across his face.

Donning an old bulky T-shirt, she slipped beneath the covers of Deb's neatly made bed. She flicked off the lamp, then drew her knees nearly to her chin, curling herself into a tight ball. She knew she wouldn't sleep, she couldn't possibly, but she closed her eyes anyway.

Arms wrapped around her knees, she lay in the dark and waited for oblivion.

Once he was certain Casey had settled for the night, Jeff rose from the bed. In the bathroom, he went through the motions of brushing his teeth and washing his face, intent on not letting memories intrude. He refused to allow the images of Casey — of her body hot against his, her moans and cries — into his conscious mind.

But when he finally lay in bed, relaxing as best he could against his body's still painful arousal, he couldn't hold the thoughts at bay. They roiled in his mind, an erotic panoply of images.

What was wrong with him? When he'd drawn Casey into his arms, he'd wanted only to soothe her fear after that episode with Zucher. And once she'd calmed enough to let go of that horror he'd had every intention of letting her go. But then she'd snuggled in closer to him, had turned to him and wrapped herself around him.

It had been like gasoline on a fire. The explosion had blown away his reservations, his control. If she hadn't pushed him away, they would have both been naked in this bed, with him deep inside her.

Jeff flipped over onto his belly, impatient

with his mind's graphic images. He had to forget it happened, had to remember their agreement. They shouldn't have started what they'd started. It was just as well she'd pulled away.

There was no reason for him to spin his wheels trying to understand Casey Madison. And his heart had no damn business aching for her the way it did.

# Chapter 11

Casey stared at herself in Deb's bathroom mirror and stuck her tongue out at her bleary-eyed image. Even her favorite T-shirt, pale blue and imprinted with an Indian girl with a face full of dreams, couldn't save her.

She lifted Deb's hair dryer to her limp wet hair, eyeing the long gray nozzle with trepidation. She always preferred showering at night and leaving the drying of her hair in the hands of the hair gods. She wasn't always happy with the results, but at least she could blame bad hair days on the fates and not on her own peril-fraught attempt at beauty.

But last night a shower had been beyond her. So she'd shampooed her hair this morning and now stood staring down the barrel of a hair dryer.

She flipped on the switch and winced at the first blast of hot air. She held the hair brush in her free hand, but since she had no clue what to do with it while the dryer was running, she simply held it out to one side.

Damp hair whipped around her face under the force of the dryer and she wondered why it always looked so easy when her stylist did it.

She heard a rap on the door and tensed. She'd managed to avoid Jeff entirely this morning, slipping into the bathroom while he was starting coffee in the kitchen. She still didn't feel quite up to talking to him.

"Yes?" she called out over the drone of the hair dryer.

"It's Deb," a weary voice said through the door. "Are you almost done?"

Casey juggled the dryer into her other hand and nearly dropped it. "Just one minute and it's all yours."

"You're not using the hair dryer are you?" Deb asked, a worried note in her voice.

"No, no," Casey assured her as she wiggled the nozzle side to side like she'd seen the stylist do. The dryer leapt from her hand and into the sink with a clatter.

"Yes, you are," Deb said. "I'm coming in."

Deb pushed the door open just as Casey burned her finger on the heating element. Casey cried out, snatching back her hand as Deb plucked the cord from the outlet. Casey's cry must have alerted Jeff because he suddenly loomed in the doorway.

"Are you all right?" He reached for the hand she cradled, but she pulled it away before he could touch her. Why did he have to look so darned devastating in the morning? And he smelled like heaven.

Deb picked up the hair dryer from the sink and coiled its cord. "Casey has a bit of a problem with small appliances. We try to keep them out of reach."

Jeff's fingers wrapped around Casey's wrist and he pulled her hand to him. "You've burned yourself," he said. Then he asked Deb, "Have you got something for this?"

Deb set down the dryer, then examined Casey's hand. "Some aloe should do the trick." She pulled a tube of the medication out of the medicine chest and handed it to Jeff. "I hate to be a crab, but could you guys vamoose and let me shower?" She nudged them both out of the small bathroom. "I might have gotten two hours sleep last night and I have to head out for another shift."

Jeff ushered Casey from the bathroom, then pulled out a chair at the café table. He gestured for her to sit.

She remained standing. "If you'll give me the medication, I can put it on myself."

His hand cupped her elbow. "Sit," he ordered, urging her down. He pulled another chair up close enough that their knees brushed when he sat.

He held out his hand, his eyes demanding that she relinquish hers. She shook her half-dry hair from her face. "Could I get a cup of coffee first? I'm dying for some caffeine."

"I'll get it," he said, rising. She heard him moving in the kitchen, the sound of the coffee pouring, the clink of a spoon.

He returned and set the mug down in front of her. He'd added so much creamer, the coffee was nearly white and she suspected he'd added the sugar to match. The fact that he knew how to fix her coffee made him all the more dangerous.

"I think it feels better now." She kept the hand curled into her.

Sitting, he held out an imperious hand. "Give it here, Madison."

She made a face at him, but surrendered to his will. As she'd suspected, the back of her hand nestled in his palm felt far too good.

He squeezed some aloe onto his fingers. "Did you sleep well?" he asked as he warmed the gel between his fingertips.

"Yes," she lied. "Very well."

With an exquisitely gentle touch, he dabbed the gel against her burned finger. "No bad dreams?"

Casey's eyes wanted to drift shut at his touch. She forced them to remain open. "Of course not." That at least was the truth. She hadn't slept long enough to dream.

Finished spreading the gel, he still held her hand. "Did you tell your sister what happened last night?"

"No." With her free hand, she hooked a wet strand of hair behind her ear. She must look like a drowned rat. "I was asleep when she came in. And she was asleep when I got up."

His brief, fleeting smile transformed his face. Casey ached to touch the lines bracketing his mouth, to press her lips to his rough cheek.

He let go of her hand and Casey felt relief and regret that now she could move away from him. But instead, his hands moved to her hair, fingers diving into the damp strands and lifting them away from her head.

"This is where the cinnamon comes from," he murmured, leaning forward to press a handful to his face. He curved his fingers around the back of her neck and pulled her closer, taking in her fragrance on a long breath.

At a sound from the doorway, he jerked back from her and rose to his feet. Deb, her hair perfectly blow-dried and a pale pink robe wrapped around her slender body, stood watching them.

"Excuse me," Jeff said as he ducked past

Deb and headed for the bathroom.

Deb sauntered into the dining room. "He doesn't mean a thing to you, huh?"

"Wipe that smirk off your face, Madison," Casey growled.

The phone bleated, but Deb just stood there. "This isn't a smirk, it's sisterly interest."

"The hell it is." The phone rang again. "Aren't you going to answer that?"

Deb grinned and continued on into the kitchen. Casey nursed her coffee as she listened with half an ear to Deb's side of the conversation. Jeff returned just as Deb hung up the phone.

"Can I get you more coffee?" he asked Casey. His solicitous attitude made her nervous. She kept wondering when Mr. Hyde would return.

"Did anyone grab the paper yet?" Deb asked, heading for the front door. She opened the door and leaned down for the *Union Tribune* on the porch. "I'll take some of that coffee, Jeff . . ."

Her voice trailed off. She stood slowly, the newspaper dangling in her hand. "Oh my God." She whirled to face them. "Casey, what happened to your car?"

Jeff crossed the living room in three long

strides. At first, it looked as if the sedan had shrunk. Then as he hurried down the walk toward the curb, he realized that all four tires were flat.

"Damn," Jeff breathed as he circled the car.

Casey followed behind him, making small sounds of distress at the sight of each flat tire. "How could they all have gone flat at once?"

Jeff had a suspicion. He crouched by the front left tire for a better look. "Slashed," he said, fingers probing the holes. He moved to the back tire and checked it. "This one, too." He looked up at Deb who stood at the end of the walk. "Have you heard of anyone's tires getting slashed around here?"

Deb's eyes widened. "Not that I know of. This is a pretty quiet neighborhood." She moved out to the curb. "Who could have done such a thing?"

Rising, he turned to Casey. Fear flickered in her face, then indignation. "Zucher," she hissed. "Damn him, he slashed our tires."

"Who's Zucher?" Deb asked.

"The card cheater," Jeff and Casey answered in unison.

He let Casey explain it to Deb, about how Zucher had been harassing Casey and chasing them since Reno. To hear Casey tell it, it had been a hilarious adventure, right up to when Zucher tried to drag her off with him. Except for the trembling in Casey's voice she couldn't quite hold back.

"We'd better find a place to get this taken care of," Jeff said, cutting into their laughter over Casey's mistaking the cell phone for a gun.

"I'll get you out the phone book." Deb headed up the walk. "Then I have to get ready for work."

It took Jeff a half hour to find a tire shop able to tow the car in before noon. His temper had been worn to a thin edge by the time he dropped onto the living room sofa with another mug of coffee. He laid his head back and listened to the muted sounds of Casey and Deb, talking and laughing while Deb got ready for work.

They appeared in the living room a few minutes later, arms around each other as Casey walked Deb to the door.

"I'm sorry we can't visit longer," Deb said, giving Casey a squeeze.

Reaching up, Casey planted a kiss on her sister's cheek. "The little bit we had was great."

Deb turned to Jeff. "You have the key. Stay as long as you need to."

"Thanks for your hospitality," Jeff said.

Deb accepted his proffered hand, shaking it with stiff courtesy before she slipped out the door. Casey moved to the front window for a final wave good-bye.

Jeff asked, "Did you want to stay here while I get the tires replaced?"

Casey turned from the window with a sigh. "No, I'll go with you."

"Then you'd better get ready." He picked up his cell phone and Zucher's from the side table next to the sofa. "I've got some calls to make."

As Casey headed for Deb's bedroom, Jeff dialed his office. "Discreet Investigations," Jim answered with the courteous efficiency of retired military.

"Jim," Jeff said. "Status please."

Jim gave him a quick update of their current cases as if he'd been waiting by the phone for Jeff's call. "Randy and Laura have it covered."

Jeff hit the recall button on Zucher's cell phone. "I have a few phone numbers I want you to check for me." He read off the ones the card cheater had stored into memory. "I'll call back later for the information. Has Mrs. Bender called?"

Jim laughed, a bulldog chuckle. "Only a dozen times."

"Just keep putting her off," Jeff said, one

eye out the front window.

A tow truck pulled up in front of the rental car. "Turns out I have to go to Phoenix."

"Phoenix? As in Arizona?"

The tow driver strode up the front walk and rang the bell. "The same." Jeff rose to answer the door. Casey beat him to it, hurrying from the other room.

Jeff sat back down, his gaze narrowing on the muscle-bound tow truck driver on the porch and the leering grin he bestowed on Casey. Jeff could only see the back of Casey's blonde head and he wondered if she was smiling in return. Her light voice shimmered into laughter as she exchanged a few words with the driver.

Something burned in Jeff's gut when the driver laid a hand on Casey's shoulder to escort her out the door. When the door swung shut, Jeff moved to the front window to watch the two walk out to the car.

Teeth clenched, Jeff's eyes fixed on the proprietary hand on Casey's back. Dimly, he heard someone speak to him, and registered that he still had his office assistant on the phone.

"What was that, Jim?" Jeff asked, his attention on the tow driver. What was he doing, leaning in so close to Casey? Why was she laughing?

Jeff caught the tail end of Jim's repeated question. "— to Phoenix?"

"Long story." Jeff moved to the front door. "Tell you when I get back."

Hanging up the cell phone, he wrenched open the door. What was it with Casey and auto mechanics? Did she have a fetish for coveralls and grease? And the tow driver — the tall brown-haired stud was eyeing Casey as if she were a hot fudge sundae dished up just for him.

Jeff felt ready to explode with anger. He scooped up his suitcase and jacket and forced himself to shut the door quietly behind him. He made his way down the front walk with a slow measured pace, acid roiling in his stomach all the while.

What difference did it make if Casey flirted with someone else? Why should he care if another man laid his lecherous, steroid-laden arm around her shoulders? He was nothing to her — he'd said as much to her several times.

Jeff reached the curb just as the tow driver finished chaining the car up in preparation for dragging it onto the truck bed. The driver seemed to spend a lot of time flexing his muscles at Casey and running his fingers through his strategically rumpled brown hair. Jeff had to restrain himself from planting a fist into the tow driver's perfectly straight nose.

"Go get your things," Jeff growled at Casey. He turned his back on her to toss his bag and jacket inside the car.

As he was reaching in to put the cell phone in the glove box, she came right up to his elbow, cinnamon drifting around her. "Should I lock up?" she asked.

"Yes," he snapped, pulling back from her. "Unless you changed your mind and want to wait for me here."

Her brow furrowed. "No. I said I'd come with you."

He turned away and strode to the cab of the tow truck. "Then get going."

As he pulled himself into the cab, he could feel her eyes on him, but he refused to look at her. A few minutes later, he heard the front door shut, heard the sound of a key in the lock. Then the slap of her sneakered feet as she came down the walk.

Her fingers curled around the edge of the half-open truck window. "I'm going to ride up top again, okay?"

He stared straight forward. "You don't need my permission."

"I guess you're riding here," she said, invitation implicit in her voice.

"Yes." He pulled his seat belt around him. "Let's go."

Her fingers slipped from the window and

she turned to the waiting tow driver. Jeff couldn't help himself; he watched the driver in the side view mirror give her a leg up onto the truck bed. She had to place a hand on his muscled shoulder and his face pressed into her hip for a moment before she gained her footing in the bed.

Jeff's gut burned. He should have been the one to help her up there. But why? he asked himself. She was nothing to him, just a necessary evil, a stepping stone for him to get back his precious negatives of a philandering Nevada state assemblyman.

The cheerful tow driver swung himself into the truck and slammed the door shut. "She says you two aren't married," he said over the roar of the engine firing.

Jeff grunted a response. The driver jammed his truck into gear and looked over his shoulder as he pulled out. "She says you're not even boyfriend-girlfriend."

He turned blazing eyes on the driver. "What the hell business is it of yours?"

"Hey, man, back off," the driver said, tossing Jeff a wide grin. "I get up to Reno once in a while and I wanted to make sure I had a clear shot."

Jeff narrowed his gaze. "Did she give you her phone number?"

"No," the tow driver said. "Not yet."

And he'd damn well make sure she didn't. Jeff crossed his arms over his chest and fixed his gaze back out the front windshield. The driver, seeming to sense he wouldn't get any further conversation out of Jeff, turned on a heavy metal station. The whine of electric guitar blared from the radio, its gaudy sound adding another twist to the tangle of emotions within Jeff.

Casey released the tight hold around her middle as they pulled into the tire shop. Before she'd even gotten the car door open, Jeff was out of the cab and around to the driver's side of the truck bed. He held his arms out to her, his stormy expression at odds with the silent offer of assistance.

She reached for him warily, planting her hands on his shoulders as he circled her waist with his fingers. She leaned into him, digging her fingers into the soft knit of his Kelly green polo shirt, enjoying the warmth of his grip as he lifted her from the truck. She expected him to quickly let her go, but when the tow driver slid from the truck, Jeff snagged her wrist and pulled her in the opposite direction.

He led her into the showroom area of the tire shop, then dropped her wrist. He conferred with the clerk on the tires, tossed out a credit card, then gripped her shoulder and headed for the door.

"There's a park across the street," the clerk called after them, "if you folks want a nice place to wait."

Jeff urged her to the crosswalk, then guided her across when the light turned green. Tension seemed to tighten every muscle in his body, as if anger or some other strong emotion held him in its grip. He wouldn't meet her eyes as he led her to the nearest park bench and sat her in it.

He remained standing. "You were certainly damn cozy with that tow driver."

She craned her neck up at him. "What are you talking about?"

Stepping closer, he towered over her. "You were snuggling up to him from the moment he arrived at your sister's."

Her mouth dropped open. "I was not!"

"And I saw the way he was pawing you."

"Pawing me?"

"He had his hands all over you!"

"He was just being friendly," Casey protested.

"Friendly?" Jeff bit out. "He was practically mauling you!"

Casey grit her teeth and counted to ten. "He wasn't doing anything wrong."

Jeff bent to place a hand on either side of

her on the back of the bench. "Are you going to see him again?" The heavy denim of his crisp blue jeans scraped the insides of her legs. "Did you ask him to come see you in Reno?"

Casey wasn't the least bit interested in pursuing anything with the tow truck driver, but Jeff's attitude riled her up, made her want to lash out. "Maybe I did," she said, tipping up her chin. "What business is it of yours?"

He leaned closer. "He's wrong for you, Casey."

"How would you know?" Casey shot back. "Are you suddenly an expert on what's best for me?"

His expression dazed, he stared at her, his warm breath curling against her cheek. She wanted nothing more than to give up the argument, to draw him the few inches nearer, to press her lips against his.

He pushed back, paced away from her a few feet, then back. "I know you better than you think."

Inexplicably, emotion clogged her throat, tightened in her chest. She didn't even know herself — how could Jeff? Yet she wanted so very much for him to know her, to understand her.

Abruptly, he turned and started down the

path that circled the park. "I'm going for a walk."

He couldn't leave, not yet. She had to ask him . . . ask him . . . "Jeff!" she called out.

Spinning on his heel, he faced her again. "What?"

What indeed? She stared up at him, casting about in her mind. But the real question wasn't there, it was in her heart.

And that would be the biggest mistake, to let her heart do the talking.

She shook her head. "Nothing. I'll wait here for you."

A moment's hesitation, then he turned again and hurried away. Casey watched him until he disappeared into a grove of eucalyptus. Then she sat back, eyes shut, and let the loneliness wash over her. For an instant, the familiar hollow ache nearly overwhelmed her.

After the brisk, half-hour walk he'd taken around the park, Jeff figured he had himself under control again. He realized how ridiculous he'd been, dumping on Casey just because of another man's interest in her. After all, if she wanted to run off to Vegas and marry the tow truck driver, it was certainly no business of his.

Then he caught sight of her, still sitting

on the bench, a brilliant smile aimed in his direction. One look at the fire in her honey-brown eyes and he was willing to slay dragons and tow truck drivers alike for exclusive rights to that smile.

Lord, he was in trouble. His best defense was to keep his mouth shut to keep himself from saying something stupid. Like how he'd love to bury his face in her hair or how he'd like nothing better than to hold her snugly in his lap the rest of the day.

Big trouble.

He gestured at her to follow and headed across the street to the tire shop. He settled the bill with the clerk behind the counter, then when Casey caught up with him, dropped the keys into her hand.

"You want me to drive?" she asked, following him to the car.

He grunted, "Yeah," and climbed inside the sedan. He forced himself not to think, not to consider the equally dazzling grin she shot at the tow driver as they left the shop. If the two of them planned to take up where they left off in Reno, he didn't want to know about it. He couldn't bear to think about it.

She matched his silence, word for unspoken word. But thirty blissfully quiet minutes later on Interstate 15, Jeff knew Casey wouldn't hold out much longer.

From the corner of his eye, he watched her fuss with the rear view mirror, then slide her gaze toward him.

Clearing her throat, she made a production out of checking in the mirror. "Still no sign of him."

Jeff knew who she was talking about, but he didn't feel cooperative. "Who?"

"Phil Zucher," she said, a faint edge of irritation in her tone. "Do you suppose he's still after us?"

"Doubt it."

She waited, as if hoping to draw more out of him. "So you think slashing my tires was enough for him? He got his revenge?"

"Probably," Jeff said.

Casey dragged in a long breath. "Look, Jeff . . ."

"What?"

She drummed her fingers on the steering wheel, flicked him another glance. "I'm not going to see him again."

"Zucher?" he asked, intentionally obtuse.

He glanced at her sidelong; she looked as if she wanted to haul off and pop him one. "The tow truck driver. I didn't even get his name."

He didn't care. Of course he didn't. Then why was that little sparkle of joy starting up inside him? "Whatever," he said, injecting disinterest into the word.

"I don't deserve this," she said hotly, eyes back on the highway.

One foot up on the dash, he tapped his thumb on the inseam of his jeans. "Don't deserve what?"

"This . . . this . . . macho attitude." She shook her hair back out of her eyes. "You're acting like a caveman. Me Tarzan, you Jane."

The scent of cinnamon wafted toward him, and for a moment his brain disengaged. He exhaled sharply, driving her from his senses.

"Tarzan wasn't a caveman," he pointed out.

"You know what I mean," Casey said. "You don't run my life. You don't decide for me who I do and don't talk to."

"You're right."

She fell silent at his quick agreement, then her eyes narrowed on him. "If I want to invite a dozen tow truck drivers to my apartment, that's my business."

Damned if the image didn't loom sharp in his mind. Casey surrounded by studly men, a finger on her chin as she tried to decide which one to choose next.

He dropped his foot to the floor in agitation, forcing the picture away. He wanted to roar at her, to tell her she wasn't to have any man near her but him. That it was *him* she had to choose.

He couldn't believe how close those words were to escaping his lips. He clenched his jaw against the onslaught of emotion.

"Feel free," he said finally, taking perverse pleasure in her outraged shriek. He glanced at her, and couldn't quite suppress a smile at the snap in her eyes, the high color on her cheeks. God, he loved to needle her. He could spend the rest of his life getting under her skin. . . .

Good Lord, where had that come from? He didn't want to spend his life with any woman, most especially not Ms. Casey Madison.

Feeling even more out of sorts, he crossed his arms over his chest and hunkered down in his seat. "Wake me when you want me to drive." That was all he needed, to catch up on his sleep. Her constant presence had him on edge, robbed of him of his rest.

But although he could close his eyes against the sight of her, he couldn't shut the sound of her breathing from his ears or her scent from his nose. Sleep was a long time coming.

Casey squinted at the car clock as Jeff pulled the rental car up to Liz's condo complex. It was just after nine. Jeff must have really pushed the speed limit after taking over the driving this afternoon.

Just as well. After hours of stony silence as they drove through the Sonoran desert, Casey thought she'd scream waiting for Jeff to say something, anything. Scream or throttle him.

Of course, if she'd put her hands on his throat to choke him, she'd probably end up stroking him, caressing him, letting her hands roam his face, his strong shoulders . . .

Knock it off!

Casey peeled her sweaty back from the passenger seat and pushed open the car door. As she stepped from the car, the muggy tail end of Arizona's monsoon season pressed in on her oppressively. The saguaro cactus in Liz's front yard towered over her like a portent in the moonlight, sending a shiver up her spine.

They'd nearly reached their goal, why did she feel this sudden sense of foreboding? She watched Jeff rounding the car and tried to parse out her unease. She'd told Liz to hold the pictures for them. Even if she and Jeff didn't leave until tomorrow morning, he'd still get them to his client by the deadline.

Shaking off the unreasonable discomfort, she dipped back into the car for her purse. Then she led the way to the bank of mailboxes and pressed her thumb to the doorbell.

"Yes?" Liz's throaty voice called from the speaker.

"It's me, Liz," Casey squeaked out. "Casey."

She jumped back at the buzz of the security door. Jeff reached around her and opened it, then waited for her to pass through.

"It's upstairs." Casey pointed upward unnecessarily. He let her precede him around the swimming pool, then up the stairs.

Liz waited at her door, lean as an athlete in red camp shirt and khaki shorts. She reached out for Casey, her long arms enfolding Casey in a powerful hug.

She put out a hand to Jeff. "Liz Madison," she said, her tone no-nonsense.

"Jeff Haley." He flinched a little at the force of Liz's grip.

She grinned at Casey, her teeth white against her tan face. "God, it's good to see you. I hate the fact that we all live so far apart."

Casey tweaked a lock of Liz's sun-streaked brown hair. "You've let it grow out a bit."

Liz raked back the bangs that flopped in her eyes. "It needs a trim."

"Where are my negatives?" Jeff asked, apparently having had his fill of sisterly affection.

Liz turned to Jeff. "What negatives?"

"The ones Casey asked you to hold onto," Jeff said, his irritation plain.

Her sister looked puzzled. "It was the *negatives* you wanted me to keep?"

Jeff narrowed his eyes on Liz. "What are you saying?"

"In the phone message, Casey asked me to hold on to the *pictures*. I thought she meant the prints." Liz said. "I sent the negatives on to Shar."

# Chapter 12

Casey couldn't quite stifle the giggle that rose in her throat. "She sent them on. Imagine that."

Jeff rounded on her, his glare incendiary. "I said to tell her to hold the negatives. The *negatives*."

"Wait a minute," Liz said, her gaze moving from Casey to Jeff and back. "You *don't* need the prints?"

Jeff redirected his ire to Liz. "Why the hell did you take her literally?" He flung a hand at Casey. "She never says what she means. You should have kept it all just in case."

Looking ready to throw a punch, Liz shifted to the balls of her feet. "I'm a photographer. To me, pictures mean prints and negatives mean negatives."

"But why the hell would I want the prints?" Jeff roared.

"How the hell should I know?" Liz shouted back. "I didn't even know you existed!"

His jaw twitched and Casey knew he was grinding his teeth again. "But why would you send off the negatives?"

Arms crossed over her chest, Liz tipped her chin up. "Shar wanted them. She planned to just make prints of the whole batch."

Casey winced. She wondered what her rather staid oldest sister's reaction would be to finding pictures of a naked Nevada state assemblyman in amongst the reunion shots.

A crazed look seemed to have entered Jeff's eye. He lay a hand on her shoulder, pulled her around to face him. "Why are you doing this?" He tipped her head up, held it there so she couldn't look away. "Why are you trying to drive me crazy? For revenge? To get back at all those men who done you wrong?"

Casey shook her head, his warm palm cupping her chin. "I'm not, Jeff. I swear. I just . . . I'm sorry," she squeaked out as his gaze darkened.

She tried to interpret what she saw in his face — anger, frustration, confusion, hot passion. She wondered which would win out — would he kiss her or swallow her whole?

Obviously kissing her in front of her

equally angry sister wasn't an option. Breathing hard, he dropped his hands from her and backed away, intent on escape. Casey jumped when he slammed the door behind him, then stood trembling in reaction in Liz's living room.

Liz reached out and slipped her arm around Casey's shoulders. "You look like you need to sit."

Guiding Casey to the sleek, sand-colored sofa, Liz nudged her into it.

Then she dropped beside Casey and tucked her long tanned legs under her.

"You want to tell me what's going on?" Liz asked.

Casey stared out Liz's front window, still feeling shivery and warm inside from Jeff's touch. "It's kind of complicated."

"I figured as much." Liz turned to Casey and took her hand. "But who is that man? And how long have you been in love with him?"

An hour later, amid a great deal of laughter and a few tears, Casey had told Liz everything — or nearly everything — about Jeff and the photos and the Nevada state assemblyman. She skipped the part about the connecting door, glossed over Zucher's frightening pursuit of her, and avoided entirely the subject of Jeff's devastating kisses.

"I had the darn things in my hand," Liz said, referring to the negatives, "that's what makes it so frustrating."

"I did, too." Casey took a sip of the spicy iced tea Liz had produced somewhere between Casey's tale of the bikers and the slashed tires. She slanted Liz a look. "Did you look at them?"

"Not a peek." She clinked the ice cubes in her glass. "Believe me, if I'd seen pictures of a naked man cavorting in a hotel room, I wouldn't have sent them to Shar."

Casey slapped a hand on her forehead. "God, can you imagine her expression when she sees them?"

Liz guffawed. "That ought to ruffle even Earth Mother Shar."

"Which reminds me." Casey set aside her iced tea and rose. "We'd better give her a call."

Liz put out a hand to stop her. "You still haven't told me."

She looked down at Liz's long slim fingers, then out the front window, anywhere but into her sister's eyes. "Told you what?"

Liz squeezed Casey's hand and shook it. "Look at me." Casey did so, but sidelong. "What about Jeff? In all that very entertaining story about car chases and Harleys, you never once mentioned what's happening between you and him."

Casey pulled her hand free. "That's because nothing's happening between me and him."

Liz didn't miss the catch in Casey's throat. "Then why is it every time you say his name you look as if you're hiding something?"

Casey pasted a smile on her face. "What would I be hiding?"

"That you love him, or —" Liz rose abruptly. "He's not hurting you is he?" Her blue eyes turned stormy. "Hitting you or —"

"No," Casey said. "Absolutely not."

"Because if he was, you know I'd punch out his lights."

Casey laughed; Liz would certainly be an even match for Jeff. "I'd beat you to it. No, Jeff's not hurting me."

She grinned, convincing herself that she really wasn't lying. After all, the only thing that hurt was her longing for something that never could be.

"Is it after ten?" Casey ducked away from Liz and headed for the phone. "Shar's restaurant ought to be closed by now."

Her bright tone didn't fool big sister Liz; she still had questions in her eyes. Casey waggled the phone receiver at her. "Do you have the number programmed? I always forget what it is."

Liz strode to the phone and pressed the proper buttons. "This discussion isn't finished, Casey."

Casey waved a hand at her as Shar answered the phone with a businesslike, "Edge of Heaven."

Turning away from Liz, Casey answered with a cheery, "Hey, Sis!" She quickly told Shar about the negatives, then asked Liz, "How did you send them?"

"Express Mail," Liz answered. "They'll get there tomorrow or Monday."

Casey relayed the information to Shar. "We'll be there tomorrow, maybe Sunday."

"Liz is coming, too?" Shar asked, curiosity in her throaty contralto.

"No, I'm with a friend." She supposed Jeff could be loosely described as a friend. "If you get those negatives tomorrow, guard them with your life."

Hanging up the phone, she briskly moved past Liz to the kitchen. "What have you got to snack on? We had some fast food around five, but I'm starving now."

Liz opened the refrigerator and tossed Casey an apple, then pulled out one for herself. "Your 'friend' *is* coming back isn't he?" she asked before biting into the apple.

Busying herself with taking a huge

mouthful, she shrugged apologetically as she chewed. Liz's eyes didn't leave hers until Casey swallowed. "Of course," Casey said, not feeling at all sure. "He has the car."

After a moment's sharp scrutiny, Liz sighed. "You used to tell me everything, every little crush, every little heartache."

Her gaze on the apple, she turned it in her hand. "There's nothing between Jeff and me, Liz." She looked up at her sister. "At least I don't want there to be."

Closing the space between them, Liz drew Casey into a hug. "Sometimes you don't have a choice."

Casey pulled away. "Of course I do. I mean, he's a pretty sexy guy — those shoulders are to die for. But even if I wanted something more, Jeff's not interested in a commitment."

Liz narrowed her eyes on Casey. "Just sex, I suppose."

She nearly choked on the mouthful of apple she'd just bitten off. "Sex?" She chewed and swallowed with effort. "I haven't . . . we haven't . . . God, Liz, I told you there was nothing going on." She dumped the rest of the uneaten apple into the trash and strode out of the kitchen. "Lord, I'm tired. I think I could sleep standing up."

Catching at her shoulder, Liz stopped her,

turned her around. "You don't fool me, Casey. You're your cheeriest when you're hurting the worst inside. I want to remind you that you can tell me *anything*. And anytime."

Casey managed a wan smile. "Thanks, Sis."

They made Casey a bed on the sofa, since the futon in Liz's bedroom was too small for two. Liz tossed down a sleeping bag on the living room floor for Jeff although she told Casey she'd just as soon he sleep outside in the car after the way he'd stomped out without so much as a good-bye. Liz was even more annoyed with him when they realized he still had Casey's bag in the car. Mumbling and grumbling to herself, Liz rustled up a spare toothbrush and a nightie so long it skimmed Casey's calves.

It was past midnight by the time Liz gave her one last hug and headed off to bed. Casey lay on the stiff cushions of the sofa, knowing she wouldn't have been able to sleep if it were the most comfortable of beds. Jeff still hadn't returned and anxiety over his safety gnawed at her.

Her mind whirling, she fell into a half-doze filled with choppy, nonsensical dreams. She had no sense of the passage of time, so that when Jeff stumbled in the door sometime in the night, she had no idea what time it was.

She lay still on the sofa while he moved around, dropping one shoe with a clatter on the tiled entryway, the other with a thud on the living room carpet. His movements seemed clumsy and awkward and Casey realized he was probably drunk.

She heard the sound of him shucking his jeans, then the near-silent swish of his shirt being pulled over his head. She opened one eye just enough to see him standing over her in the last of the moonlight, watching her. He had to have seen the sleeping bag on the floor, she could see one of his shoes atop it.

But he didn't settle onto the sleeping bag. Instead, he tugged up the corner of Casey's blanket and sat beside her. Nudging her over with his hip, he stretched out alongside her on the wide sofa.

For an instant, Casey froze in shock, despite the sharp pleasure of his hard warm body against hers. Then he insinuated one of his hair-roughened legs between hers, hiking up the hem of the nightie so that his thigh rested against the juncture of her legs. He pressed against her, his arms pulling her tight against his chest.

Then his mouth covered hers, and the smoky scent and taste of whiskey filled her senses. His tongue slipped inside her mouth immediately, dipping and thrusting while his leg pressed snug against her. She felt an exquisite sensation between her legs, a throbbing at the center of her. She trembled from the feel of it.

Then seconds after the kiss began, it ended. Jeff eased slightly away from her, still keeping his arms securely around her, one hand tucking her head against his chest. His leg between hers went lax and a moment later, she heard the gentle snore that told her he was asleep.

Every nerve ending in her body stood at attention. She lay in his arms, hands pressed against the mat of hair on his chest, certain she'd never fall asleep.

But moments later, the heat of his body seeped into her, and the security of his arms soothed her into sleep.

The Arizona sun, cruel and vivid, pierced Liz's front window and peeled back Jeff's eyelids. He'd been enjoying a marvelous dream — in which Casey lay hot and willing in his arms — when the brilliant light jolted him awake. Like a demon, a whiskey hangover swooped in after.

But the dream of Casey lingered. The pounding in his head a monstrous distraction, it took him a moment to realize that the sweet weight across his chest was the woman herself. Then she shifted in her sleep and her breasts, shielded only by a nothing of a nightgown, slid against him.

He was hard, getting harder by the second. Her leg had burrowed between his, pressing against his manhood so that he had to swallow back a groan. One of her small hands splayed across his shoulder, the other rested dangerously close to his hip.

He was thoroughly disgusted with himself. Had he taken her last night in a drunken stupor? That he might have taken advantage of her only added to his self-revulsion. Not to mention he felt utterly stupid blacking out what had to have been an incredibly pleasurable experience.

His left arm lay wedged between the back of the sofa and Casey's slender body. He could tell he still wore his briefs — which meant nothing since in his younger, more randy days he'd accomplished the act fully dressed. But what about Casey? Was she still wearing panties?

Cautious, he lifted his hand from where it nestled in the small of her back. Feeling along ever so lightly with his fingertips, he tried to sense what she was wearing under the filmy stuff of the nightgown. His fingers reached the swell of her bottom and his breathing caught. He stopped for a moment, dragging in air as he fought the urge to cover the fullness of her rear with his hand.

Casey moved again, fitting herself more snugly against him. This time he did groan as he struggled against the urge to thrust against her. He forced himself to lie still, counting specks in the ceiling, reciting the Pythagorean theorem in his mind. Finally, he was able to move his hand a little lower. He sighed with relief when he detected the top edge of Casey's panties.

He was pretty certain that if he'd loved her last night, her panties would be nowhere near her person. So his vague memory of having come in late and lain here with her was accurate. He wasn't quite as low a creature as he'd thought himself when he'd first awakened.

Which you couldn't prove by Liz who stood glaring at him from the entryway. He stilled, acutely aware that he'd pushed away the blanket in the course of checking Casey's behind. Now his hand lay in full view, limpet-like on that luscious mound.

Moving as gently as he could, Jeff eased Casey off his chest and slid out from under her. Once free of her body, he nearly rose before remembering he wore only briefs, ill concealment for his state of arousal. So he perched on the edge of the sofa, blanket demurely across his lap, until he could snag his jeans with his toes and tug them on.

At least halfway dressed, he stood and confronted the reproach in Liz's blue eyes. "Good morning," he mumbled, feeling the same way he had facing his parents the first time he'd stayed out all night with a girl.

Her icy, "Good morning," could have made a Popsicle of him, despite the Arizona sun creeping into the window. He turned away to pluck up his shirt and had to suck in a breath at the searing pain in his skull. God, he was too damned old to be going out and getting drunk.

"This isn't how it looks," he said, feeling stupid for wanting to defend himself.

"I'm sure it isn't," she snapped, her gaze flaying him.

He enjoyed a momentary escape by pulling on his shirt. "We didn't . . . We haven't . . ." Hell, he was a grown man, why was he standing here explaining himself for Casey's older sister?

"I try to keep out of Casey's affairs," Liz said, her harsh voice barely above a whisper, "but when I see someone causing her pain and in my own damn house —"

A sigh alerted him that Casey had woken.

He looked down at her as her fluttering eyes drifted to Liz. "What's up, Sis?" she asked, her voice still soft with sleep.

A pain unrelated to hangover lanced through Jeff in the vicinity of his heart. She looked so sweet lying there, he wanted nothing more than to scoop her into his arms, older sisters be damned.

Liz faced Casey, patently excluding Jeff. "Just wondering if you'd like to go out to breakfast before you get on the road. There's this great pancake place near here."

"Sounds wonderful." Casey sat up and stretched like a particularly slinky cat, her small breasts outlined by the thin nightgown. She turned to him. "Jeff?"

He shoved his hands in his pockets to hide his inevitable reaction to Casey's unselfconscious sensuality. "You two go ahead. I'm not hungry."

Casey rose, so that the blanket fell away, revealing the curve of her hips, her small slender feet. "Or do you think we should get going?"

Jeff backed away a pace. "Go ahead and spend some time with your sister. I need to make a couple phone calls anyway."

"Thanks," Casey said, her gown swirling around her as she turned toward the bathroom.

Leaving Jeff alone with Liz again. She smiled, an unpleasant baring of teeth. "If you hurt her, I will beat you into a bloody pulp," she said with false sweetness.

Which she looked fully capable of, with her long strong limbs in no-nonsense purple tank top and matching running shorts. "That's not my intention," he said.

"Just so we understand each other." Liz reached for the front door handle. "Are Casey's things still in the car?"

Jeff nodded, then endured another of Liz's long, narrow-eyed looks. He finally took an easy breath when she headed out the door.

The sisters laughed and chattered while Casey dressed, their gentle noise only ceasing once when the phone rang. He heard Liz's voice, then Casey's, speaking on the bedroom phone, the words too soft to make out. A short while later, they reappeared, then headed off to breakfast.

Torn between calling Jim and a shower, Jeff voted for the latter, and headed down to the car to retrieve his own bag. A strategically placed rock kept the condo complex security door open for his return.

When he laid his hand on the car door handle, a tingle danced up his spine. His garment bag still lay on the back seat where he'd left it, but the zipper was partially open, and a bit of the contents protruded.

He pulled open the door. That Liz might have rifled through his bag he immediately dismissed; if she'd wanted to search his things, forthright Liz would have done it right in front of him.

Ducking into the back seat, he opened the bag the rest of the way. His neatly hung shirts and folded socks were all disturbed; the plastic bag he used for laundry had been opened and its twist-tie not quite shut again.

Someone had been through his things, that was damn certain. They might have searched Casey's as well, although Casey probably wouldn't know the difference since she kept her clothes in such disarray.

A simple burglary? He'd had nothing of value in his suitcase. He popped open the glove box. His cell phone still lay inside.

But where was Zucher's?

He remembered putting the phones in the glove box together, back at Deb's house. If someone had burglarized the car, they would have taken both phones, not just Zucher's.

Unless it was Zucher himself. Damn, Jeff had thought the man had given up in San Diego. The card cheater was more of an inconvenience than a threat to Jeff now that he knew Zucher wasn't armed, but the card cheater's continued pursuit would frighten Casey.

Jeff didn't want to consider too deeply his concern for Casey's feelings or why he was no longer angry with her. Somehow last night, between one shot of whiskey and the next, he'd decided that Casey was only being Casey — she couldn't help herself. He didn't have to let himself be sucked into her baffling logic, but he didn't have to crucify her either.

So he wouldn't tell her about Zucher, he decided as he closed the garment bag and tugged it from the car. He could handle the card cheater; there was no need to worry Casey about it.

He returned to Liz's condo, feeling a greater urgency to discover just who Zucher had called on his cell phone. But when he called Jim at home, his wife reported he was off coaching his grandson's soccer game. That information would have to wait.

He showered quickly, relieved to change into a set of clothes that didn't smell like whiskey. Then, figuring to earn back a few brownie points with Liz, he tidied up the living room and gathered up Casey's things in the bathroom. He felt like a real pervert when his fingers lingered on the silky material of Casey's panties just before he tucked them away in her bag.

When Liz and Casey still hadn't returned, Jeff sat down with the *Arizona Republic* newspaper and a black as death cup of coffee. He nearly gagged on the coffee when he saw the page ten photo of Assemblyman Bender grinning and clasping the hand of the Arizona governor.

Seeing Bender's picture reminded him of Mrs. Bender, which reminded him of the negatives, which reminded him of Casey. Jeff rubbed at his eyes. Who was he kidding? Everything reminded him of Casey these days. He could probably find a connection to Casey in a book of Latin grammar.

Footsteps on the walkway outside jarred Jeff from his morose thoughts. He tossed aside the newspaper and rose just as the door opened. Casey paused in the doorway, backlit by the morning sun.

Damn, he'd been waiting for her. Without even realizing it, he'd been killing time until she returned. And now that she stood before him, her curves outlined by a brilliant turquoise T-shirt and softly worn jeans, his heart was doing some pretty undignified singing.

He snatched up his coffee cup, turning away from her as she walked inside. Liz didn't miss the slosh of coffee on her pale rose tile floor; before he even had a chance to clean it, she'd grabbed a napkin from the table and swiped it up.

Casey seemed lighter after her visit with her sister, as if she'd laid her problems at Liz's feet and felt all the better for it. Of course, Jeff suspected the bulk of those problems had to do with him, which clued him in to why Liz was still shooting him daggers.

He poured the remainder of the sludge in his cup down the drain, then assiduously rinsed both cup and sink. "We'd better get going."

The joy in Casey's face dimmed just a watt. "Sure. Just let me get my things together."

"Already done." Heat rose in his cheeks as he remembered the panties.

Casey looked at her sister then, her regret at leaving apparent in her face. "Guess this is it, Sis," she said as she threw her arms around Liz.

Jeff didn't anticipate Liz would give him a warm good-bye. More like a kick in the butt to urge him out the door. Why Liz's approval of him suddenly mattered so much he didn't want to ponder.

She didn't plant her foot on his rear, but as she shook his hand she gave him a look that spoke volumes. *Hurt my sister and I'll hunt you down.* He acknowledged her message with a tip of his head.

Her purse and her sports bag acting as ballast for her small frame, Casey gave her sister one last hug, then followed Jeff out the door. She moved along quietly enough in his wake, waiting until they'd reached the sidewalk to tell him, "Liz doesn't like you."

"So I gathered." Jeff took her burdens from her and dropped them into the back seat.

"Very odd," Casey said thoughtfully as she slid into the passenger side.

*I don't want to know,* Jeff told himself as he circled around the hood. Yet as he swung shut the driver side door, he heard himself asking, "What's odd?"

"That Liz doesn't like you."

"I suppose Liz likes everyone," Jeff muttered as he started the car up and pulled out.

Casey flipped down the visor to peer into the mirror behind it. "No, just men." She must have realized how that sounded, because she added, "All her friends are men, but that's really all they ever are." Casey tapped her chin. "Yet she doesn't like you."

*With good reason.* Jeff slanted a glance at Casey. He damn well better clear the air about climbing in bed with her. "About last night," he said.

Casey shot him a worried look. "What about it?"

"About what happened." His eyes searched out the entrance to Interstate 10.

She tipped her chin up. "You mean when you accused me of intentionally driving you crazy?"

It took Jeff a moment to remember the scene he made before he stomped off to a bar. "I've decided to let that go for now."

Her eyes widened in indignation. "Don't do me any favors."

This wasn't going well at all. He finally caught sight of the freeway sign. "Could we just get back to last night?"

"What about it?" Casey said, her tone wary.

He caught a glimpse of her chewing on her lip before he breezed past the Interstate 10 entrance. "Damn!" He fixed his eyes ahead, searching out a place to turn around.

"I think I'll do a little reading." Casey ducked beneath the shoulder strap of her seat belt so she could retrieve her purse. She pulled out a dog-eared romance novel and immediately buried her nose in it.

Occupied with finding an intersection that allowed a U-turn, then busy locating the Interstate 10 entrance, Jeff's focus slipped away from their conversation. An hour later, when the Sonoran desert's endless miles of saguaro, brush and boulders had numbed his mind to everything but the memory of Casey nestled in his arms, he should have brought it up again. But by then, Casey had fallen asleep, her face pressed against the window, arms tucked tightly around her.

He reached across her to lock her door, his arm brushing against her face. Her lips tightened at the touch, as if she slept very lightly. He imagined her kissing him there, her tongue flicking out to wet his skin. The rumble of warning bumps under the tires jerked his attention back to the highway.

The unchanging vastness of the Sonoran desert didn't help his efforts to keep his focus fixed on his driving. At least his sharp awareness of her beside him, the sweetness of her cinnamon scent, would keep him from being lulled to sleep by the unvarying landscape.

He couldn't help the spurt of joy he felt when she woke and smiled at him. "Want to play States and Capitals?" she asked.

*I want to pull over to the side of the road and drag you into the back seat.* Out loud, he said, "It wouldn't be much of a contest."

Her languorous stretching was a hazardous distraction to his driving. "I can start you off with the easy ones," she said.

He slanted her a look. "I won first place in a seventh grade geography bee. I am unstoppable."

She lifted her chin, a clear challenge. "We'll just see."

She proved to be a formidable opponent, quick to answer when he shot out the name of a state, nearly as fast when he gave her a capital to match. He'd always prided himself on his knowledge of U.S. geography, but he had to admit she was strong competition.

When they'd exhausted States and Capitals, they moved on to the alphabet game. But there were so few highway signs along the way, it was difficult to find the sequential letters of the alphabet. So Casey suggested a variation — match mileage numbers to the corresponding alphabet letter. A sign showing them thirteen miles from Blythe yielded an M, twenty-three miles from Coachella they had a W.

As rush hour traffic slowed their progress through San Bernadino, Jeff wondered how a woman as seemingly scatter-brained as Casey could be so quick with games of mental skill. Then he thought back, to those long nights discussing strategy, planning

Zucher's downfall. Her logic hadn't been straight and linear like his — she'd tended to jump from idea to idea with no apparent pattern. Yet, time and again, when he threaded together the sense of what she'd said, the result was often brilliant.

He realized with chagrin that if she'd been a man, he would have just considered her absent-minded, not scatter-brained. If Laura, one of the investigators in his office, got wind of his sexist train of thought, she'd have his head.

The traffic finally lightened when they reached Interstate 15. Jeff headed north, grateful to have glare of the setting sun to his left instead of directly ahead.

"Were we going to stop?" Casey asked. "I'm starving."

"Can you hold out a little longer?" He checked the rear view mirror, relieved to see no sign of Zucher. "I'd like to get to Highway 395 before we stop for the night."

"I can wait." Her stomach rumbled to give the lie to that assurance. She laughed, and him with her. He felt altogether too happy.

By the time they reached Adelanto on Highway 395, the sun's light had faded to a purple-pink on the horizon and the spiky leaves of the yucca trees stood as stark silhouettes in the growing dark. Jeff pulled into the first motel he saw, glad to see a coffee shop within walking distance. His stomach had joined Casey's in protest a good twenty miles ago.

In the motel lobby, the desk clerk looked up from her computer terminal. "Can I help you folks?"

"We'd like two rooms." Jeff twisted his back to work out the kinks.

"Sorry," the woman said, a hand up to brush back her salt-and-pepper bangs, "only one room left."

Jeff sighed; he hadn't wanted to have to search for accommodations. "Can you tell me where else I could go in town?"

"There are only two other places — the casino and one other. But they're full up."

Jeff was not liking the sound of this. "How can everything be full?"

The woman shrugged. "A movie crew's in town. Filming at the old Air Force base. Do you want the room or not?"

Jeff's stomach growled, reminding him that he was taking far too long with this negotiation. "How many beds in the room?"

The clerk took a look at her computer. "One. A king," she answered.

Jeff sucked in a breath, aware of Casey's attention on him. "We could go back to Victorville." He kept his gaze on his hands gripping the counter.

"We could," she said, her voice small.

He flexed his arms and rocked back on his heels. "I'm exhausted."

"Me, too. And starving."

He slid his gaze to her. "A king is a big bed."

"Sure." She worried her lip. "Lots of room in a king."

"Then we'll take it," he said, although it was a question.

She nodded wordlessly. He turned back to the clerk who waited expectantly. He dug out his belabored credit card, his fingers squeezing the thin plastic. The raised numbers were probably leaving indentations in his fingertips.

"We'll take the room," he said.

He knew he was making a mistake. He only wondered just how huge.

# Chapter 13

This is a mistake, Casey thought. She stared down at the vast expanse of king-sized bed tucked into a corner of the motel room. A huge mistake.

She flicked a glance at Jeff, took in his set jaw, his narrowed gaze. He seemed as transfixed by that room-dominating mattress as she, and a lot less happy about it.

After slinging their bags onto the foot of the bed, he stepped back as if he didn't want to get too near it. Hands shoved into his pockets, he turned to her.

"Dinner or showers first?" he asked.

Even if she hadn't been ravenous, she would have pounced on any excuse to escape the intimacy of this room and its monster bed. "Definitely dinner."

He moved with alacrity to the door. "Coffee shop okay?"

She was right behind him, purse clutched to her side. "Fine. Let's go."

He was silent during the short walk to the coffee shop, quick to step aside as he held the door open for her. So Casey withstood the gauntlet of locals at the counter first, six faces that turned in unison to look her up and down. *They know,* Casey thought irrationally as she passed that line, *they know about The Bed.*

She was only too happy to creep to a booth in the back, to hide behind the menu the waitress brought. Of course, the waitress took that back when she returned to take their order, leaving Casey exposed again to the counter sitters' scrutiny.

"They're staring at us," Casey whispered as she fiddled with the condensation on her water glass.

Jeff looked over his shoulder to follow the direction of her gaze, then turned back to her. "They're staring at their dinners."

Casey ran a thumbnail along a gash in the table. "No, I really think they're looking at us."

"Casey." Jeff put his hand briefly on hers, stilling her aimless movements. "Forget about them. I want to talk to you about last night."

Lord, she'd hoped he'd given up on that. "What about it?" she asked brightly.

He kept his eyes focused on hers, his gaze intent. "I wanted to apologize."

She widened her eyes, forcing a disingenuous expression on her face. "For what?"

"For being drunk as a skunk."

She busied herself with sipping her water. "You're a grown-up. You don't have to apologize for tying one on."

"Not just that." He watched her carefully. "Also, for doing . . . what I did when I got back from the bar."

Casey tried on confusion. "What did you do?"

His eyes narrowed. "Do you remember when I came back to Liz's?"

She shook her head, wincing inwardly at the lie. "I'm a pretty sound sleeper."

He studied her a long moment, his jaw working. Then he averted his eyes. "Never mind."

Casey sighed in relief. She'd just as soon he believe she never knew he was there. It would be difficult enough to get through sleeping with him in The Bed without re-membering the heaven of his arms last night.

When their dinners arrived, Casey's ap-petite had vanished. She picked at her sea-food platter, poking at the tartar sauce with the crispy fish pieces, leaving the mountain of fries untouched. Jeff seemed to spend more time cutting up his top sir-loin than eating it and he never even broke open his baked potato.

Then the waitress dropped the check on the table. The slip of paper sat between them like a challenge, an announcement that the meal was over and in a few minutes they would be returning to the motel room. To The Bed.

Jeff's hand closed over it. Casey couldn't help the little sound of dismay that escaped her.

He snatched his hand back again. "You're not finished?"

She wanted to say no, but she couldn't have stuffed another piece of fish in her mouth if her life depended on it. She shrugged and slid from the booth. She waited while he paid the bill, then followed him from the coffee shop.

Her first sight of that big bed again and she thought her knees would give way. It seemed as if there was nothing else in the room but that massive mattress.

"You want to shower first?" he asked at her elbow, making her jump.

"No, you go ahead." She retreated until she whacked her hand on the worn dresser. "I want to let my dinner settle," she added, as if she'd eaten any.

He shrugged, then opened his suitcase and pulled out a pair of black sweatpants. She sagged with relief when he disappeared into the bathroom.

As if it were a pit of alligators, Casey approached The Bed. Figuring she ought to get used to the feel of it while Jeff was still in the shower, she sat on its edge, then lifted her feet onto it. Leaning back against the pillows, she scooped up the remote control and turned on the television.

She heard the sound of the shower starting up, then the scrape of the shower door sliding open. She could all too vividly imagine Jeff, gloriously naked, stepping over the edge of the tub into the shower. The water would run in rivulets down his chest while he soaped himself up, ran his hands over his body. . . .

She cut off that line of thought as she flipped through the channels. She barely focused on the images on the screen before switching to another channel.

She looked down at the remote in disgust. Nothing even half-way decent on television to distract her from her tantalizing images of Jeff.

An inscription at the bottom of the remote caught her eye. "Turn key to view Channel 8." She looked up at the television curiously, saw the small black box atop it with a key protruding.

She dropped the remote on the nightstand, then padded to the television. She turned the key, then returned to the bed. Grabbing up the remote, she selected Channel 8.

The sound registered before the picture on the screen. The high-pitched moaning, deep-throated grunting, the sickly music. Then the antics of the couple riveted her, held her in guilty thrall.

Good grief, could people really do that? she wondered idly, as the naked bodies cavorted athletically in a bubbling hot tub. And could a man really be that . . . humongous?

Despite the crassness of what she saw, the blatancy that turned the act of love into sheer mechanics, she reacted. As she watched the movie, her thoughts of Jeff in the shower segued into imaginings of her with him, of her hands on him, skimming over his soap-slicked body.

Her breathing grew shallow, she felt a tightness between her legs. She knew she ought to turn the darn thing off, felt embarrassed that she was watching it at all, but her mind had overlaid a new image on the screen. It was Jeff she saw naked in that hot tub, and herself in his arms.

She didn't even hear the bathroom door

open, or Jeff's near-silent footfalls into the room. His sharp intake of breath drew her eyes to him, and she couldn't look away.

His bare, still-damp chest heaved, his black eyes burned into hers. When her gaze of its own accord drifted down his body, she saw the moisture nestled in the dark curls on his chest, the whorls of hair that trailed into the waistband of his black sweatpants.

*Don't do it,* she told herself. *Look away.*

She didn't. Her eyes drifted lower. To his unmistakable arousal, jutting under the soft material of his sweatpants. Her breathing grew even shallower, and her tongue crept out to wet too-dry lips.

He uttered a vicious oath and with a slap of his hand turned off the TV. Then he turned to her, face stormy.

"What the hell were you doing?" he ground out.

Swallowing, she fixed her eyes with tremendous effort on his face instead of the enticing evidence of his manhood. "It was an accident," she gasped.

"An accident that you turned it on?" he asked. "Or an accident that I caught you watching?"

She waved the remote toward him. "There was a note, you see, about Channel 8, and I wondered . . ." Her cheeks burned as he narrowed his gaze on her. "So I turned the key and I switched it to . . ."

His gaze moved to the box on the television. With an impatient flick of his wrist, he turned the key back to the locked position, then tugged it from the box. He carried it to the dresser and dropped it in the bottom drawer.

With the Bible, Casey noted, catching a glimpse of the drawer's contents. He rounded on her. "No more accidents," he said.

She scooted from the bed and grabbed a sleep shirt from her bag. "I'll go shower." Then she escaped from his intense gaze.

But snips of images from the movie, intermixed with her own fantasies of Jeff, followed her into the shower. As she bathed, she felt so sensitized it almost hurt to touch herself. The ache between her legs was a constant throb.

Her sleep shirt didn't seem nearly long enough when she pulled it on. The short-sleeved fuchsia plaid flannel didn't cling to her curves as Liz's nightie had, but the sides seemed much higher cut than she'd thought they were. The shirt left her legs exposed nearly to her hip.

She considered pulling her jeans back

on. But then what? She couldn't sleep with her jeans on; she'd have to pull them off eventually. Maybe if she waited until the lights were out. . . .

She shivered, her wet hair chilly on her neck. Maybe the sleep shirt wasn't so bad; the front and back dipped to a decorous enough length. If she just kept her sides averted from Jeff, she'd be okay.

Gathering up her jeans and T-shirt, she crept from the bathroom. Jeff was bent over the bed, his back to her. She moved crab-like through the room to where he'd set her bag on top of the dresser.

She stuffed her clothes into the bag, then raised her eyes to the mirror over the dresser in time to see his gaze burning into hers. She realized suddenly that by bending over, she'd probably revealed the bottoms of her panties. She stood bolt upright and whirled away from the mirror, the sides and buttoned front of the sleep shirt gaping open.

His eyes drifted, just for a moment, to the length of leg from thigh to knee exposed by the shirt. Then his gaze rose to her face.

"You don't have anything else to wear?" he asked. "I mean, so you'll be warm enough."

The sheen of sweat beaded his forehead. She shook her head. "Nothing but blue jeans."

"I couldn't sleep if you . . . weren't warm enough," he said. He turned to stare down at The Bed, fingertips rubbing at his brow. Then his eyes lit with something akin to relief. "I have an idea."

He grabbed up the bedspread, then stripped back the top sheet and blanket. Then he laid the bedspread over the bottom sheet and rolled one edge of it up until the thick roll bisected the bed from head to foot.

"That should be more comfortable," he said, a faint flush staining his cheeks.

"I'm sure it will," she murmured as he pulled the top sheet and blanket back over his makeshift bundling board.

"Are you ready?" he asked, then ran his hand over his eyes. "To go to sleep, I mean."

"Sure," she said, peeling back the blankets. Although she would have had to be ten times more tired to drift off to sleep with him inches from her on the bed. A six-inch concrete wall wouldn't help, let alone that little barrier of bedspread.

Moving so that the sleep shirt wouldn't ride up too much, she slipped under the covers. She scooted down and lay stiffly on her back, the underside of the bedspread scratchy against her legs.

She looked up at Jeff, still standing over the bed. He gripped the blanket and sheet, as if steeling himself to pull them back. Then he climbed gingerly into the bed, switching off the light before he settled under the covers.

"Good night," his voice rumbled close to her ear.

"Night," she responded into the darkness.

She heard his breathing, even but with an edge to it. Her fingers itched to reach over the roll of bedspread to trail through the crisp hairs on his bare chest. She squeezed her eyes tightly shut as if to force temptation away.

She shifted restlessly, her foot sliding across the sheet. Before she realized it, her toes burrowed under the barrier, skimmed across the warm fabric encasing Jeff's leg. She froze a moment, before snatching it back to safety.

"Sorry," she whispered.

"No problem," he answered softly.

But it was a big problem for her because now she could think of nothing but that brief sensation of his warmth against her foot. It didn't help that she had an acute case of Popsicle toes that no amount of chafing her feet together would help.

How would it feel to tuck her feet under his strong legs, to warm them with his heat?

An altogether too-appealing thought, one to be filed away with the one of dragging her fingers across his chest.

Resolute, she turned on her side, away from him. That increased the distance between them another six inches, even more when she scrunched further over onto her side of the bed. As she wriggled away from Jeff, her knee jarred the wall against which the bed rested, and she felt a trace of alarm at the closeness of the space. But claustrophobia, she decided, was a small price to pay for more real estate between her and Jeff.

Despite her heightened awareness of him, the warmth of the bed and the sound of his breathing sifting into her ears soothed her. Her erratic sleeping patterns of the last few days overwhelmed her with a sudden lassitude. Just before exhaustion claimed her, she thought about pushing away from the wall, that she really didn't like the feeling of being in a box.

But in the next moment, her brain shut down and she slept.

Intellectually, Jeff knew he damn well had to sleep. He'd been doing most of the driving and if he didn't get some rest, he'd be running them off the road tomorrow.

But how could he sleep with Casey within

arm's length on the bed? How could he rest with her scent fogging his senses, her heat palpable even a foot away? How could he ever hope to drift off with a constant aching hard-on?

Jeff turned away from her on his side. Why did she have to keep making that soft sighing sound when she breathed? He clapped a hand over his ear, but the sound had insinuated itself into his brain so that he could think of nothing else. His ever-willing imagination took her deep regular breaths and transformed them into the mewing pants of a woman on the edge of ecstasy. But not just any woman — his mind supplied the sounds Casey would make just before he brought her to climax.

Jeff growled deep in his throat. Why did she have to have that damned movie on? His sexual tastes had never run to X-rated films, but no man could watch such blatant images without reacting. Especially when the woman who could fulfill those fantasies lay curled on his bed, lips parted with her own arousal, eyes smoky with sex.

He clenched his fists, letting his fingernails bite into his palms. It didn't help to know exactly what she felt like. That the picture of her draped across his chest this morning still lay crystal clear in his mind.

While showering tonight he'd had to switch the water to ice-cold when fantasies of Casey joining him painfully roused his flesh. Fat lot of good that had done when he'd left the bathroom and found her enthralled by an X-rated movie.

Jeff ignored the first faint whimper from the other side of the bed. He stiffened his shoulders against the sound, figuring in another moment Casey would relax back into sleep. Then the whimper stretched into a cry, still soft, but laced with fear. Breath held, Jeff listened, every sense attuned to Casey.

She seemed to struggle in the bed, her limbs banging against the wall. A strangled sob escaped from her as her movements became more frantic. He could feel the bedclothes move and shift as the sounds of her distress grew louder.

"Don't want . . ." she moaned, "don't want . . ."

She thumped the wall again and suddenly Jeff understood. She'd boxed herself in against the wall and probably tangled herself in the bedclothes to boot. The length of bedspread under the sheet probably wasn't helping matters either. He'd been stupid to lay that barrier there — it brought him no peace of mind and had only added a layer to Casey's unconscious fear.

Moving quickly, he reached under the sheets and pulled at the bedspread. She'd wrapped herself in it and it took several sharp tugs to free her. He tossed it aside, then grasped Casey's body to slide her away from the wall. He pulled her clear to his side of the bed, then eased himself over her so that she'd feel open space at least on one side.

He thought she'd wake, would complain about his hands on her, demand an explanation. But she only drifted deeper into sleep as her tension dissipated. Her breathing grew regular again and her restless movements stilled.

But not entirely. Before he could retreat, she scooted back against him and plastered her body from shoulders to feet against his. Her back pressed against his chest, her legs tangled with his, her rounded bottom nestled against his groin. It was heaven and hell all at once and he knew he'd never get to sleep now.

Might as well be damned as a sinner instead of a saint. Snuggling against her, he snaked his arms around her, one under her head, the other curving against her breasts. He'd be hard all night, he wouldn't sleep a wink, but he welcomed the opportunity to enjoy her body stone-cold sober.

He didn't have as much of an opportunity as he might have hoped. It took only a few moments before the blissful warmth of Casey's body soaked into his limbs and edged him into sleep.

Casey gazed across the breakfast table at Jeff, his thoughtful expression sending off warning signals. She'd grown accustomed to his anger, but this quiet pensiveness unsettled her. From the moment she woke to find him hovering over her, already dressed, an unreadable light in his eyes, she'd felt thoroughly off-balance.

But what in the world could she have done during the night to bring that considering look to his face? She'd slept more soundly than she ever had, not even waking once, best as she could recall. She had a vague memory of an old nightmare visiting her, one that had stalked her throughout childhood, that even now popped up bogeyman-style occasionally.

Was that it? she wondered as she swirled a bit of her chocolate chip waffle in a lake of syrup. Had her restless tossing and turning during her bad dream woken him, interrupted his sleep? That might explain how she'd ended up on his side of the bed and why he was up and dressed long before her.

Maybe she should apologize. She forked up the bite of waffle and raised her eyes to his. "Did you sleep well?" she asked by way of broaching the subject.

Surprise widened his eyes, then a faint smile curved his lips. "Very well."

Suspicion curled inside Casey at his amiable response. "I wasn't too restless?"

He cocked a brow at her. "Why would you be restless?"

She gestured with her fork. "Sometimes I have nightmares. My sisters tell me I moan in my sleep and thrash around, so I thought —"

He returned his focus to his eggs and bacon. "It wasn't a problem, Casey."

"I did moan, didn't I?" she asked, the heat of embarrassment rising in her cheeks. "And I bet I kicked you or punched you or — did I push you out of bed? Is that why I was on your side this morning?"

He lifted his gaze to her. "I traded with you during the night. You didn't seem to like being trapped against the wall."

Why did his expression have to be so tender now, his tone so gentle? It was easier to keep from falling for him when he was mean to her; but when he acted as if he cared. . . .

Realization lanced through her with the sweetness of a new breath, with the pain of fresh grief. She wasn't falling for Jeff. God save her, she'd already fallen.

Eyes squeezed shut, she tried to shut out the reality of her monumental mistake. But no amount of hiding could save her from the truth.

She loved him. Sweet Lord, she loved him. And no amount of time, no sensible words or arguments was going to change that.

She'd fallen in love with another Mr. Wrong.

In another moment he'd see it in her face. She bent her head to her waffle, and picked up her fork although her stomach turned at the cloying sweet taste.

"One more bite." Her voice was a shred of sound. "Then we ought to get going." She forced another mouthful of waffle down her throat, pushed her plate aside. "Ready?"

His eyes were still fixed on her, his jaw working. For a moment, she thought, *Oh God, he knows!* Desperate for a distraction, she stretched her lips into a grin and winked at him.

He didn't scowl as she'd expected, just gazed at her contemplatively before sliding from the booth. Casey rose and slipped past him where he stood at the coffee shop's register. She retreated to the car to wait for him, holding her newfound knowledge inside her like a guilty secret.

Her chattering started the moment he climbed into the car. She started with tales from her childhood, embroidered to make the dire seem humorous, then moved on to hilarious descriptions of her card-playing customers' peculiarities — Mr. Fleet who wore the same unwashed socks whenever he gambled, Mrs. Baumgartner who spoke to her dead husband at the table.

Jeff took it all stoically, keeping his eyes on Highway 395 as they traveled north. Each time he might have inserted something into the one way conversation, Casey's stream of words bulldozed over whatever he might have said.

Casey wasn't sure what kept her talking — nervousness, fear, excitement. For any other woman, discovering she loved a man would be cause for joy. But Casey knew better. For her, disaster was just another step away.

Then they hit Inyokern, and the stream of words stopped. She sagged back in her seat, eyes closed to block the sight of him. That left her nursing a dull ache centered in her chest.

His voice rumbled in her ear. "Do you want

to take a nap?" he asked.

She couldn't miss the hopeful tone in his voice. "Don't worry, I've run out of stories."

He chuckled, the warm sound tightening in her chest. "I like your stories."

She looked at him sidelong. "You sound like you wish you didn't."

"Maybe I just wish there were fewer of them," he said, his tone laced with humor.

She laughed with him then, enjoying the way he threw back his head, his carefree grin. Then as he slowed for the Highway 14 junction, a smile still lingering on his face, he turned to her.

He only glanced at her, offered her just the briefest glimpse of his eyes. Yet for a startling instant, Casey saw something in his face that teased her with the possibility of a miracle. That he might — against all odds — love her back.

But before she could grasp that hope, a door closed, his expression shuttered. He looked away again, and Casey's laughter became painful in her throat.

And for the rest of the long, long trip up Highway 395, she couldn't think of another thing to say.

# Chapter 14

Casey opened the car door, her eyes on the rustic wooden clapboards of *Edge of Heaven*, Shar's inn and restaurant. Behind her the late afternoon sun hovered over the jagged peaks of the Eastern Sierras; just beyond the inn lay the stark Mono Lake basin.

The deceptively calm blue surface of the lake was a good metaphor for her own emotions, Casey thought wryly. Underneath that mirror-smooth surface, Casey knew, craggy tufa towers lay. Formed when fresh water springs at the bottom of the lake bed mingled with the acrid saline of the lake water, they grew and thrust higher until they lurked just below the surface.

Turning, she reached into the back seat for her purse just as Jeff leaned in to pull their bags out. He surprised her with a brief smile, all the more devastating for its unexpectedness. Ordering her rebellious heart to slow, she hesitated there with her hand on her purse as Jeff backed out of the car.

Then she rose and fixed her gaze out onto

the lake again. She'd be safer navigating those murky tufa-laced waters than the depths of her own traitorous heart. Loving Jeff threatened her well-being far more than those towers of calcified rock would endanger an unwary boater.

Jeff pulled open the ornate front door to the inn, then turned to her. "Coming?" he asked with another one of those heart-stopping smiles.

When did he get so darn cheerful? He'd barely spoken during the last leg of the trip, although the long, silent stretches hadn't seemed uncomfortable. Now he was grinning like an idiot at every opportunity.

Feeling uncharacteristically cross, Casey slipped past Jeff and marched into *Edge of Heaven*'s lobby. It was more a front parlor than a lobby actually, furnished with an eclectic mismatch of antique chairs, tables and sofas. A wrought-iron chandelier hung from the ceiling and roses decorated the carpet beneath their feet.

"Casey!"

Casey turned at the sound of her oldest sister's melodious voice. Shar rushed down the last of the stairs and unceremoniously dumped a handful of linen on the nearest chair. Then she enfolded Casey in a soft, warm hug.

Shar drew back, hands still linked with Casey's. "I'm so glad you're here."

Shar's motherly warmth chased away Casey's blues. In the tumultuous household in which they'd all grown up, Shar had taken the mother role early on. Even now she looked the part — a generous bosom, ample hips and short light brown hair a halo around her head.

"You're an archetype, you know that?" Casey said laughingly. "I suppose you have fresh-baked cookies waiting for us in the kitchen."

"Guilty as charged," Shar said agreeably. "But then, I always serve them to the guests at afternoon tea."

The sound of Jeff's shifting feet registered and Casey tugged Shar around to face him. "Jeff Haley," Casey strove to keep her voice neutral, "this is my sister Shar Phillips."

His brow arched slightly at the difference in surnames. He took Shar's proffered hand and shook it. "Beautiful place you have here."

Where Deb was suspicious and Liz confrontational, Shar's warm heart let everyone in. Unless someone hurt her sisters, then the transgressor was courteously, politely, tossed out on his duff.

She smiled, her gold-brown eyes steady on

Jeff. "Thank you. About your negatives . . ."

"You have them?" Jeff asked.

Shar shook her head. "They didn't arrive yesterday."

Jeff rubbed at his brow with his fingertips and Casey wondered if he was beginning to wear a dent there. "Monday then," he said.

Why did he sound relieved? She would have thought he'd explode at being thwarted yet again in taking possession of his precious negatives.

Casey studied his face, seeking a clue to his change of attitude. But he wouldn't meet her gaze, instead focusing on the profusion of cabbage roses woven into the carpet.

Voices on the stairs pulled Casey's attention from Jeff. Shar snatched up the pile of linen, bundling it in her arms.

"The guests are coming down for tea," she said. "Casey, I fixed you up in your usual room." She began backing out of the parlor. "The rest of the rooms are full, though. We'll have to figure something out for Jeff."

Shar whirled and disappeared through the doorway that Casey knew led to the utility room. A family of four — husband, wife and two boys — had reached the foot of the stairs and were eyeing them with friendly curiosity.

Casey smiled and nodded, then turned to

Jeff. "Let's take these things upstairs for now."

She led the way to the sunny, spacious room at the end of the hall that Shar always tried to reserve for her. Tall windows on one wall overlooked the expanse of Mono Lake, misty blue in the dimming light. The double-sized brass bed boasted a patchwork crazy quilt. Tapestry-covered occasional chairs flanked a mahogany side table with a dry sink and pitcher.

Jeff dropped their bags to the floor by the bed and scanned the room. Up to now, she'd managed to close herself off from him, to keep a certain distance between them. But now, in the intimacy of this comfortable room, she felt helpless against the pull of love within her.

Why did his black T-shirt have to look so soft to the touch, his muscles flexing beneath it so tantalizing? Her eyes wanted to drink in every inch of him, her lips ached to explore each angle of his strong body, her fingertips wanted to glide across the planes of his face, to soothe that tension in his jaw.

He turned to meet her gaze. She was naked before him, despite the vivid purple T-shirt and jeans she wore, despite the barrier of her arms across her middle. Her love for him had stripped her bare. Perceptive as he was, he would see it, would know her secret. Then he'd be cross with her, or worse, he'd tell her kindly, gently, that he felt nothing for her in return.

He did neither of those things. His face seemed to fill with a lightness, a joy. But only a whisper of joy, and only for an instant. Then something seemed to wash it away, leaving that same, carefully neutral expression on Jeff's face.

"We'd better go back downstairs," he said, turning his back on her. He stood rigid, eyes on the distant reaches of the lake.

"You go ahead," she said. "I'm going to lie down for a bit."

He drew in a long breath, then headed for the door. He looked back at her once, briefly, before slipping out of the room.

Casey sank onto the side of the bed and leaned against the brass footboard, the metal cool against her cheek. It had happened again. Despite all her admonitions, despite the lessons she should have learned so many times, she had fallen in love again. This time with a man who would never love her back. . . .

She had a sudden, desperate need to call Pearl, her Little Sister. Maybe by talking to Pearl, listening to her uncomplicated perspective on life, she would be able to figure out what to do about Jeff.

Slipping off her shoes, she scooted back on the bed and lifted the receiver of the old-fashioned French phone. The first sound of Pearl's sweet voice was a balm, the girl's excitement over her upcoming birthday a distraction. They talked until the cuckoo in the clock on the wall had made its appearance three times and shadows usurped the sunlight in the room.

When Casey finally hung up the phone and settled back on the plump lace pillows, a calmness suffused her. She understood that as much as she might want to, she could not control Jeff, could not create a love for her that didn't exist.

What she could do, though, was tell him the truth. She could tell him she loved him. He would probably reject her — however gently or kindly. But at least her heart would be eased by telling him all that lay within it.

She snuggled deeper into the pillows, the growing darkness in the room cloaking her, setting her mind adrift. Her thoughts coalesced and then dispersed, forming endless patterns. Just a few more moments, she thought to herself, then I'll go find him and tell him everything.

Jeff gave the pipe fitting one last turn, then

wriggled out from under Shar's dishwasher. "You want to give it a try? I'm pretty sure that's where it was leaking from."

Shar slapped shut the sliding doors of the dishwasher, then flipped the ON switch. A rush of water sounded inside the metal cylinder.

Jeff grabbed a grimy towel from the stainless steel counter, then hunkered down underneath to dry the fitting thoroughly. He watched the repair site until he was certain there was no more seepage.

He straightened and tossed the towel aside. "That did it."

Shar smiled, her gratitude clear on her face. "I can't tell you how long that's been leaking. Thanks so much."

"No problem." Jeff brushed off the knees of his once pristine jeans. "I'll go grab a shower now if you don't mind."

"Just be back by seven," Shar called after him as he headed out of the kitchen. "I'm cooking up something special just for you and Casey."

Jeff nudged through the swinging kitchen door, guilt at Shar's generosity twinging within him. If Shar knew what kind of thoughts he'd been entertaining about her younger sister lately, he'd be wearing his dinner instead of eating it.

The cot Shar had promised him sat folded up at the foot of the stairs, the bedding for it tucked inside. He hefted the contraption upstairs, then set it on its wheels when he reached the landing. He slipped inside the now dim room, towing the cot behind him, taking care not to bang it against the door.

Casey lay asleep on the bed, her hands curled by her cheek, her stocking feet tucked against one another. Her bright purple T-shirt had crept from the waistband of her jeans, revealing a swath of satiny flesh. He wanted to brush his lips along that bare inch of skin, to wake her and hear her breath catch at the sensation.

How would it feel if she loved him? The thought came unbidden, and on its heels a rush of triumph washed over Jeff, filled him before he could squelch it. Shame followed, shame at his eagerness to take without giving. Because he knew he would take Casey's love and never give it back. He just didn't have it in him to love her.

Casey stirred, turned to her other side. Unable to bear the exquisite sight of her another moment, he grabbed his garment bag and swiftly eased out of the room. He found the bathroom three doors down, thankfully unoccupied. He needed desperately to stand under the warm spray of water, to have it wash away the confusion that had him tied up in knots.

A fool's wish, he knew. He could swim the breadth of Mono Lake, let its saline water soak him to the bone and never clear away the joy of Casey's love, the ache to have her always at his side.

The water ran cold by the time he turned off the shower. He had a feeling he'd be hearing from Shar about that; she'd already warned him about her faulty water heater. Maybe he'd fix that too before he left, a roundabout way to please Casey.

He dressed quickly, donning the one dress shirt he'd brought, shaking wrinkles out of the moss green fabric as best he could. The forest green gabardine slacks had fared better; he didn't look like a total slob at least.

He hesitated in toweling dry his hair. Why was he dressing up in the first place? For the special dinner Shar had promised? But she'd told him jeans and casual shirts were more common in the rustic dining room than suits and ties. Yet despite his certainty that Casey had nothing in her sports bag but jeans and T-shirts, somehow tonight, their last night, he wanted to look nice for her.

That didn't bear considering, Jeff decided as he gathered up his things and carried them back to the room. The cuckoo clock called out the half-hour just as he entered and Casey roused, a shadow sitting up in bed. She snapped on the bedside lamp and its yellow light turned her all honey-golden.

"What time is it?" she asked, blinking sleepily.

Would she taste as warm as she looked, as sweet as the honey in her eyes? Jeff turned away, busying himself with drawing the drapes. "Six-thirty. Shar said she'd have dinner ready at seven."

"You're all dressed up," she said.

"It was all I had left," he lied. He turned back to her, keeping his gaze hooded. "Don't worry about it. Wear whatever you have."

Her expression grew thoughtful, then she smiled, the gesture plucking at the knot of his heart. "Give me a few minutes to wash up. I'll meet you downstairs."

Something in her face clanged a warning inside him. He shut the door behind him as he left, unease and anticipation warring in the pit of his stomach.

Shar was watching for him in the dining room, her chocolate brown shirtwaist flattering her ample figure. "I saved you a window seat." She led the way through red-covered tables set for two and four, pulled out a chair with a flourish.

"Casey's still getting ready," Jeff said as he lowered himself into the chair.

"I figured as much," she said. "Can I get you something to drink while you wait?"

"Whatever you have on tap." She hurried off, and Jeff sat back in his chair to look out the window. The moon had just broken the far horizon, silvering the black surface of the lake with a long, glittering stripe. Barely visible a dozen feet from the window, gnarled trunks stood as sentinels between him and the lake.

He nursed his beer when it arrived, marking time, waiting for Casey. The buzz of voices lay in the background, his only reminder that others were in the room. His thoughts all centered on her. His world had paused on its axis, awaiting her arrival.

He caught her scent first. He'd been gazing out the window, idly observing the reflections of the waiters in the glass when the spice of cinnamon sifted toward him. The fragrance pulled him around in his seat, dragged his eyes to where she threaded through the dining room. Thunderstruck, he watched her close the distance between them.

She was a fragment of dream, a shred of heaven fluttered to Earth. She wore a confection of white lawn, pleated demurely across her breasts, flowing out in a spill of creamy white past a fitted waist. The snug sleeves just covered her delicate wrist bone and a pink satin sash cinched her waist, its ends hanging nearly to the hem of her dress.

She'd done something with her hair he wouldn't have thought possible with such a short cut. Two ornate silver combs tucked back her hair, framing her face.

She smiled, a small, mysterious gesture he ached to resolve. "I'm sorry to take so long," she said, standing over him.

Stunned, it took him a moment to stumble to his feet and pull out a chair for her. He cupped her elbow and guided her into the seat.

She arranged the folds of the skirt around her, then fussed with her sleeves. "It's an antique," she said, as if he'd asked. "Shar has a whole set of them."

Jeff wondered why his tongue felt ten times its normal size. He swallowed, tried to summon up an appropriate response. "You look beautiful in it," he said, the words inadequate.

Eyes downcast, she blushed. "Thanks." Her laugh was a nervous sound. "It's a girl's dress. I'm the only sister puny enough to fit into it."

He didn't bother commenting on her self-deprecation. He was too captivated by the high collar with its edging of crochet. He wanted to draw his lips across it to seek out her beating pulse. Then slip a fingertip underneath the lacy edge to feel the warmth of her flesh.

The modest dress — its flowing skirt only suggesting her womanly hips, the bodice hinting at the curve of her small breasts — inflamed him. He burned to know, to touch what lay underneath. The wash of rose across her cheeks, the banked fire in her brown eyes, incited him further, until he teetered on the brink of control.

He couldn't have said later what they'd talked about, couldn't have described even one mouthful of Shar's carefully prepared meal. He had a vague memory of something Italian and something sinfully chocolate for dessert. He only remembered the chocolate because he entertained a brief fantasy of lapping the rich, creamy stuff from Casey's breasts.

They left the dining room side-by-side, his hand on the small of her back, her hip brushing his as they walked. She seemed to hold herself on a breath as they moved up the stairs, the air escaping in a gasp when they reached the room and he shut the door behind them.

Shar had sent someone to make up the cot. Jeff stepped around it, advancing on Casey, who stood reed straight at the foot of the brass bed, the lamp on the nightstand illuminating her softly.

"You tell me what you want," he said softly, running his finger along the shell of her ear. "Everything."

She swallowed, her eyes widening. "I don't know," she whispered.

Stilling his hand, he tried to understand the message in her words. "Don't know, as in you don't know what you want?" he asked, his voice rough. "Or you don't know if you want this at all?"

Her eyes shut, revealing a pale smudge of lavender on her eyelids, another enticement. Then she gazed up at him again. Her voice was a mere breath of sound. "I want this."

His heart thudded to a start again. "Thank God."

He dipped his head, her eyes on him all the while. They fluttered closed just as his lips brushed hers, the brief touch jolting his entire body. Fire chased through him, driving him to swallow her in his arms and take her to the bed. He wanted to cover her body with his, to have her now, as fast as he could.

Pulling back a fraction, he dragged in an unsteady breath. He'd waited too damn long to waste this moment with Casey in a flash-fire of lust. Forcing his trembling hands to be gentle, he threaded his fingers through her hair. They snagged on the comb, nudged it loose.

The silk of her hair slipped across his palm, stoked the fire again. He cast about for a way to distract himself from his headlong rush toward completion.

He tugged the comb free. "Where did you find this?" He ran his thumb across the ornate metal.

"Shar collects them." She leaned her face against his other hand, rubbing against it like a cat, undoing his good intentions to slow down.

He tossed the comb onto the cot, then sent its mate spinning in the same direction. He closed his mouth on hers again, urging it open this time, sweeping inside with his tongue, tasting chocolate and Casey. His tongue sought her crooked tooth, and the feel of its imperfection after all his fantasies sent a hot shaft through him.

Giving in to his earlier temptation, he traced his fingertips along the lacy edge of her collar, then dipped inside with his thumb. He found her pulse point, and his urgency shot up another notch at its crazy, erratic rhythm.

Her hands rested lightly at his waist, as if she felt too shy to touch him more boldly. He wondered at that, until she leaned closer and her breasts pressing against him seared thought from his mind.

His fingers skimmed lower, past the slender blade of her collarbone, moving slowly down along the folds of white lawn. When he would have cupped her breast, he dipped between them instead, the blade of his hand traveling that tantalizing valley.

He let his hand curve beneath one breast, just where the flesh first rose in its soft mound. He felt just a hint of that softness brushing against the back of his hand.

He imagined her nipple beading against the white lawn, ached to confirm her response. But he kept his hand away from that center, moving it along the periphery, prolonging the exquisite agony.

He could do this, he could maintain control. Yet no sooner had he entertained that proud thought than Casey clutched at his hand, drew it up and over her breast. She pressed him against her so that the tight bud of her nipple burned into his palm. His hips bucked against her, an agony of sensation suppressed.

Stepping back, he tugged his hand free and closed it around hers. "You're making it very difficult for me to take this slow," he said hoarsely.

"Do we want to go slow?" she whispered, pressing her lips to his chest.

He groaned aloud. "I want it to be good for you."

She pulled her hand free and embraced him, splaying both hands across his back. His blatant arousal pressed against her soft belly, sending a shudder through him.

"Any way would be good with you," she said softly.

There was a secret hidden in those words, a mystery his mind told him he should unravel. But his body only heard the meaning, the invitation to do just what it wanted. Moving of their own accord, his fingers sought the fastening of the dress, racing along her spine, seeking buttons or zipper.

She laughed, only the edge of nervousness in the light sound. "It's here," she said, "on the side."

Turning away from him, she lifted her arm. From the top of her ribcage to her hip lay a row of what seemed like hundreds of tiny round buttons.

"A plot," he said, his wry chuckle raw with need, "to drive men wild."

She brought her hand up to his chest. "Do I? Drive you wild?"

Taking her hand, he pressed a kiss into her palm. "God, Casey, you know you do."

Her eyes were luminous as she gazed up at him. Then she took his hand, pressed it to the row of buttons.

He fumbled with them at first, her cinnamon scent a sweetness along his tongue, confusing him, making him clumsy. As he struggled, a brief, entirely unworthy thought occurred to him to throw the dress up around her hips, pull down her panties and take her that way.

But he pushed aside that consideration, bringing both hands to the problem and releasing each round button with as much patience as he could muster. He discovered the exercise was an erotic dream in itself, as each inch freed exposed more of her warm, sleek flesh.

Savoring each new touch, he slowed as his fingers discovered the firmness of her ribcage, the curve of her waist, the softness of her hip. Once he'd undone all the buttons, he drew his knuckles along the opening, enjoying Casey's uneven breathing, the tightening of her fingers on his shoulder.

"Aren't you going to take it off?" she whispered.

His hand curved around to her narrow back, his thumb drifting just at the edge of her bare breast. "I will, soon enough."

There was something unbearably erotic about having his hand inside her dress like that. To have her still clothed, yet to be able to stroke along her waist, to tease the soft mound of her breast.

She shuddered each time his thumb brushed the swell of her breast, moaned softly when he neared her turgid nipple. His senses were full of her — her silky skin, her luminous eyes, her tantalizing scent, her ragged breath, the flavor of her lips still clinging to his tongue.

Her hands moved to his waist again, and she began tugging at his shirt. "I want to feel you, too," she said, a tremor in her voice.

His hand spanned her ribcage, his thumb resting just under her breast. "Do you?"

"Yes," she said. "Please."

She freed his shirt from his slacks and he obliged her by taking it off. She scudded her hands up his chest, fingers threading through the thick hair.

She sighed, stroking him with her lips. Her breath warmed him, seared him. "I've wanted to do this for so long," she murmured.

Her fingers meandered down his chest, then trailed along the waistband of his slacks. He fisted his hands for control as she traced and retraced that path.

He waited for her to dip inside with her fingers, to move to the front and unfasten his belt buckle. But she didn't. She slipped her hands around to his back and nestled them there as if waiting for him to make the next move.

He had wanted to let her set the pace, to let her lead. But there was something tentative about the way she touched him, a lack of confidence. As if this were new to her. As if she were dipping into untested waters.

But all those men she'd mentioned, all the relationships gone bad — surely she'd been intimate before now. He thought back to the times he'd kissed her and realized how untutored she'd seemed, even as he'd reveled in her sweetness.

Oh, Lord, she couldn't actually be a virgin, could she?

That thought sent a cacophony of emotions through him — lust, fear and joy chief among them. And he realized he had to know, had to be certain.

"Casey," he said, his lips buried in her cinnamon-scented hair.

"Yes?" She snuggled her face into his chest, shattering his thoughts for a moment.

He took her head in his hands, tipped it back. "I have to ask you something. Please don't take this the wrong way."

Her brown eyes gazed into his. "What?"

Dragging in a breath, he postponed the question, not sure if she'd be blazing mad or horribly mortified. But there was no avoiding it. "Have you done this before?"

She stiffened in his arms, giving him her answer. "Have you forgotten Roger, Steve and Tom?" She shifted her gaze to the blackness outside the window.

He smiled. "No. But did Roger, Steve and Tom —"

"No." The painful embarrassment was clear in her tone. "Never. Or Ian either."

He drew a fingertip along her face so that her eyes met his. Her openness took his breath away. "How did they ever keep their hands off you?"

She shrugged. "It wasn't that they didn't try. It was just that . . ."

"Just that?" he prompted.

"It was me, really." She dropped her gaze. "The claustrophobia thing."

"What about it?"

"Sometimes when they put their arms around me, I felt trapped. I couldn't respond." She slanted a sideways look at him. "So they just sort of . . . gave up."

His lips brushed across her brow, her cheek, her chin. "Damn idiots. All of them."

Her sigh went straight to his core. "Jeff?"

He kissed the corner of her mouth. "Yeah?"

She wriggled closer. "Is it that obvious?"

He touched the tip of his tongue to her lower lip. "What?"

"That I'm . . . that I never . . ." She let the word trail off.

"Only to me," he assured her, kissing her fluttering eyelids, "and only because . . ."

Because what? Because he'd been so close to her over the past few days, he'd learned to sense her every emotion, could read her body like a road map? Because he felt more connected to her than he had to any woman, his ex-wife included? Because he'd come to care for her, to want her, to —

He cut short that impossible train of thought. She gazed up at him, waiting for him to finish, an expectant, hopeful look in her eyes. A dangerous look.

"I just knew," he whispered. He grazed his thumbs along her temples. "So, do we continue?" He held his breath, his body screaming for a "yes," his better sense telling him to run the other way.

A slow smile lit her face. "Most definitely."

And Jeff knew he could never run now.

# Chapter 15

A thousand emotions clamored inside Casey, threatening to overwhelm her. Fear, excitement, arousal. Embarrassment still stung, but Jeff's easy acceptance, his gentleness with her, soothed that pang.

Love surged foremost within her, perilous, impossible love. And to have her first time be with this man she loved so dearly filled her heart to bursting.

Not sure what to do next, she closed her trembling fingers around his belt buckle, worked at it awkwardly. He pushed her hands away. "I'll do it," he said.

He undid the belt and zipper and hooked his thumbs in the waistband of his slacks. He shucked his pants, but left his briefs in place. The white cotton barely contained his blatant arousal.

She struggled with her dress, managing to pull it up around her waist, but her arms caught in its folds. "I guess I need some help here," she said, her laugh breathless with nerves.

She held her arms out to her sides as he moved closer. He tugged at first one sleeve, then the other, pulling the snug fabric past her hands until he'd released her arms. There were three more buttons at the back of the neck; he slipped each one free, then pulled the dress over her head.

Still shy, she crossed her arms over her breasts, clad in only her high-cut panties. He ran a tantalizing finger down her cheek.

"Sit down," he said softly.

She sat at the edge of the bed and he bent to her feet. His hand wrapped around her ankle as he tugged off first one white satin slipper, then the other. She never would have guessed having her shoes removed could be so erotic.

He pulled back the covers on the bed. "Get in." He watched as she slipped beneath them, pulled the blankets up to her chin.

His hot gaze remained on her and she realized he was waiting for her invitation. She slid to the other side of the bed, then flipped back a corner of the covers. "Come here," she whispered, her arms beckoning him.

Slipping off his briefs, he knelt on the bed beside her. "Wait," she murmured, astounded at her own boldness.

He raised one brow expectantly. She shifted in the bed, her own body's heat making her restless. "I want to look at you," she murmured.

He let her look her fill, his manhood swelling even more under her scrutiny. Then she crooked her finger, inviting him to lie with her.

As he pressed her body against his, he groaned, his hand closing over her breast as if he couldn't wait a moment more. "God, you feel so good."

She reveled in the feel of her nipple nestled in his palm. She wanted to know every part of his body, to explore every inch.

"Jeff?" She stroked his back, up along his spine, to his broad shoulders.

"Yeah?" he rasped out.

"I want to touch you," she said.

He kissed her brow, her cheek, the corner of her mouth. "You're doing fine."

"I mean," she said, a flush warming her cheeks. "I want to touch you . . . your . . . I mean, I never have."

As understanding dawned, he went still. "Go ahead."

Her hand dipped deeper under the covers, retracing its path along his spine, enjoying the feel of his flesh. She moved along his hip, then to the front of him. Her hand brushed against the thick curls there, her fingers circled him.

It was like hot steel encased in satin. She stroked him with her thumb, enjoying the velvety feel of the tip of his manhood.

She squeezed him lightly, and he sucked in his breath on a gasp. "Does that hurt?" she asked, loosening her grip.

"No," he said, his voice tight. "But I'm going to explode in your hand if you don't stop."

She smiled and drew her hand away, but slowly, running a fingertip along his length as she did so. He growled and pushed her gently to her back.

"Turn about is fair play," he said against her throat. He nipped at her ear, sending a shiver clear through her. "Now we'll see who squirms."

Moving with slow deliberation, Jeff skimmed his hand across her belly, then lower to the juncture of her legs. She couldn't seem to lie still under his touch and when he cupped her mound, a little cry escaped her lips.

He moved his fingers gently between her legs, then dipped inside her panties. He brushed his fingers across her center, through the silky hairs, testing her. Casey thought she would scream at the sensation of his fingers moving against slick, wet flesh.

"You win," she gasped out.

"But I'm not done yet," he said, bringing his hand back up her body.

Moving with excruciating slowness, he skimmed his palm higher, until she thought he'd brush it across her beaded nipples. But just as he should have teased that sensitized flesh, he circled them instead, keeping just out of range of the aching peak.

"Is this what you want?" he said, his voice rough. He raised his leg, slipped it between hers, pressed his knee against her center. "And this?"

Her head lolled back and she thought she might come apart right then. "Yes," she murmured, "all of it."

"On one condition." His thumbs brushed against her nipples, the briefest of contact. "If you start feeling uncomfortable and want to stop, tell me."

She ran her hand up his arm, enjoying the rough feel. "Believe me Haley, I won't want you to stop."

He pulled his hands away from her breasts, settled them at her waist. "Promise you'll tell me."

She fixed her gaze on his, saw he was dead serious. "I will," she vowed. "If you'll promise something in return."

"What's that?" He gathered her hands in his.

Her cheeks heated at what she was about to ask. "You tell me if I'm doing something wrong. Or that what I'm doing feels good."

He leaned close to brush his lips against her forehead. "That shouldn't be a problem."

Drawing away, he lay back against the pillows, tugging her with him. "Light on or off?"

"On," she said. "I want to see you."

He tucked her against him, his left arm under her head. "For now, I just want to touch you. If anything feels uncomfortable —"

"I'll tell you, I'll tell you," she assured him. "But what do I do?"

"You can touch me," he said. "Anywhere you want to."

She pressed her hip against his blatant arousal and he groaned. "You might want to steer clear of that particular part of my body for now."

She couldn't help the satisfied smile at her effect on him. But then his palm brushed across her breast, wiping the smile from her face.

"Do you like this?" His palm lightly circled over her nipple. She could only nod. He brought his lips close to her ear. "How about this?" he whispered, then his tongue flicked out to tease the shell of her ear.

She groaned and her legs moved restlessly against each other. "Yes," she said, the word drawn out on a sigh.

His hand moved to her other breast, skimming against her nipple until she thought she'd burst with sensation. His mouth left her ear and moved along her jaw line to her lips, his tongue dipping inside her mouth only briefly before he moved on.

He kissed the point of her chin, then sipped along her throat to her collarbone. He hesitated there, then rose on his elbow to continue down toward her breasts. When his mouth pressed a kiss between her breasts, she brought her hand up to grip the back of his neck.

She wanted . . . she wanted . . . she couldn't form the words, or even the thought. She just prayed that Jeff would know.

The first feel of his lips closing gently around her nipple jolted through her like lightning. Her hand flexed on the back of Jeff's neck, until she was afraid she might hurt him. Then his tongue crept out to lave her nipple and she didn't even care as long as he never stopped.

Her free hand stole up to curve around his back, ran along the taut musculature until it seemed she could never feel enough of him. She dipped as low on his back as she dared, fascinated by his narrow hips, the muscled curve of his backside. Each time she felt the brush of his erection against her thigh she ached to touch him there, to feel the sleek turgid flesh in her palm.

She felt wet between her legs and so hot she thought she'd burn up. Her panties felt too tight, constrictive. She wanted them off, but the lassitude in her limbs had stolen her energy.

Jeff's hand left her breast and moved lower, shivering across her ribcage, pausing on her belly. Then his fingertips reached the top of her panties, traced along the elastic. Casey felt relief; Jeff would take care of them, slip them off so he could bring her even closer to him, to relieve the ache growing between her legs.

But he was in no hurry. His palm skimmed over the silky knit, teasing a moan from her. When his fingertips grazed the sensitive tops of her thighs, she gasped, gripping his head tightly to her breast.

"Jeff," she pleaded, not knowing what for.

She heard the low rumble of his satisfied laughter. Finally, when she thought she'd have to grab his hand to force him to, he hooked his thumb into the top of her panties.

He skimmed his thumb slowly back and forth, the tender skin of her abdomen rippling in reaction.

He shifted his hand, his fingertips easing under the elastic of her panties, dipping inside. She trembled, her breath catching at the new sensation. He skimmed lower, his fingertips just brushing the triangle of curls between her legs.

His voice rumbled in her ear. "Take them off."

Casey wanted to rip them off, but forced herself to move slowly, reaching under the covers and easing the panties from her hips. Jeff watched her every wriggle, his dark eyes growing even blacker.

She tossed them aside with a trembling hand. "Now what?"

"Now we try something," he said, his voice rough. "I want you to hold my wrist. Follow along with me."

Tentatively, she circled his wrist with her fingers. Her hand moved with his as it drifted from her face, down along her throat, skimming between her breasts. Fire followed in the wake of his touch, rekindling the heat low in her belly. He made his leisurely way down her body, taking a moment to tease her navel, then exploring the curve of her hip.

Once, when she felt just a trace of alarm, a faint sense of feeling trapped, she tightened her grip on his wrist. He immediately withdrew, his harsh breathing the only indication of the toll that self-discipline took on him. She pulled him closer again, elated by the sure knowledge of being in control of her own body.

When his fingers first slipped between her folds, she jolted, not out of fear, but in reaction to the unexpected sensation. Jeff instantly pulled away so that Casey had to bring him back with an imperious tug on his wrist.

She felt, rather than heard, his growl of satisfaction. Then his thumb began stroking the sensitive nub between her folds and her whole world centered there. Her grip on his wrist loosened, then fell away entirely as wave after wave of sensation rolled through her body.

Her legs thrashed on the sheets, her hips thrust up against his hand. A moan started low in her throat, coming out in a gasping pant. Pressure began to mount between her legs, an expansion of exquisite awareness. She was reaching, reaching for something that she hadn't even known existed before now.

Keeping up the tantalizing rhythm of his

thumb, Jeff slipped a finger inside her, driving a groan from her. "Don't —" She couldn't form words, even her thoughts were fragmented. "God, Jeff, I'm so wet."

"I want you that way," he growled in her ear, "wet and hot."

The blankets were too heavy on her, she tried to push them off. Jeff obliged, stripping them from her body. "God, you look so good," he said, and she shivered at his appreciation.

Then he dipped down to her breast again, his mouth closing over her nipple. She shuddered at the first touch of his tongue and felt a coil within her tighten another notch. The pressure between her legs built, the agony of sweet pleasure beyond bearing.

The first burst of heaven stole her breath, then she was floating, flying, free of the bounds of Earth, in a universe of brilliant light and sensation. Her body throbbed with it, her muscles clenching around Jeff's finger, her legs tightening to hold him there. She thought she might die of the incredible rush of feeling and die happy.

Then the shudders in her body eased, her breathing slowed as a sense of well-being washed over her. Jeff's hand slipped from between her legs, stroked up to settle at her waist.

His voice rumbled in her ear, laced with humor. "Was that okay?"

She released an exasperated sigh. "That was a couple hundred light years beyond okay, and you know it."

He laughed softly. "I thought maybe you enjoyed it."

She didn't miss the edge of tension in his voice. She nudged him away from her so that she could see his face. "It's your turn now." She hoped she sounded more confident than she felt.

"Are you sure?" he asked, his eyes searching her face.

"No," she told him honestly. "But I very much want to try."

"We'll take it slow." He moved his hand back between her legs to part them. Rising, he lowered himself between her thighs.

She tensed at the first feel of his rigid flesh against her belly. "Not yet," he murmured, "just want you used to me here."

Resting on his elbows on either side of her, he lowered his mouth to hers. He drew his lips across hers, teasing at the seam with the tip of his tongue so that they parted of their own accord. Emboldened by the triumph of her body, Casey chased his tongue with her own, thrilling at the feel of it against hers.

The insides of her thighs felt unbearably

sensitized where they rubbed against his powerful hips. She found herself wanting to wrap her legs around him. When she moved one leg up, stroking it along Jeff's thigh, he encouraged her, pulling her leg up around his back. She locked her heels at the base of his spine, and cradled him between her legs.

His breathing grew more ragged and Casey felt driven to take him over that same precipice he'd taken her. She began exploring him with her hands, running her fingertip along his muscled back, down the notch of his spine, to his firm backside. She pulled his hips toward her, feeling her own pressure mount as his tongue dove deeply into her mouth, battling with hers.

His erection pushed against her belly and she ached to have him inside her. She was incomplete, an emptiness pulsing inside her that only he could fill. She writhed against him, trying to relay her silent message.

A long groan slipped from Jeff's throat. "Casey —" he said brokenly.

"I want you inside, Jeff. Now," she said, her body seconding the motion.

"God, I thought you'd never ask," he rasped.

He shifted, pulling back so that Casey felt him pressing against her. She felt a flutter of fear — would he be too big for her, would it hurt — then she saw his face. Woven with the arousal sharpening the lines of his face was concern and caring and something so near the love she held in her own heart, tears pricked her eyes seeing it.

Jeff would never hurt her. Assurance flooded her, filled her with joy, anticipation of the pleasure she would give him.

She nodded, a nearly imperceptible movement. The strain of his control showing in his face, Jeff pushed inside her, slow and tantalizing. His arms trembled with the effort of holding himself back, his eyes burned into hers.

At the last moment, Casey thrust up to meet him, sighing with satisfaction as he filled her. She ran her hands up Jeff's rigid arms, snugged her legs more tightly around him.

"Are you okay?" Jeff rasped out.

She felt a catlike pleasure. "Tight," she whispered. "But you feel so good."

Jeff swore, the oath pungent. "Damn straight I do."

"Move, Jeff." She couldn't bear his stillness another moment. "I want to feel you move inside me."

With a long groan, he obliged her, his hips pulling back, then thrusting forward. If she'd thought he'd brought her to heaven before, now it seemed he'd invented a new paradise. She felt he was climbing inside her, deeper and deeper into her soul. Her arms, her legs surrounded him. In another moment, surely he would merge with her, become a part of her very being.

He kept his eyes fixed on her, intent on his own pleasure, but searching for hers as well. Each thrust nudged her, like a boat teased by river currents toward the rapids, toward the dizzying rush of excitement. She wanted more of him, faster, and she gripped his hips to urge him on.

He responded to her signal, the current catching him in its urgency. Her world stretched, expanded to encompass him, to fill her universe. Then with the shuddering surge of his climax, the sound of her name torn from his lips, she reached her peak, went spinning again into space. Lost in the roiling rapids of her soul, she clung to him, joined in intimacy, in brilliant love.

Jeff watched Casey sleep, secure in the curve of his arm. The still-burning lamp cast a golden light across the soft angles of her face, made dark crescents of her lashes. The sheet had slipped from one perfect breast and Jeff ached to touch it, to urge her to arousal and climax again, even as he cursed himself as an idiot.

*Damn, what the hell had he done?*

It had been the most spectacular experience of his life and the stupidest. Because now he felt ties to her more durable than tempered steel. Because now walking away from her would devastate her.

He'd seen it in her eyes. *She loved him.*

A softness spread within him at the thought. He clenched his teeth against it until a spasm tightened in his jaw. That was lunacy that didn't even bear thinking about. Because tomorrow, when she woke, he would have to make it clear to her that their making love hadn't changed anything. They would still part company once he had his negatives in hand and they returned to Reno.

*Why not let her love you?* a little niggling voice inside asked.

Because it would be a lie. Because she would want his love in return, an emotion he was incapable of giving.

He felt an ache inside, a wishful longing that he could love her. That the urgency he felt to be with her, to have her always at his side, was love. Love, not lust mixed with arrogant pride that he'd made her love him.

No, he didn't love her. So it was best not

to let this go any further, best to break the ties right at the outset. In fact, if he wasn't such a damned coward, he'd climb out of bed right now and crawl onto that cot that still waited for him on the other side of the room. But it felt too good to hold her, and his hope for another chance to make love to her proved too great a lure.

Holding her snug against him, Jeff reached over and snapped out the light. In the deep black of the room, he could pretend anything was possible, could believe his heart might somehow learn to love. He could keep her body near him, could breathe her cinnamon scent and let it soothe him into sleep.

And while he slept, he could dream, he could believe two people could love each other and love could last forever.

# Chapter 16

*Why did she have to be so damn beautiful?*

Jeff kept his hands tightly wrapped around the wheel of the car, his eyes fixed firmly on the curves of Highway 395 leading to town. He didn't dare let his gaze stray to the soft, warm woman at his side, or his thoughts to last night's ecstasy. Because in a few minutes he'd have his negatives and a few hours after that, they'd be in Reno and she'd be out of his life again.

A couple more miles to the post office; he could manage to keep his eyes off her for that long. Her scent he couldn't do a damn thing about, he could only try to suppress the memories the spicy cinnamon teased in him.

He'd taken her again during the night, this time entering her in one sure stroke, her hands on his hips guiding him in. Tangling in the shadows, he'd brought her to a quick climax with just the fierce urging of his body. Then with the first of the early morning light glazing their bodies with rose and gold, they

340

came together again, like two lovers lost in a dream.

A pungent oath escaped his lips and he felt Casey's eyes on him. He ignored her, as he'd ignored all of her questioning looks since he'd returned from his shower this morning to find her gazing up at him from bed. He'd cursed then, too, since he'd hoped to escape to the post office before she woke. Instead, he'd had to struggle through breakfast with her across the table from him, Shar's delectable vanilla French toast like ashes in his mouth.

And now he had to deal with her tantalizing, agonizing presence beside him in the car. He slowed at the outskirts of town, then followed Casey's soft-spoken directions to the post office. Once he'd killed the engine, he tossed out, "Stay here," before climbing from the car.

As if he'd really expected her to listen to him. She nearly made it to the door of the post office before him. He glowered at her to no effect, then opened the door for her. He gave her a wide berth as they crossed the small lobby and approached the counter.

The postal clerk stood with her back to them, sorting handfuls of mail. Casey jostled his elbow as she leaned over the counter. "Hey, Gina," she called out.

The postal clerk looked back over her shoulder, then smiled. She threaded her way through mail sacks toward them. "Hey, when did you get into town, Casey?"

To forestall one of Casey's lengthy explanations, Jeff cut in, "We need to pick up a package."

Her smile fading, Gina narrowed her eyes on Jeff. "What's the name?"

With an effort, Jeff softened his tone. "It was addressed to Shar Phillips. It should have arrived today."

"I haven't finished putting up today's mail," Gina said. "I haven't come across a package for Shar yet."

Casey stepped forward with a smile. "It's a really important package. I know it's a big imposition, but could you look for it?"

"Sure, Casey." Gina turned and made her way back through the obstacle course of mail, then disappeared into a back room.

Casey stirred beside him. "This is it, I guess."

"Yeah." Jeff ran a hand over his face, trying to understand the emotions roiling in his belly. "Assuming she finds them. Assuming they haven't disappeared in a cloud of fairy dust." Why did a part of him wish that very impossibility were true?

"I'm sure they're here," Casey said with a

sigh. "Then we return to Reno and get back to our lives."

He heard her underlying message. She understood that this was the end of their reason for being together, the fulfillment of their goal. In her hopeful tone, she was pleading for something more, an "us" beyond their return to Reno.

But no way would he add fuel to that fire. "Thank God," he said heartily, although he felt anything but thankful.

Not wanting to see the disappointment in her face, he kept his eyes fixed on the doorway to the back room. Gina finally reappeared brandishing a manila envelope.

"On the bottom, of course," she said. She made her way back to the counter and handed it to Casey.

Casey's hand trembled a little as she accepted the package, stared down at Liz's black scrawl across the front. Then she turned to Jeff, held it out to him.

For a moment, he got tangled in her soft brown gaze and he wanted to forget about the damn negatives, to say to hell with Mrs. Bender and her philandering husband. Then he shook himself loose and took the package from Casey's hands.

Tearing the top from the padded envelope, he plucked the glassine negative sleeve from it. Holding the top row of negatives, he let the strips accordion out, then held them to the light. A quick scan of the last half-dozen strips told him he'd finally gotten his hands on his negatives.

It seemed a lifetime ago since he took those shots and somehow, seeing them now made him feel dirty. He quickly ripped his negatives from Casey's, tearing along the perforations in the glassine sleeve. Somehow, it seemed the product of his labors would contaminate Casey's innocent family shots if they were conjoined even a moment longer.

He handed Casey her negatives. "Let's get going," he said brusquely as he headed for the door.

If only he could leave her behind here, so he would no longer have to face the hope in her eyes, in his own heart. But of course, she followed him to the car. His moment of reckoning had yet to come.

She was itching to tell him.

Jeff knew it the moment they topped Conway Summit, when Casey made a big show of oohing and ahing over the view of Mono Lake. Up until then, he'd been focused on squirreling the sedan up the long twisting grade, too focused on Highway

395's tricky turns to notice Casey's long looks at him.

Then as they negotiated the tight curves of Walker Canyon, she was just too damn bright and cheerful — effusing over every red-tail hawk circling above them, declaring each bend of the rushing Walker River alongside the highway more beautiful than the last.

She'd been quiet enough on the drive back from the post office, downright taciturn as they packed their things at Shar's — which for Casey meant she only spoke a dozen words to each of his one. She damn well glowed as she said good-bye to Shar, all but broadcasting the fact that she'd been thoroughly loved the night before.

Now she was working herself up to telling him she loved him. And if she did, if she got the words out, it would only make his inevitable good-bye all the more painful and embarrassing for her.

So he stonewalled her, tossing out noncommittal grunts when she attempted to draw him into conversation, answering outright questions in monosyllables. Which only seemed to increase her determination to get him to talk. By the time they reached Gardnerville, her sweet warm voice had wrapped itself around his every nerve. He would have reached over to stop the flow of words with his hand if he didn't know how much trouble that would get him into.

It was his cell phone that finally quieted her. He snatched it up in desperation at a stoplight and dialed the car dealer. He killed nearly twenty minutes on hold while they tracked down the service writer, then the mechanic, to confirm they'd received his fuel injectors and they'd be installed by the time he and Casey arrived. Next he called the rental agency to arrange for them to pick up the sedan at the car dealer. Finally, he dialed his office and asked Jim about the calls Phil Zucher had made on his cell phone — one to his mother, two to a bookie — dawdling on the line as long as he could.

That got him as far as Carson City. But before he could call Time or Nevada Road Conditions to fill the last thirty miles, Casey's slim hand covered his on the phone. "We have to talk," she said firmly as she plucked the phone from his hand.

"No we don't," he muttered under his breath. Aloud, he said, "About what?"

"About last night," she said in a very un-Casey-like tone of reasonableness, "about you and me."

"There is no you and me."

"There could be."

346

He tightened his grip on the wheel. "There shouldn't be."

He heard her reaction to that, a quick intake of breath. Her hand curved around his upper arm, the gentle contact an agony. "Last night meant more to me than I could even express."

"Don't make more out of it than it was," he said, squelching a bubble of happiness. "I'm not."

"I'm not either." Her fingers stroked his arm. "Jeff, I love you."

Damn it, she'd said it. And the words shot straight to his heart in a jet of pure joy. It took him a moment before his more logical mind regained control. "You don't," he said flatly.

"I do," she said.

He pulled his arm free of her hand. "It's a reaction to last night, that's all."

"It's not," she insisted. "I love you, Jeff."

He shook his head. "I'm just another Mr. Wrong."

She laughed, a low, sexy sound. "Then you're the right Mr. Wrong."

Temptation overwhelmed him. *Do it,* a little voice said inside, *let her love you.* Take her devotion, her heart, her love. It doesn't matter if you have nothing to give in return.

And damn his own dark soul, Jeff listened.

He considered his sterile life alone, weighed it against the unconditional love of a woman. He could take it, and be a happy man.

And destroy Casey. A shaft of pain cut through him at the thought of hurting her that way. He couldn't, wouldn't do that to Casey.

His eyes flicked to the Reno city limit sign. Mentally he counted the minutes before they reached the Starlight Casino and he could drop her off, put distance between them. He had to say the words now, to cut the link immediately.

"It doesn't matter how you feel," he said as coldly as he could. "I don't love you."

She gasped, pain laced in the sound. "You might learn to, if you gave it a chance." She gave him a threadbare laugh. "I'm not entirely unlovable."

He saw the Starlight's glittering marquee, a beacon in the distance. "I won't be with a woman I don't love," he said, managing an indifferent tone. "I tried that with my ex-wife. It didn't work."

"But couldn't we give it time?" she said, a pleading note creeping into her tone. "Couldn't we —"

"No!" he said more harshly than he'd intended. "No," he repeated more softly. He pulled into the casino lot, stopped behind the red compact. Leaving the engine running, he turned to her. "We've been in each other's pockets these last few days. And last night . . . it was special, Casey, believe that."

Tears brimmed in her eyes. "Then why won't you —"

"Shh," he said, his fingertips over her soft mouth. "Let's just leave it."

Before she could say another word, before he drew her closer for a kiss that wouldn't end with just a kiss, he climbed from the car, rounding it to open her door. She got out without looking at him, took her bag and purse from him wordlessly. As he shut the car doors and returned to the driver side, he tried to pretend he didn't see the tears coursing down her face.

He edged the sedan out of the way of the red compact, then waited to be sure her car started. He forced himself to face forward as she pulled out, suppressed the urge for one last look in the rear view mirror. By the time his willpower gave out and he turned to catch another glimpse of her, she was gone.

Casey guided her red compact out of the Starlight parking lot with one hand, swiping away the tears slipping from her eyes with the other. Teeth gritted as she drove, she managed to hold back further tears until she shut her apartment door behind her.

She gave herself permission for a good ten minutes of maudlin crying, gasping against the tightness in her throat, scrubbing at her wet, swollen eyes. Then she ruthlessly cut off her emotion like a tap, realizing she wouldn't get anywhere sobbing like a lovesick girl.

Damn Jeff Haley and his stiff-necked, overly noble attitude. So intent on saving her the grief of being locked into a one-way love affair, he couldn't see the truth she saw so clearly. There was nothing one-way about their relationship because he loved her too, she would bet her soul on it.

She marched herself into the bathroom to splash her face with cold water and drag a brush through her hair. She had to find a way to enlighten Jeff as to how he felt about her. She'd camp on his doorstep if she had to, roost in his office. She'd waited long enough for the kind of love she felt for Jeff. This was real, entirely unlike the pallid emotion she'd felt for her worthless boyfriends. Damned if she'd give Jeff up without a fight.

Just as she grabbed the hem of her sweatshirt to pull it off, the doorbell buzzed. Her heart rattled into double time, a thrill shooting through her as she realized it must be Jeff, come to his senses. She considered stripping off the sweatshirt and greeting him at the door topless, but then thought better of it.

For which she was extremely grateful when she wrenched open her door and saw who stood on her door step. Phil Zucher, evil grin and all.

She tried to slam the door shut, but he blocked it with his foot. "Got ya," he said, stepping inside.

Then she noticed the gun.

Even as he watched the negatives slicing through his office shredder, Jeff wasn't quite sure what had come over him. His temporary insanity was composed of equal parts Casey's tears, his own yearning for her love, and his disgust over the Benders' whole sorry mess. When he left the car dealer and drove to his office, he had a single-minded goal — to destroy the negatives he'd gone to such great lengths to recover.

He walked back to the outer office where Jim sat at his desk. "Where's the check?" he asked his assistant.

Jim handed it over without comment. Jeff scrutinized the amount. "This is everything Mrs. Bender's paid us?"

Jim nodded. "Every penny."

Jeff scrawled his name to the check. "I

want this delivered immediately."

He handed the check to Jim, then wandered back to his own office. A dull ache ground away inside him, like a fist beating at his chest. He settled in his chair, then swivelled it to the credenza behind him where a black-and-white portable sat. He switched on the television, then flipped aimlessly through the channels.

When he settled on a midday newsbreak, it took him a moment to register the image on the television screen. Will Bender amidst a sea of reporters and television cameras. Lola Marks close beside him, her plain face radiant with joy as she gazed up at her lover. The reporter's voice-over announcing both the retirement of Assemblyman Will Bender and his imminent divorce.

Jeff grinned, inordinately pleased that his grand gesture with the negatives was unnecessary. On the television, Will Bender beamed down at Lola, his love for her clear in his face. Love that said this man would do anything for this woman, sacrifice his career, his self, his heart.

Jeff stood pole axed as a realization struck him with the force of a lightning bolt. *He would do the same for Casey.*

He would sacrifice anything — his pride, his ego. His fear.

Oh my God, I do love her.

A burst of laughter exploded from him. *He loved Casey!* The logjam in his chest began to shift and he felt giddy with joy.

Turning on his heel, he strode out the break room door. "Have to go," he told a startled Laura.

He dimly heard the ringing of the phone as he shoved open the door to step outside. Jim called after him, "Mrs. Bender on line two."

"Take a message!" Jeff tossed over his shoulder, hurrying to his car.

He jammed the sedan into gear and squealed into a U-turn. Mentally mapping out the route to Casey's apartment, he rehearsed what he would say, how he would tell her that yes, she could love him. Because he loved her, too.

Casey's first reaction was bemusement that she had ever mistaken a cell phone for a gun. Because now that she saw the real thing, she realized the two items bore absolutely no resemblance to one another. Her second reaction was despair that it wasn't Jeff on her doorstep and her third, belated, response was a very sensible fear.

Zucher waved the gun at her, his hand visibly shaking. "Where's yer boyfriend?" he asked as he shut the door behind him.

"Boyfriend?" Casey squeaked, playing dumb. Her eyes riveted on the tidy bit of black steel in Zucher's hand. It was barely larger than his palm; how could something so small be so deadly?

"Haley," he hissed, gesturing with the gun.

Watching his hand flopping around, Casey realized that Zucher was just as much an amateur at guns as he had been at card cheating. Except where a marked ace couldn't kill her, a gun in the hand of a stupid man was downright deadly.

She had to protect Jeff at any cost. "He's gone," Casey said quickly. "He went to . . . to . . . South America."

Zucher's brow furrowed as if he was trying to work out the sense of what she'd said. "I'll take care of him later, then." He thrust the muzzle of the gun into her ribs, and Casey thought her heart would stop without benefit of a bullet. "C'mon."

"Where are we going?" Casey asked, stalling.

A long pause, then Zucher blurted, "Don't ask stupid questions."

He grabbed her arm. Casey snatched it back. "You don't know where we're going, do you?"

Zucher thrust out his lower lip. "Course I do. C'mon."

She crossed her arms over her chest. "I won't."

Another jab of the gun nearly collapsed Casey's knees. He was looking scared now and that was infinitely more perilous.

"Okay, okay," Casey said. "I'm going, I'm going."

She thought quickly as he gripped her arm, tugged her toward the door. She'd probably be safer out on the street anyway; more opportunity to escape. Thank God Jeff hadn't stayed with her, thank God he was safely away from here.

She nearly stumbled as Zucher dragged her down the stairs, one hand clutching her arm, the other jutting the gun into her back. He slapped open the front lobby doors, then took a quick look up and down the street before heading for his pickup parked in front of a gray sedan.

At first, Casey's terror clouded her recognition of the lean form climbing from the gray car. Then joy slammed into fear as Jeff's eyes met hers and in an instant he took in her peril. Even as she was shaking her head to ward him off, Jeff was leaping over the hood of his car, slamming Zucher's body away from her with a roar of rage.

They hit the pavement with Jeff on top and the impact jarred the gun loose from

Zucher's hand. Casey lunged for it, tried to kick it clear, but Zucher got to it first, snatching it clear of the sweep of her foot. Straining against Jeff's weight, he fumbled with the weapon, trying to get his fingers around the grip.

Casey screamed as Zucher swung the gun up, but before Zucher could aim, Jeff closed his hands around Zucher's wrist. They grappled for the gun, Zucher pounding at Jeff with his free hand while both of Jeff's were occupied in keeping the gun from his head.

Casey dashed to Jeff's car, found the cell phone on the seat. She punched in 911 with trembling fingers, reported her location in a shaky whisper. Then Jeff's cry of pain whirled her around.

His face in a tight grimace, Jeff arched his body protectively as Zucher drove another knee into his groin. Jeff's grip on Zucher's gun hand weakened, and Casey watched, stunned as Zucher scrambled out from under Jeff and brought the weapon closer to his head.

*What do I do, what do I do?* Zucher was going to kill Jeff, kill the man she loved. She raced to her car and wrenched open the passenger door, her gaze roving the interior for a weapon.

Her gaze and her hands fell on the cans of motor oil in the back seat at the same time. She grabbed up two and pelted to where Zucher had pinned Jeff to the sidewalk.

She lifted the first can high over her head, and with a cry of white-hot anger, flung it onto the back of Zucher's head. Her aim was bad and it glanced off his ear, rattling to the pavement and rolling toward the street. She hefted the other, this time driving it onto Zucher's back.

Then she watched with a distant kind of terror as Zucher pivoted his head toward her, his eyes crazy. He snarled at her, the sound chilling her straight to her soul. If the meanness in his eyes could have killed, she would have been dead right then.

But Zucher had taken his eyes from Jeff, and that was enough for Jeff to heave a knee of his own between Zucher's legs. That weakened Zucher's grip on the gun so that it clattered to the pavement. This time Casey was able to kick it away, across the sidewalk into the oleander.

His fists driven by fury, Jeff struck Zucher once, twice in the face, until the other man slumped to the pavement. Rolling to his feet, he looked ready to kick the prone body for good measure.

"Jeff?" Casey called, the aftermath of fear

trembling in her voice.

He strode to her, swept her into his arms. "Oh God, I thought I'd lose you."

"Never," she said, her cheek pressed to his chest. "I love you, Jeff." She pulled back, tipping her head so she could see him. "And you love me."

"Is that right?" he asked, but she knew from the smile he tried to hide that he wouldn't deny it anymore.

She poked a finger to his chest. "And you're going to ask me to marry you."

His eyes widened and he threw back his head with a burst of laughter. "Am I now?" he asked, although a tenderness gentled the tone of his words. "When I do, what will you answer?"

"Yes," she whispered. "As soon as possible."

He drew her close to him again, holding her tightly against his chest as the sound of sirens clamored up the street. "I love you, Casey Madison," he said fervently.

"And I love you, Jeff Haley," she said, just as devoutly. "Forever."

As he bent to kiss her, uncaring of the chaos as police and neighbors surged around them, Casey reveled in the joy in her heart.

# About the Author

**Karen Sandler** fulfilled her lifelong dream of becoming a full-time writer when she moved with her husband and two sons from the congestion of Los Angeles to the beautiful Sierra Nevada foothills.

After four years of submissions and rejections, she sold her first two romance novels. She has since sold six other novels, one science fiction, one young adult and four more romances. Also a screenwriter, she's produced one short film and has plans to write and produce other projects.

Visit Karen's web site at: www.karen sandler.net

The employees of Thorndike Press hope you have enjoyed this Large Print book. All our Thorndike and Wheeler Large Print titles are designed for easy reading, and all our books are made to last. Other Thorndike Press Large Print books are available at your library, through selected bookstores, or directly from us.

For information about titles, please call:

(800) 223-1244

or visit our Web site at:

www.gale.com/thorndike
www.gale.com/wheeler

To share your comments, please write:

Publisher
Thorndike Press
295 Kennedy Memorial Drive
Waterville, ME  04901